Y0-CCW-774

in the breeze of passing things

a novel by nicole louise reid

MacAdam/Cage
155 Sansome Street, Suite 550
San Francisco, CA 94104
www.macadamcage.com

Library of Congress Cataloging-in-Publication Data

Reid, Nicole Louise, 1973—
    In the breeze of passing things / by Nicole Louise Reid.
    p. cm.
    ISBN 1-931561-42-7 (hardcover : alk. paper)
    1. Fatherless families–Fiction.
    2. Mothers and daughters–Fiction. 3. Sisters–Fiction.
    4. Girls–Fiction. I.Title.

    PS3618.E54515 2003
    813'.54–dc21

                                                    2003013010
Manufactured in the United States of America.
10 9 8 7 6 5 4 3 2 1

Book and jacket design by Dorothy Carico Smith.

Several chapters of this novel have appeared elsewhere, in slightly
different form, in the following publications: *American Literary
Review*, *Apalachee Review*, *Asylum 1928* (Fish Publishing, 2001),
Black Warrior Review, *Confrontation*, *GSU Review*, *Indiana Review*,
Karamu, *Other Voices*, *Quarterly West*, *Rain Crow*, *Washington Square*,
Willow Springs, and *Yemassee*.

in the breeze of passing things

a novel by nicole louise reid

MacAdam/Cage

For Matt, Julianna, Daddy, and Mom
and
for other truths in my life —
those that stay, those that pass me,
and those I pass by.

There are things you can't know but you feel. Like the way your heart moves blood. How a baby sister breathes like the leaves holding on just a day or two more, the loose ones, the ones waiting to fall. That he is gone.

None of these makes any sense. You couldn't draw it. But you know it's real.

Sometimes you think it's like swallowing water. Or like being born too soon. You think you remember the way your daddy sounded in the hospital hall, the way he echoed and wouldn't leave you, wouldn't go home for anything. You used to think it was fresh-baby you who made him collapse to the tile waiting to touch you, to sing to you, to memorize the shape of your brand new mouth. But all those later nights, you a big sister now, when he called or didn't, when you waited up in bed—counting or rhyming just to stay up— when Mother would shut your sister in with you and go off searching him out, you couldn't make that one work in your head, so what you told yourself was he's lost.

What you feel, though, is like walking neckdeep in water, when it's warmer than your own skin and is singing and making pillows and tipping you back, and showing you the moon with its crisp lower point and halo of the rest you can't see, with your knees bending, lowering you because that's easy and feels nice like someone's catching you, grabbing hold of you. When you're breathing in that salty dank and wanting something, actually feel yourself wanting the single thing wanting you back right then, what you feel creeping up your spine is that it's never been about you at all.

Mother pulls from a box the wrinkly sheets of packing paper that she smoothed and folded and saved after our last move. She hands them out sheet by sheet, licking her thumb to be sure she's got just one page. First a sheet for Mally, then one for me. Mother is the keeper of the paper; she runs this show.

"Wrap everything," she tells us. "Even balls of socks. And help your sister," she says to me.

Her hair's up in side-combs today, neat and pretty brown. And because of how lovely Mother looks when we start packing, I hate to say a word of anything to her, hate to think I could change the way she smells of buttered lemons, the way when she squeezes me to her, I can feel the softness of her cheek on mine for hours, and I rub it and touch my hands to each side to know the difference.

But I can't keep this back, not even for her. "I don't want to go," I tell her.

"I'm going, Iva," says Mally. "You have to go."

"Everyone wants to go, see?" Mother says, happy and decided. "It'll be fun, Tennessee."

Sometimes she just talks and talks and I wonder if she knows what she's saying because the way she looks is like a robot with no idea what the sounds mean. And she couldn't possibly think I want Hopewell, Tennessee, or anything other than Daddy in the Nacogdoches house.

"We'll make stops and see things on the way," she's going on, "who knows what we'll find, but anything we like the look of, we can pull over to see better. And you'll love the mountains. Pretty as all."

Even though she's talking to me, she reaches to Mally's hair, a piece sitting wrong from sleeping every which way. Sometimes I'm not sure what Mother really looks like. And lately I'm not even sure how I look 'cause no one ever stops to see.

"Everyone loves mountains," she says, but I'm nowhere near believing her. "Think of it as an adventure, like you and Daddy wading Laguna Madre shallows grabbing at fish just like the pelicans."

"That was different and you know it," I say.

"Everything's different these days."

"You can't make me go."

"It's done, Iva." She shows Mally, who's only five, how to twirl sheets and sheets of the wrinkly pages around shirt stacks and pants rolls, and even Mally's blanket—which Mother wonders about but lets her keep on sucking and silking anyhow.

"Does he know we're going?" I ask.

Mother hums and nods, unrolls the package of Mally's pants even though she'd just finished wrapping it. Mally puts her mouth around the word *who* but doesn't give it any air.

"Does he know where?" I ask, and Mother's quiet. "You have to tell him where, Mother. You have to."

"Hush now." She won't look at me.

"How will he know where to come for us? You have to tell him so he knows where to go."

Mally makes another *who* in her mouth.

"Zip it, Iva. Don't upset your sister."

But Mally's calm as can be, giving no more thought to that word than she is to what this house will mean to her once we're gone from it. She is folding, folding again, wrapping several sheets at a time around single balls of bobby socks, sandal socks, knee socks. Kneeling on the floor of her bedroom, Mally is smiling, smiling wide, grinning even. I squint my eyes at her, so hard I think they'll suck right up into my brain, and still she won't look up at me.

"Do something," I say to her.

Mother shoots me a face says I'm bigger and know better, says I'm skating the ice with her.

"Say something," I tell my sister, but she goes on with her socks and her smile, looking dumb as kids who ride the special bus to school. I holler at her, "Are you empty?"

Mother grabs at me. "That'll do, Iva."

I throw the stack of Mally's T-shirts I just finished wrapping. They fall out of the paper before reaching her. When Mally looks at me she's only afraid, not thinking it through. I can't stop myself: "Are you just nothing?"

"Enough!" Mother shouts, picking up the blues and reds and greens of Mally's clothing.

"He's your father, too," I say, stomping near enough

Mally's toes that she curls them under like toads gone under a rock.

It's done.

I go to the sofa in the big room off the kitchen, sit upside down because Mother worries my head will explode when I sit with my feet flat against the wall, my head just beginning to hang over the cushion's edge.

So we are going again. Mally isn't even in school yet, and we are packing, packing, packing. Mother and I are only going from here, from Tyler, not wanting to, just doing it; Mally is leaving. The two don't match up and it hit me square the other day. Mother says Daddy left her—over and over—and only went from us. But she's positive wrong. She says he's still with Mally and me like morning milk in your belly 'round noon, but I'm not sure because I don't feel him there and by lunchtime I'm thirsty for more. She says there is a difference between people who do the leaving and those who are left. And she says whatever you do first is what you do from then on. She says she is always going to be the one who is left. She says Mally and I don't know what we'll be yet, but we'd better try to be careful never to get left like her.

None of that matters, though. I know he'll come.

* * *

When Mother's satisfied that I've forgotten who said what, and all that Mally owns is wrapped and boxed, they both come into the kitchen. I'm still sitting upside down, though to be honest I stopped midway because I thought my head would explode, but now I'm back into position for Mother's benefit.

"Oh, Iva," she says, and I have to push my cheeks to keep them flat to fight against a good, hard grin.

Mally runs over to me, fascinated by the way my face looks upside down. I cover my eyes and move my mouth around for her. "Now me," she says and climbs up onto the sofa, upside down beside me. But I don't get up to study her, just stay lying here as I am. Mally turns her head to me, and it's Mother's eyes she has. Cheeks fat as a carving pumpkin. The memory of a newt—as Mother says when she forgets and puts the sauce on the raw meatball mix by mistake, which she does a lot because she *just can't be expected to keep everything on track.*

On my back beside her, her knee wobbling over onto mine, our feet climbing the back of the sofa, I grab at Mally's nose, then kiss her cheek for her newt-sized memory.

"Tonight is pizza on paper," Mother says. "All the dishes and silver's in boxes, so there's just no getting around it, is there?"

Mother slices and Mally grabs two of Ground Beef-Extra Cheese, fussing "Iva got one of my cheese blobs." But in another moment she's forgotten. "I love pizza," she says, swinging her legs under the table so fast I feel a breeze on my toes. "I could eat it every day."

"Me, too." I give Mally one cheese blob.

"Mother, can we eat it every day in Tennessee?"

"Whatever you say, baby," says Mother, wiping her fingers in the paper towel. "Your daddy hated pizza. He was fastidious. Used fork and knife for everything."

"He isn't dead," I say.

She pretends to cut her slice into tiny bites before eating, flinging her left hand up in the air, flipping her chin this way and that for us 'cause she's trying to look fancy. "He used to scrub at his teeth with a napkin when he couldn't get home to brush," she says. Mally laughs. "And I mean scrub." She scours her front teeth with the napkin like they're the front windshield of the Impala.

I hate Mother like this. When she's feeling theatrical. When she's making up stories to prove a point that's not even true. I don't feel much like eating anymore.

Instead, I remember the zoo. Daddy and me making faces at the proboscis monkeys and their making faces back. Taking pictures of the newborn rhesus monkey still in its incubator, diapered and silent and curled to one side—not like Mally when she was fresh-born and I was only five. I was premature, and when we saw the baby monkey Daddy asked did I remember anything like that. Somehow I knew I did when he said it, same as how I feel my lungs push open, shut. He said he'd worried about not touching me there in my fish tank incubator, but no one would let him. The nurses tucked blue spray bottles into their waistbands and every time they walked past, gave a squirt to rub out how much he'd been pressing himself to the glass. He worried I'd grow up not needing anyone's hands. Mother says they're all I've ever needed. If you ask me, I need a whole lot more than that.

From the kitchen Mother calls to us, "Last night in beds." I hear her foil-wrapping leftover pizza for the drive tomorrow. I roll my eyes.

Mally's on her stepstool flossing. I stand behind her combing out my hair.

"Do you think we'll like the new house?" I ask, not really caring what her answer is; it won't change my mind.

He never lived in this house, this one we've been rattle-people in. This is the first one he never lived in—and Nacogdoches, where we were perfectly whole, is only a scootch over two hours away. But Mother said no he couldn't come in. He'd stand on the lawn and sometimes, if I was fast enough I got to run out the back around the house to him. But with Mother screaming at him he never held me very tight. So he's never once been inside here. Never once seen where I sleep and eat. Where I turn Mally's toes into happy toads or hiding toads, depending on my mood. Twenty-three weeks in this house and only his checks each month.

Mally's in her flannel nightgown, flowered and ribboned, and happy for it all. She doesn't remember the last truck, though the movers let us on before all our stuff was shoved to the back corner. They sat Mally on the tower of furniture blankets and let us walk, even run, up and down the ramp. We played pirates and I made Mally walk the plank.

I thought Daddy would be here, at this house when it was new. Mother never said so. It just seemed the natural thing: he'd just gone on ahead, scouting, Mother would have said if she were saying anything at all then. While I looked for Daddy, trying every door 'cause maybe it was a joke, Mally chose her room; she got the one with mirrored doors, yellow shag, and a wall of windows. I didn't even notice such things. Mother made his favorite Stroganoff, and still he stayed away. I walked the halls, opened and reopened every door, thinking he was the ghost and this was the graveyard.

Tonight I read to Mally, *Make Way for Ducklings* and *Pezzetino*. To show her what it's like to be lost, to get her thinking. These are Daddy's books, from his branch where sometimes he'd sit me behind the desk with him and let me be the one to collect whatever came in through the drop-slot in the brick. These are my favorite books—with his stamp and spine label I've rubbed clean of its code. Mally doesn't understand what I'm telling her. She likes the covers, she giggles when Mrs. Mallard quacks at the cars and the policeman comes running. They're just noisy ducks crossing a road, just colored pebbles. I tell her, "We'll be all right," but she doesn't understand that either. "He knows we miss him," I say.

And this time she says it: "Who?"

Mother tucks Mally into bed, leaves me on top of the covers. She wants to read to us, but I show her the books tossed down onto the floor; she's too late. "These are the ones you kept out for the car?" she asks. Mally nods though she had nothing to do with the choosing. "Well we're just like those duckies, aren't we? Making our way to a new home," she says and rubs noses with Mally.

"No, we're not," I tell her, because we've got no father to find us the right spot. "That's only in dreams," I say. "We are Pezzetino." Tiny broken pieces.

Mother leans over Mally, touches her nose and kisses her. "Your sister's quite the philosopher, isn't she?" Mother says to her, but gives me a strange look, like maybe I scared her. "Iva Freud, is it?"

I go to my own room, to my own bed. I read *By the Shores of Silver Lake*, which he gave me last year. I wonder if he knew then that she'd take all his going as being truly gone. I try counting out all the late fines and wonder if they're docking his pay like when I couldn't part with the *Free to Be...You and Me* record we'd sing to every night. Maybe now he's allowed to check out as much as he wants for as long and as far away as he needs.

Mother doesn't come talk to me. I think to dream of Daddy tonight. I pull out my picture of us, the framed one he set beside my bed one morning like it was a basket on Easter Sunday. I can't really see him clearly without it anymore; it's been two years since we didn't know any better, the undoing of things. We were on Padre Island, building white sand and shell mountains out of each other. It seems to me now that no one else was there, that it was our beach, our water and gulls. That all the air passed from him to me and back again. He listened and spoke and neither one of us could sit beneath the shoveled sand long enough to get past the knees. So we wriggled our toes and the surface beach cracked dry and soft over us until out came our feet and legs and we were free in the sun. I remember no camera, no sister, no mother.

❀ ❀ ❀

Trying to dream of someone is difficult. Each time my eyes go quiet I worry it won't be him in there with me, so I wake up. Now I can hear Mother and think she's just finishing up wrapping her knickknacks, but what it sounds like is whispering. The crackling of the old paper sheets becomes words and I can make out a way Mother used to know how to talk.

"Yes, I remember," she says sweetly, like when she loves Mally and me and is trying to go easy on us. She says, "I miss hearing my own name now. I know it's ridiculous, but I don't think this house has ever even heard it once."

I step from bed, go to her bedroom door, my toes shrinking up on the cold tile.

Behind the door Mother laughs like there's nothing in this world to hurt her. "Seven years ago," she says, "but I remember that night, I do.

...

"Yes."

...

"I think about it all the time. I miss that, but—"

...

"Lonesome. Mmm," she hums, like to catch her breath.

...

"We're past that, aren't we? Not any chance for us."

...

"Some nights I can't bear knowing it."

...

My tongue's big in my mouth, at the back. I swallow, swallow again.

She had a routine in the Nacogdoches house: first lock the front door, then unlock the back, pick up Mally's sweater or socks on the way into the kitchen where she switched off the phone. Late some nights he'd call. He'd be stuck somewhere, lost or aching. Some nights she'd bring Mally from her crib to my bed, kiss Mally first then me, and lock us in the room sleeping or not. I could see the lights from her car bright on the ceiling, then gone.

I'm stuck here in the hall with my little toes going purple and my big tongue getting caught in my throat. And I cannot move.

"So it's working?" she says. "You're taking the medicine alright now?"

...

"That's good." Her voice comes up high and tight, then real quiet. "Regularly?"

...

"Well it doesn't work if you stop and start all the time. I can't even believe we're having this conversation. Nothing's new here. You're just the same."

...

"You loved me then too. It didn't keep you on your pills."

I push open the door because I want to touch her hair or press my hand over her eyelids like sometimes when we're playing blindman and I get near enough to breathe her in and then can't pull myself away. Those are bad days because she gets cross with how tight my arms can go, she says *Stop it, I can't even breathe.*

She's hard. Sitting on the bed facing her wall now, doesn't even know I'm here. She's very tall, I think. Very tall how she sits.

"You did this, not me," she says. "You left all of us: your three girls, remember that? Your three darlings?"

...

"Yes, you were coming back, but Jameson, how many nights later? Out driving, looking for whatever it is you're missing. You always feel you're missing something. I can't be put through it anymore. And the girls."

...

"It's not ever your intention, I know that. If you could just keep yourself regular on it."

...

"Well you don't have to like the way it makes you feel, just fill the prescription and take it."

...

"You made a choice then, and you're still making that choice. Do you like where that leaves you?"

I push the door open another two inches but stop because she's quiet a minute. And what I see through the door is her arm come 'round her front to grip her side. She sits with an old shoe box on her lap, curled bright photographs scattered about her on the bed. She begins turning down each and every picture on her quilt.

I back away because the room is too quiet for her not to notice me. But even past her doorway, I know Mother's answering questions now. She says, "Tomorrow, first thing."

...

"No, don't. They're settled into it now, don't give them any hopes."

...

"I know. Hush, hush, please," she says like she's holding me. The way Mother breathes is so low and uneven, so bent and swayed that she's losing balance just sitting on her bed.

I hear "When?" and "Iva?" and "No."

Her fingernails find the grooved seam along the telephone. "You think that's the way to bring me back? You think that'll help one lick, wrecking what they've got left in this world?"

...

"You can't separate them—even if I'd let you have her." She's tugging at her elbow, tugging, tugging until her skin stands tented over her bone. "You call here with your *Lilly this*, and *Lilly that*, just to see how easy I am to break clear in half? And I am easy. So easy. But you're only playing jokes."

The way I feel is swords through the wicker basket, only the magician doesn't miss at all but plunges every blade straight through me.

"No court would give her over. To you? You are nothing. Nothing. Not one damn thing to those girls. Mally doesn't even remember last week let alone two years ago. Iva couldn't care less."

I have dreamt my father into being. He's here and wants

me. I never doubted him. Never.

I run to the kitchen phone. "Don't listen—"

"Iva," Mother yells. "Off this phone. Now."

"You're coming," I say.

"Now, Iva!"

I haven't even heard him yet. "Daddy, Daddy—" I mean to call his name again, as many times as it takes, but the word tastes strange. In my head, I'm running through all the ways I know he loves me. But he won't speak. There is nothing: no crinkly paper, no words, no beat of him breathing, no father. He's just gone.

Mother's here. She pulls the phone from me. She hangs up on him. She walks me back to bed. And she's talking, but all I hear is the nothing from the telephone. She pulls the covers to my chin. I kick them off. She bends to kiss me but I turn to the wall, pinching my knees tight in all my fingers.

"You and I, we know things, right?" she says.

I know nothing.

"We know this happens. We know he forgets things, what's possible and what's not. We know he loves us."

Nothing at all.

Her face is mean tonight: angular, rough, crisp. She leaves.

Her theory is wrong.

❊ ❊ ❊

Mother wakes me first this morning. She says, "Baby, we should talk."

My mouth isn't working yet, and I'm glad because suddenly I recall who she is.

"You're my girl and always will be," she says. "He didn't mean it, that you could go live with him. He's just trying to upset me." She's holding my earlobe and looking down into me. Her mouth doesn't want its smile. Her eyes don't want it either. "You wouldn't like it there anyway."

I don't give her any words but wonder where he's gone now and somehow she knows, says: "Pascagoula, Mississippi. He can't stay anywhere long. Right on the water, and your roses don't want wet toes all the time."

I'm through with roses.

"He's poor now or ought to be. And besides, even if it weren't entirely out of the realm of stars," she says, "Mally needs you, and he can't have you both."

Why not?

She doesn't say.

❋ ❋ ❋

I go to Mally's room, climb in bed with her. She's still dreaming, I can see; her eyelids twitch and her hand opens and shuts. I slide in behind her. I whisper, "Go to Pascagoula with me." I tell her, "We can make the movers put our boxes on another truck." I kiss her blond streaky hair. But she sleeps and I know Mother won't let Mally go. I step on her getting out of bed.

For breakfast, mother wants me to eat oatmeal from a waxy Dixie cup. I want pizza. She gives in. She wants to warm it. I want it cold. She holds it out to me. I wait until she sets it down on the table before I take it. She storms off to her room, and I hear the shower. Mally pads in from bed rubbing her eyes and blinking. She points at my pizza, but I give her the oatmeal, tell her Mother said so. I eat standing but say Mally has to sit down. I tell her "chew with your mouth shut," and "elbows off the table."

The phone rings and Mally jumps up to answer it. This

is her latest thing. Every call, we have to let Mally get it or else she'll throw a tantrum. But I'm taller and I push her.

"Lilly?" he says.

"No." For just the splittest second I can't say a thing. I'm more certain than I've ever been about anything in the world. "I know who this is," I tell him.

"Can I talk to Lilly?"

"This is you," I say.

I hear him breathing. "I need Lilly."

"No you don't."

He won't answer.

"I know you."

"No."

"You are coming, aren't you?" I ask.

"Iva," he says, but I can't recall him saying my name like this at any other time. I-va, slowly, like he's not sure he's right, like I might be anyone else in the universe.

"I love you, love you, love you!" I say, and Mally starts smooching it up all over my elbows, like this is the black-eyed monster boy, Petie, she loves from next-door.

"Please don't," he says. "Get me Lilly. I need her."

"She's in the shower."

"Oh, Iva! You're not supposed to say!" Mally squawks and runs down the hall. "I'm telling Mother. Just you wait."

"Come now."

"Plum," he says and I know he remembers me.

"It isn't right, you not here. I want to go. I'm packed, for Tennessee. Come right now, Daddy."

"We shouldn't be talking. She won't like this," he says. "I didn't know I'd get you so early. She won't like this one bit."

"Are you nearby? Come on before the truck."

"I need your mother," he says. "Where is your mother? I can't talk to you. We have rules. Where's Lilly?"

I remember Mother's Ls all over his tongue like that. "In the shower. Come right now!"

"I'm in Mississippi."

"Well how will we get there? Is there a bus? I've never been on a bus. Mother says it's wet and I can't grow my roses there—I don't care."

"What's this all about, Iva? Is your mother there?"

I turn to the wall, cup the phone between my chin and chest. "I can come alone," I say.

"I need your mother. Please."

"She's in the *shower*," I say doing my best not to raise my voice at him. "You want me, right?"

He doesn't answer.

"Last night, you told her you want me."

I can even sort of see him. My daddy breathes once deep into his lungs and belly and even toes, then blows it all out through his bristly face. I hear it. I know it. I can see him making up the plan. How much he wants me. All those handprints on my glass.

"I don't remember," he says, shaky. Afraid.

I drop the phone.

I go to my room. I don't look at my photograph of us at the Gulf. I don't look at any photograph in my head. I put him somewhere. I set him aside, every bit of him I know enough to draw, every bit of me that is him: the stringy yellow hair, the way he strokes his chin and so I do too, the way he gave me a razor without the blade to touch up our whiskers standing at the foamy sink on Sundays, that now I want to rub my teeth clean after eating pizza. I fold these bits, turn them and crease them tighter into something so small it's invisible. I wrap it in the noisy paper from our moving day seven months ago. I set it in a box lined with more scrunched-up paper. I shut the flaps in order, bottoms then tops. I squeeze the lid shut, tape the lid down.

Mother comes finally, her hair in a towel on top of her head. She leans over me and water drips from her fingertips onto my skin. But there isn't enough of me here for her. I was mostly him, so now I am mostly gone. I wonder if it's possible to leave my own self.

She says "I love you," and another voice should be there, too. She kneels on the floor, wraps her arms around me and presses her cheek to mine. Steamy water sucks me to her. "I want you," she says, and the hole splits wider. "I will always want you no matter what."

But there's no way to know for sure anymore.

"Won't you speak?" she says, and I won't. "Nothing, not even for your mother?"

And I say nothing, not even for my mother.

"I remember when you were born," she says, "and all I could wish for was that you'd keep on breathing." She stretches her fingers open across my face, touches my lips and cheeks and eyes. "You were small enough to fit in my hand, well almost," she says. "You climbed up my arm like a monkey. Covered in stiff, white bristles."

She looks at me a minute. "Daddy cried every night we left you in the hospital. He took it harder," she says. "He couldn't make sense of the rules. He frightened all the nurses yelling, then crying. That's your father. Oh Iva, I wish for things."

I want to know what but still don't speak.

"I wish you were only mine so no one else could hurt you. I wish you hadn't always been up on his shoulders, learning to love him more. I wish you were young as Mally so you wouldn't remember him wanting to be so near. I wish we were gone already and that he didn't know our new telephone."

Mother takes a deep breath and I think she's taking it hard, my hair and hazel eyes and every way she's ever shown me I'm him. Not like looking at Mally. "I wish I had seen the signs sooner," she says.

I don't know what she means.

"If he had been honest. You know the very first thing out his mouth to me was a lie—born in a *lake*, my foot—like it mattered a bit to be from water instead of Texas. An only child—ha!" She sits back on her feet folded under her, and is so still I watch myself in her eyes. "I never would have married him. He's unstable, irresponsible, he's crazy. I still love him."

"Is that allowed?" I blurt out before I can stop myself.

"Of course," she says. "It just hurts more that way." She lifts my bangs from over my eyes. "But it's human."

"It hurts."

"You're lucky, though," she says, "he's in you—in your yellow hair, your tiny toes, your thick voice. I have no hold on him like you do."

I think of my box.

"The picture you keep in that drawer there," she says, "maybe that's all you'll ever get—just that day, and some others before now. Before this year. Maybe that'll be it. But you've still got him." She fingers the selvage rim of my bed sheet like Mally fussing over her blanket. "I'm no part of him at all. Do you see? You're the lucky one."

"I don't know if I want it. What if I don't want him now?" I stare up into my mother's face and it is the most beautiful face I have ever seen: glistening and peach. "He didn't know me," I say. "He didn't even know me."

"Oh, love." She lets out so much air in one quick breath. "I wish hard but five hundred miles from us is way too near, he can do so much still. You'll see in Hopewell, you'll see the difference. New house, new world."

"I don't want him in me."

Mother holds me to her and rocks me slowly. Ten years, eleven months is way too old for this. She should know better. But I let her go on. I even set my cheek to her shoulder, let her have some of me. Take a little in return.

"I do," she says, and I think she's hoping enough silence sleeps between our words that I won't know what I said and she's answering.

"Lilly," I whisper, touching her skin.

She turns away from me, her arms wrapping 'round her. "Don't say that," she says, shaking her head.

I want to say it again.

"That's not for you, Iva. Don't go looking for me."

We're still figuring out how tight our arms can hold and still let us go on breathing when Mally walks in clutching her blanket with her thumb in her mouth. Mother's arms go to her lap, reach out for Mally, so I guess the two of us are hiding this all away.

"I thought you'd packed it," Mother says.

Mally only nods and comes climb in my bed with us, whispering, "Is it safe now?"

Mother says, "Always," and Mally believes.

"I ate the pizza," Mally says.

"You ate the pizza?"

Mally grins.

"Every last slice I foil-wrapped for lunch?" Mother asks, her eyes wide.

Mally nods.

"All the cheese, too?" I ask her.

"Every blob," she says, sitting right on top of me, not even seeing the way we can look only at her.

The truck pulls up, throws down its ramp, and Mother is still in her robe, Mally and I in our jammies. We race around in Mally's room, rewrapping everything she'd ruined to get at her blanket—sweaters and curtains and shoes. Then Mally and I play in the truck, and I let her make me walk the plank. The neighbor kids come out to watch the truck fill. Petie won't speak to Mally and I won't let anyone but us up onto the truck. They stand in a straight line on the curb: Petie, his little brother, and a girl who has Campbell's Kids paper dolls and once let me play with them. All the kids are tidy and quiet watching our table and beds, the few chairs and lamp, our neatly labeled boxes packed in. In the gape of their mouths, I can see them wondering who we are to stay so short, to go so soon.

They haven't the slightest clue that one of us is leaving and two of us are stuck. We are only going from this house he's never breathed in, though he's hollered and cried on the front lawn some nights. Our boxes taped and ready for another house he will probably never breathe in or even see, though bits of him will sleep there.

something fierce

Mother, Mally, and I were off to her sister's house in Galveston. This was three years ago so I was seven, Mally two. It was January, I know, because we'd just banged New Year's saucepots the night before. Daddy banged the copper bottom like a drummer that morning watching Mother back us out the drive in her Impala wagon. Mally was just to turning two so she was sleeping or cranky or silky-smooth but nothing in between. Stretched out on the bench seat because Mother hated for her to sleep sitting up. I was in the backseat making sure she didn't fly off, my fingernails cutting little grooves in the Naugahyde in between reaching for her every time Mother suddenly got stuck behind a truck of chickens and Mally'd roll forward like a floppy sack of rice.

Mother was wearing pink that day. I remember that. Bright pink on her lips to match. A black scarf covered in red poppies tied around her hair. She was happier then to have Mally, I think; she was somehow more interesting and interested than when it was just us three. Relieved to have a favorite of her own. "How're my girls?" she asked, and I liked being part of something of Mother's, even if only a part.

At some point I sat on the floor behind Mother's seat to keep Mally from landing there. Mother played games.

"Where's Iva? Where's that girl of mine?" she said, 'cause sometimes she didn't know to treat us different. "Did she fly out the window?" She looked all around her. "No, windows are all shut. Did she jump out the tailgate? No, that's locked and I would've heard her thumping on the road. Where could she be?"

I couldn't help giggling, so loud Mally woke and shot right to silk. Mother called back to me, "Oh, Iva, I thought I'd lost you forever!"

That's what I remember of this drive, the way I laughed so hard my ribs ached. I couldn't help that sort of cry that comes over a person, sneaking up in good times then just won't quit. Still laughing, I cried and then Mally cried because she didn't know any better, and Mother sang every song she ever knew.

I don't remember Galveston or Mother's sister. I don't remember my uncle or their daughter or that Mother's sister was pregnant. I could swear that I never even went inside their house because I don't recall a single thing about it. The one thing I know as clear as the taste of pink in bubblegum ice cream is that Daddy came for us.

That night, Mother woke me in a twin bed paired up to another but nobody was in that one. Mally was asleep on her hip and shoulder, one loose arm swinging down into my hair when Mother bent over me. I don't remember finding it strange she was waking me in the dark, or that we were leaving through dark hallways, no hugs or sendoffs—didn't feel one bit strange. I climbed into the way back of the station wagon to fall back asleep. Mother laid Mally beside me in a nest of sweaters and nightgowns. I didn't even know he was there until we were on the road.

I was in and out of sleep, counting the grooves in the pavement between lampposts so I'd know when to shut my eyes to the blast of white. Thirty-four. In between I watched the moon on the stars.

I heard Daddy and Mother talking and thought nothing of it then, though in daylight things would be different. But in the dark on that drive, of course I heard Daddy with us, in the front seat of the car.

"I just couldn't wait," he said.

"This is a problem," said Mother.

"I'm sorry."

Mother was driving. I didn't peek out over the middle seat, but somehow I knew Mother was driving and Daddy was leaning against her, maybe even with his head in her lap, the way I'd seen them do so many times. Like the sight of him is gone in me now, he was gone in that car. I couldn't see him, I only knew how his skin was up against her—had to be up against her. And that he was somehow there.

They talked so tender, not quarreling at all, so soft. "Why not drive the Pontiac down here at least?" Mother asked.

"It'd be just as bad being in separate cars driving back. I need to see you, hear you."

"It's dangerous. Anyone could have picked you up. You're too trusting."

"Yes," he said.

"Oh, Jameson," Mother said.

"I know."

"But you've got no qualms leaving us, go looking for water," she said.

"I got qualms. Let's don't talk about that."

"Hardly a word to where you are, when you're coming back."

"I don't want to," he said. "It comes over me. I start feeling him around and it just comes over me—who we were together, his face turned back over his shoulder to be sure I was there. It all just spins me."

"You can't stand for us to go down to my sister's for the weekend. That baby's coming soon. Just two nights is all you'd have to suffer. She just wanted me for *two* nights."

"Just two nights," he said.

"And so here we are. You've got us. And now you could go, you could run off and where does that leave me?"

"You're right."

"Am I supposed to chase after you?"

"Course not," he said.

"'Cause I won't do it. I won't live like that."

He was quiet a minute and I thought maybe she was letting him sleep now, giving it a rest with so much of her back and forth.

"I was scared," he said real quiet. "I didn't know what I'd do there. If I went. I didn't know what I might do."

"Sweet," Mother said.

"It comes over me."

"You have to fight that."

"I have to fight it."

"Can't you do that for me? Give me that?"

"It spins me."

"Well stand still," she said. "You've got to stand still. Iva's older now. She'll start to wonder where you go. She'll start to feel betrayed."

"I don't want to hurt anyone."

"I know you don't," said Mother.

"I don't think it's controllable," Daddy said. "I don't think it is."

"She'll start to feel betrayed."

"I just couldn't be alone tonight. I just couldn't be without my three girls. It was so dark in the house. It was cold. I sat under the cottonwood. I leaned against it to wait for morning because then it wouldn't be so bad, maybe."

"Shush, baby," Mother said, and I knew she was stroking Daddy's cheek and beard. I knew Daddy was collapsed in Mother's lap. She drove with one eye on the road and one eye on Daddy. Prickling her fingers against his stubbly cheek, smoothing his pink lips. "You need to conquer this feeling. When it comes on you, you're no good—"

"I know, I know."

"You get crazy."

"I get so nervous."

"It was only going to be for the weekend."

"I know, I know. I get so crazy. I get so nervous. I start thinking I'll never see you again. Lilly," he said, "I get to feeling I'll never see you again. And the girls. That I'll go there and I'll step in after him."

"No," she said. "No. Hush."

All I could understand was the sound of their voices. That she was cross and then sad. That he was in one of his panics and then she was able to quiet it, some. The rest was just words I knew but places they made no sense. My name, that Daddy could ever hurt me, that thinking on me was trouble. In daylight, I understood even less. I forgot the sense of the night, the way he was naturally there because he couldn't be anywhere else. I forgot to wonder what's wrong with him. I forgot it all.

Back in Nacogdoches, he woke us by opening up the tailgate and it was like magic. That there was suddenly bright sunshine everywhere. That it was oven-hot morning and we were together and home. Mally squealed to see him there, jabbering the second word she ever learned, "Dadda, Dadda, Dadda!" But he'd come for me, too, and with Mally swung 'round his neck holding on with a fierce baby-grip to his navy-blue turtleneck sweater, he reached for me. He was looking at me. Green eyes that day, green calm eyes. His hands were big, soft, his cheeks rosy above his caramel-colored whiskers.

"There's my girl," he said.

And I was his girl.

"You're a sight, Iva," he said. "A real sight." Mally was squawking still and he tickled her until she turned out loose and scuffing around on the driveway in her footie pajamas.

It was me he wanted.

"Did you have a nice visit?" he asked.

I nodded, though I could not recall anything happening outside of the car.

He reached in for me, kissed me square on the nose, then swooped me up over his shoulder so I hung upside down. *"Here I come with a sack of potatoes,"* he sang carting me along, tossing me left, right, up, down. *"You thought you were a sack of tomatoes."*

Daddy gave me a squeeze so tight I sucked against his shirt for air. He tugged me up from swinging against his back, slid me rightwise so my face and his face were touching and kissing. He went on gripping me tight as Mally gripped him, so tight I could feel it rising in him, something climbing his nerves. "I missed you something fierce," he said. "You won't leave me again, will you?"

Before I could swear away my life — and I wanted to — he'd fought it off.

"Didn't know I'd see you back here this morning," he said, starting to hum again. "Mother cut the visit short again? You know your mother."

Yes, I thought. I knew my mother.

I steal the maps we're done with from the stash of papers and planners underneath the driver's seat of the station wagon. Mother shoves them under, I pull them out when Mally's not looking. Texas, Louisiana. I'm waiting for Mississippi— where he is—waiting, I'm not sure what for. Either I'll rip the creased and tattered thing into shreds or slip it deep inside my pillowcase to sleep with him near. Can't tell which way my mood is blowing and if it weren't so dark out there I'd roll down my window, lick my thumb and see if the wind knows.

Pascagoula. Like a gulp of water at the back of my throat. Like smiling while drinking from a fountain. Pascagoula, Mississippi.

Daddy and I both come from Nacogdoches. Nacogdoches held us whole. We're not even going to be in the same state this time. We're leaving it all.

Soon as we've crossed into Alabama, I'll find the Mississippi coast, leave a crooked finger there on the spot of green all day long. We're long gone from Texas, blinking through dribs and drabs of light and darkness on I-20.

Mally is sleeping wedged into the door and seat. She doesn't want the way back this trip, she's been too worried she'll miss something, she's so excited. All I can think of is the way back that night going home from Galveston when Mother held Daddy to her, drove with him curled like Mally or like me, like any baby of hers sleeping across her lap. We're crossing the corner of Alabama now and I've got Pascagoula in my pillowcase, got Pascagoula in my head.

Mother has been hurrying us along. We've stopped only for bathrooms and three different waffle houses, each time Mother ordering the same thing for us all—like to want something different would complicate who we are, who we love.

"For efficiency," she said the first time we stopped, clapping shut Mally's menu, then mine while I was scanning the listings of eggs and sausage and hash browns. "For solidarity—we're a family, for pity's sake."

So it was Belgian with strawberries at the first place, Belgian with blueberries next, and Belgian powdered with bananas and syrup last.

Across from me in that last booth, Mally had scratched at her head and then her elbow. Her brow grew tight and she made her face pointy at me, wanting me to ask for us both. She tucked the tip of her knife in and out of the cubbies of her waffle, making sure each one got its due of butter. She stopped a second, looked at her plate, its brown waffle and red scatter of berries mashed around. She dipped the tip of her knife into one of the little squares again, but this time she brought it to her mouth and sheepishly licked the butter from it. She glanced at Mother who was busying herself positioning and repositioning her clean fork and knife just right on either side of the plate and not eating.

Mally's knife went back for more butter. She touched each square, tucked the tip of the knife between her lips after each one. She knew I saw her; she wouldn't look at me. She reached out her hand for the knife to scoop into the porcelain butter cup.

"Mally, gross!" I said.

Mother looked up from the napkin she'd pleated over her thighs. "Girls," she said and that was enough, except Mally had to stick out her tongue at me and I kicked her shin once pretty good.

She shrank back against the seat, watching the table next to our booth, the women older than Mother with white hair and lumped bellies. Mally couldn't take her eyes off them, their digging in to the piles of crispy fried potatoes before each of them. Her head lolled to one shoulder and her mouth pushed forward and then open with what was about to be her whining. I slumped down in the seat to reach her under the table and poked the tines of my fork into her leg— just the slightest pricking, no more. Beside me, Mother's eyebrows tugged together in nearly a single dark line across her forehead. Fried potatoes might have been the very edge for her.

So we ate. Our matching waffles. The two of us did. Mother took the bill to the counter to pay and sent me with Mally to the bathroom where I gripped her by the wrists, her soapy hands turning red 'neath the too-hot water. She didn't say a word.

The three of us walked out the restaurant door and the

sky was streaky white with clouds like so many jetstreams. "Look," I said, coming up behind Mally and gently tugging a bit of her hair. "Up there." Her head tipped back and she stood still a moment to take it in. Her square little sneakered feet wide apart for balance, arms at her sides, butter-lips mouthing the word *pretty*. I kissed her cheek.

We took hands and followed Mother to the car.

Now we drive and drive. It's late. Mally sleeps. I watch and wait. Mother is quiet. She pulls one hand off the steering wheel at a time, flexes it open and shut in the air, stretches her long fingers. She rubs her eyes, slaps her cheeks lightly just to keep herself awake. She hums something softly with the radio. She punched every button to tune in something other than static what seems ages ago, has settled on a faint signal from Memphis.

The front seat is a different universe. One where I do not belong. The light's different, bluer, silvery. The air is cool. Watching the back of her head, the way she stretches her neck to one shoulder then the next, seeing her touch her hair but decide not to readjust it, I have a word for her. She is *exquisite*. Daddy used to say so. And when I asked he'd say, *like a queen, she's regal and perfect.*

Yes, exquisite.

I believe she may know French and every song ever written. Her hair's falling from its side-combs and now she does decide to replace one. She pushes it up into her dark hair and flips it back on itself to hold. I've seen her do this a zillion times. I've seen her slender wrist turn 'round on itself, her long fingers push-pull-push, as if the entire procedure of setting her hair back to its exquisite perfection were nothing. As if she didn't even know her hand were moving. As if all it were was a heartbeat that goes on without any thought or choosing.

I could count grooves in the pavement between lampposts, but instead go to her. I climb into the front seat. I sit straighter up here, my lungs small inside my ribs. Somehow, I believe my being near will change the way she's sighing and humming and feeling glum.

"Iva," she says to me.

I look at her, lamplight quick on her then gone for twenty grooves.

"Long drive, isn't it?"

"Mm-hmm."

"We're closing in on our new home," she says and smiles like when there's no time to rebraid Mally's hair and there's a big snaggy loop sticking up out of one of the sides. "Come on now, sweet-thing, lie down." She puts her hand to my face and pulls me near her.

All I wanted until this very moment was to lie in her lap like Daddy, for her to want me to lie in her lap like him. But there is a way Mother has of breathing, like it's trouble, it's work, but she could go on for centuries without sleep or air or love. So I sit. I sit beside Mother. A stream's low in the gully by this highway, following us silver-touched by moon and stars. I push my pillow into the tiny hollow our bodies are making not quite touching. I lean into it, let her lean, too.

Pascagoula sleeps between us but Mother and I slap our cheeks and hum to stay awake.

faith

Daddy was out the door, already creaking the car door shut, when Mother screamed. I ran for ice for her finger instead of running for him because I needed something sure and at least ice took some time before melting. But there he was kneeling with her over the old strips of nightgowns she was trying to make into something early this morning. Kissing her. Speaking to her. Holding my ice to her even though the cold or the cut or him coming back was making her shake and cry and look like there was rain in her eyelashes. "You promised," she was saying, and all he could answer was "Love."

She'd slipped while cutting three flannel layers at a time, snipped off the tip of her fourth left finger with the pinking shears. Now what remained was jagged and she was turning white with towels and ice wrapped so thickly she looked like a boxer. Mally was draped across her, kissing Mother till she fell asleep mid-smooch, lips suctioned to Mother's chin.

So Daddy and I were on a mission to save her and

wherever he went, he went fast. Ordinarily I was dragged so my tennies turned black on the toes. But that day I was keeping up 'cause I couldn't bear to think of Mother's bit of finger lying in the sink. We were speeding to the Aldey Street stores; he'd promised me something I can't recall. I was seven, I think—maybe some bit less or more but near seven because that was the way I parted my hair there in the glass of the Krest window. Down the middle, a tight fancy French braid on either side of my head. Red yarn ribbons 'round the bottoms because Daddy braided me this morning before he decided to go and Mother decided to pull out the mending, and red was his favorite.

"Will she be all right?" I asked.

"Fine."

"She should go to the doctor."

"You heard her. She won't go."

"Will it stop bleeding?"

"Eventually."

"Will it grow back?"

Daddy stopped to look at me like I'd had a very good idea.

"Starfish do," I said.

"I'm certain of it," he said, his voice high like a chittery sparrow. His hand snug around mine.

"You shouldn't go on your trips," I told him. "We always end up needing you."

He didn't answer that, just tugged me into the Krest, and walked right to the man in a white smock at the back counter. The Answer Man, that's what Daddy called him. I was supposed to get gauze and wraps and bandages and anything that came in a glass bottle with a dropper. Daddy forgot his promise and I said not a word, though I'd already picked out a banana Laffy Taffy from the rack by the register. I set it back in its box without him seeing. He paid for the sack of supplies and we were off up the street again. He said I was smart, knowing to go for the ice. I stretched that like taffy yellow and gooey on my tongue and it was just as juicy-good.

❋ ❋ ❋

When we got home, Mother's face was wet. Daddy peeled Mally off of her and laid her down onto the foot of the sofa. He unwrapped Mother's glove, kissing her sticky cheek when she gasped for air. She was waving her good hand back and forth like a light bulb flickering.

"You sure you want to see this, Iva?" he asked.

"I'm not sure *I* want to see this," said Mother.

I nodded, felt green, nodded again. He touched the top of my head and sort of shook it a little, looking up at me, squinting some to take me in. "I got the ice," I said on my behalf.

"You got the ice," he said, flashing me his big white teeth through a grin off to one side.

He went back to work on her, got down to the soppy red of the dishtowel I'd wrapped the ice in. Some of the watery blood ran down Mother's wrist. He pried off the last bit of washcloth and I fell a little, ended up sitting on the rim of the couch.

"Easy there," he said to me. "Oh, it's not so bad, Lilly."

She started to look so he twisted her hand away from her. She leaned back again.

"Just the tippiest of the tip," he said. "Iva's convinced it'll grow back."

"I don't believe it anymore," I said.

"It's that bad?" Mother strained to see again.

Daddy was oozing all sorts of ointments over the tip of her finger—every single one I'd taken from the shelf: first a white cream, then clear gel, a liquid brown, and finally something pink and foamy from its tube. She was a mess but with all that muck covering up the wound, her finger ended up looking a half inch longer than it should have been before the scissors. He folded gauze over the tip, then began winding it up in a stretchy ankle wrap.

"Will I live?" Mother asked once he had kissed her again and was done.

"You'll live," he said. "Iva, clean up this mess for your daddy."

I picked up the boxes and plastic wrappers. I loaded them into the Krest sack with all of the dribbly mess in the bottom. When she sat up there was some color coming back into her face. I went after Daddy to tell him she was feeling better and found him bent over the toilet coughing and wiping at his mouth with a perfectly folded washcloth. "We saved her," I said. He nodded and shut the door.

* * *

Mother didn't cook for a few days. She poured the milk and juice but Daddy was the one feeding us, making his special rice and chili and hotdogs all those nights. Soon she was down to just gauze over her finger and after we finished putting away the lunch dishes one day, she felt up to washing her shears. I sat on the counter, holding them under the water. She was scrubbing at the dried blood with her good hand, looking hard, studying each point and V along the blades for where she went wrong.

Her left hand was on the rim of the sink, trying to keep

out of the water. I twisted my head to the side to see if blood had soaked through. I touched my finger to her knuckle, walked it up the bandage.

"Careful," she said, still looking at the pinking shears.

I felt the strip of white skin across the base of her finger. It was softer, so slick to be almost sticky when I traced it. I pointed my finger to that spot. "Did you lose them?" I said.

She picked herself up from leaning, looked at her hand, seemed to have to concentrate to know what it was I was saying. "They're in my jewelry bowl."

"Can I?"

"*May* I," she corrected me, then relaxed her shoulders by rolling them back one at a time. She liked to work on her posture and thought of it at odd times. Her eyes settled on me. "If you play nicely," she said, then took the scissors from me, gripping them awkwardly with her bandaged hand—just looped around her thumb, dangling in midair like they were too dangerous to hang on to.

Mother's tiny and I'm not, so her rings fit my index finger then and that's how I wore them. Daddy always said I've got his bones, that I'd be tall and strong and it was 'cause of the milk and him; Mother liked to say I was well on my way and she'd give a little sigh and start checking the lines of her bankbook. One ring was her engagement ring. It was old, and had been somebody else's first. It read *Faith* on the inside, and Mother said she was never sure if that was the name or the promise that first went with this ring. She liked to think it was the name, because, "love shouldn't be about hoping on promises." Daddy once said hoping's all there is. This ring had two small diamonds sitting up high in a rectangle off the band. The wedding ring had a few tiny diamonds, with nothing written in it. When I get married I want a ring that says *Faith* because it's the hope not the name.

That night I ate supper wearing Mother's rings. Daddy'd made tacos which he said were to be festive; he was pretending it was my engagement party. Each time I set down the chip basket or cheese dish on the table, he asked me to get up and curtsy.

"Whewee," he said. "That thing could poke out an eye. Just who are you loving so much gives you a ring the size of Mars and Mercury held together with a kiss?"

"Just for tonight," Mother said, "then right back in the bowl." She watched me eat taco after taco, making sure I wasn't going to eat her diamonds.

Mally made a mess in the highchair tray, of lettuce and cheese strips and canned corn. I scooped up a bite on a taco chip for her and moved the rings to my other hand under the table, then fed her the chip and Mother about lost her mind thinking Mally'd swallowed her rings.

"Ta da!" I held up my other hand where they were sparkling away at her. Daddy laughed, Mally looked to Mother and made that face she had just before she'd cry a fit-and-a-half.

"Enough, Iva," Mother said. "Put them back now." She petted Mally's hair, stroked her out of the storm before it started.

"Lilly, ease up."

"*Now*, Iva," she said.

"If you're not wearing them…," he started but then just looked at her.

She lifted Mally out of the high chair and started clearing the table, Mally squirming on one hip, tugging at the air wanting something more. Daddy tried to wipe at Mally's cheeks and hands, but Mother swung around so he couldn't get at her face. Still, he scrubbed away at her fist until she gave a whimper and Mother shot him a look. He went back to the table for more dishes.

"And don't let the baby see where you put them," Mother said to me, setting Mally up on the counter over the dishwasher, so I couldn't figure how she was a problem. "Last thing I need's her choking on a cloudy old set of mismatched diamonds."

Daddy stood alone in the doorway. He watched her working at the sink and took a step back from the room and from her. Then he changed. To her back he gave half a smile and went to her. Slid his arms around Mother and held her from behind. The two of them swaying side to side like there was music. He whispered and loved her. For me, I knew; he was doing it to make her kind again. "Easy," he said low to her.

"Stop it," she said. She unhitched his arms, and handed them back. "Doesn't change a damned thing."

I went to their room. I even sucked the salt and cheese smears from the band and rubbed both rings clean in my T-shirt before dropping them into the bowl, *clink-clink*.

❀ ❀ ❀

In the morning, Daddy came to check on me in bed. He was going on another mission—taking the good car, Mother's car, the car that ran properly then, and going somewhere we didn't know. I wasn't allowed to go because he said someone had to watch Mother.

"Her finger might grow back," he said, trying to tuck the sheet up under my chin but I pushed it back down. "Just like you said, and someone's got to be here to stop it from getting too long—you know your mother has a hard time saying no."

I giggled at the picture in my head of her fourth finger dragging to her knees, and because "no" was certainly not what my mother had trouble saying. He tickled my belly. I kicked him in the back—couldn't help it. So he sat plop on my wriggly legs.

"How will I know if it's grown back?" I asked.

"I just performed the unveiling. No more bandage."

"Did it?"

"I'm leaving that to you," he said, covering his eyes. "I didn't look."

"Don't go," I said, gripping his thumb.

"Got to."

"Where?"

"A little lake."

"Why?"

"Got to."

"Why?"

"You know me."

"Why?" I said too loud.

"Hush," he whispered, his finger to my lips.

"Let me come."

"No, lump," he said, rubbing noses. "It's early. Be back for lunch."

"Today?"

He shut the door behind him. My room was dark gray. The bed long and sheets suddenly too hot. I kicked them off. I lay on my back. I flopped to one side. I heard the front door, the engine start up, and felt my belly drop like at the bottom of a hill if he drove it fast enough without braking at the bottom even though the sign said STOP.

✿ ✿ ✿

I went looking for Mother because she wasn't in the kitchen. The house was cold. The lights were out, and there wasn't any sun coming through the curtains. I went to her bedroom, the door shut like maybe I'd dreamt it and they slept now. I listened at Mally's door: quiet, too. I went back up the hall, put my hand on the knob and it was warm. I eased open their door and saw the bed unmade. She was at the window watching the road, sitting on the bench with her feet up and her arms around her legs, the pile of nightgowns and the sewing box open at her feet. She had the pinking shears in her hand and was holding her left hand over the closed blades, working them open inside her hand, feeling the metal.

"Did it grow back?" I asked.

She looked at the tip a minute, then held it out for me. "No, baby, it didn't. I think there's only so much a body can take." She looked at me a funny way, with big full eyes like I wasn't the one she was seeing. "But I never thought it would heal so fast."

I held her hand beneath my face, one hand to each side of it, checking the end of her finger. It still looked chewed, red and ragged, and still a hair shorter than her right fourth finger. I went to her jewelry bowl for her rings.

"Not today, Iva," she said.

"Not for me," I said, "for you." I started to slide them back up her finger.

But she stopped me at the first knuckle. "Not today."

"It still hurts?"

"Mmm," she said, taking them off over her fingertip. "Insult to injury and all that." She was fitting her fingers one by one inside the shears, not even watching, clamping the bite of the blades down around a knuckle, then the next and the next until she started over at her first finger.

"Mother," I said.

She wouldn't look at me. "This one on purpose," she said, pulling her ring finger out of the shears. "This particular one. But still he goes." She studied the end. "It's not even truly healed yet."

"Will it scar?"

"Certainly. It already has."

I showed her the smears of smooth white skin across my knees where I'd skinned them falling too many times. "Just like this?" I asked her because I thought those scabs and the new skin they made were lucky and sometimes ran my fingers over the patches, wishing on them at night.

"No. Meaner. Uglier looking. Gruesome and awful."

I walked away from her. I knew my mother and so I walked away from her before I could make it any worse, make her anymore hateful. But there was the dark hall and there was the bed. I checked her clock: 4:14, it said. I climbed in their bed, snuggled into his pillow. I could smell him there in the covers. Thick and warm, the way he smelled before dressing. I was still holding on to her rings, fingering the worn-smooth inside, the name or the word, setting my first finger just so it held on to that little bit of something. "What will we have for lunch today?" I asked, feeling dreamy.

She didn't answer, just stayed at the window working her shears until Mally cried and I woke and the three of us started up another day waiting.

Mother says Tennessee like she means it, with all the Ns and Es. But our boxes sit four to the ceiling and we've been here four months. Tennessee in autumn is cold where we are, and I like that. These days, Mally runs around in galoshes without socks, and long underwear. I launch paper-boat notes to Mother in the creek.

When she comes to tuck us in, Mother says, "Hopewell," like it's the name of a poem she's about to read to us. "I chose it for the name, you know. We'll last here," she says.

I'm not so sure and give her a look to tell her so.

"You'll grow up here," she says. "This one will count; we'll make it the one that counts. Now go to sleep."

Mally's got the shredding satin binding up to her chin. She squeezes her eyes shut, pretends to be asleep.

"This," Mother says, her arms spreading wide in a formal show, "is our transition house—though we'll stay in Tennessee forever. It's cramped here, I know." She's kneeling over our bed, smiling big and wide and trying to make me believe her. "The two of you sharing a room is only temporary," she says. "We're saving."

We are in a permanent state of temporary.

I hear things in this house the same way I did before Daddy left us or maybe we left him—things of who did what to whom aren't so clear as Mother says. Back then I'd go to them, to Daddy and Mother, because the voice said so—just a kind of buzz in my ear, a kind of absence of sound. I felt it in me like a shadow covering only face. They'd be reading or in bed or cross with each other and refusing to talk, so she'd send me out to play or back to bed. Sometimes Daddy winked and said, "Just this once, sugar-pie." Sometimes Mother wouldn't shake out the paper at me.

It's clear, I think, that I'm losing him. I can't remember how he said goodnight anymore—if it was a kiss or hug or both. Mother says she can't recall not being alone. So when I slip into her room because the buzzing voice has made me need her beyond all else, and I'm extra quiet or she's extra deep, I don't wonder if she thinks I'm him. Even sleeping, she says *Iva* and turns back to her dreams.

Mally and I share my bed here and I don't like it one bit. She slobbers her pillow and elbows my ear. She flops and kicks all night, throws off the covers then grabs back at them. It's not in the night she pees herself, but at school. She's having trouble there. And the nurse always calls me down like I'll know what to do with her. I just stand still watching while Miss Lobell pulls off her bottoms and hands her a clean set of underwear and pants. When she's busy writing notes in the other room, Mally says, "Sometimes I just can't make it there in time."

"Ask the teacher to let you go," I say, knowing how dumb it sounds as any sort of a fix.

Mally scratches her side where the new wool pants make her itchy first. "I don't want to bother everything," she says.

Since we moved here, Mally looks very round—always tucking in to herself like a hedgehog, but she's got no quills.

Miss Lobell's notes for Mother are a daily occurrence. When I walk Mally back to class in someone else's bottoms, she says "Could you keep it?" I say nothing but fold the *Dear Mrs. Giles* into a paper-boat like Daddy used to show me. On the way, Mally watches me set each one afloat in the creek that walks us home.

Only on the first day she came home in new clothes did Mother ask Mally about the blue and white checked pants, the matching vest. "What're you in, love?" she asked, picking pills of rolled lint off Mally's shoulder and then a side-seam.

"Oh," Mally said, looking down at herself, "I got the wrong ones after nap."

"What a silly," Mother said and Mally walked to the kitchen for a bread and butter sandwich, moving slowly like to go unnoticed.

Mother did not seem to wonder then or now why Mally's taking off her clothes for morning nap, just washed and folded the outfits for Mally to take back to school the next day. And she does not notice the way Mally walks and stands—with legs apart, twitching away from the rash burning the insides of her legs. Or that she turns her back to Mother when stepping into the tub with me on shower nights. Mother doesn't notice a thing. I never see Mally with a bag of the clothes; her own from that day sit buried in her closet and Mother says our room smells like cat. Mother is peculiar here and some nights I tell Mally what I've been noticing, but she doesn't want it in her head so she scrunches up her eyelids some more and rolls up tight in a ball beneath the covers.

❊ ❊ ❊

"You're racing tonight, Iva," Mother says. My forehead is clammy and Mother pulls away her hand quick, quicker than she means to. Her fingers go to her side, wiping on the edge of her wraparound skirt. But she doots my nose once with her fingertip, like she used to, when I was younger. She bends over us, over me first. Her face hovers there like a spaceship going to land, her coming in for a kiss. But it doesn't. She doesn't.

She folds more of the blanket up under Mally's arms. "Was school okay?" she asks. I don't answer because she isn't even listening for my voice. She looks at me like she hasn't seen me in two years. There aren't any clues to what she wants. She stares with dark pupils overtaking the color of her irises.

Mother turns off the light and leaves.

"Sometimes," I whisper into Mally's hair, "I wish she were different."

Mally doesn't answer.

"Sometimes," I say again, "I wish she were him."

She kicks me once, hard, and then turns to the wall.

❊ ❊ ❊

This morning the nurse calls me down from Music class. Mrs. Harris stops "O Shenandoah" right in the middle of the round she'd worked so hard at timing. "Iva, Miss Lobell wants you," she says. It's beginning to weigh on me, the number of times I'm pulled from class. The girls with satin ribbons in their hair have been giving me dirty looks for some time now. And the girls with yarn ribbons have just started to watch me in the same way. No doubt they're all thinking disease: flu, strep, lice.

I walk quietly to the office with Miss Lobell, who does not speak one word to me, but smiles when she turns around. Her shoes squeak on the checkerboard floor. Her stiff white pants whistle. She opens the clinic door but Mally isn't there, standing in soaked pants or in new pants. She isn't there at all.

"Iva, I haven't heard a word from your mother," says Miss Lobell. "What she intends to do. About Mallory." She stops there like I'll know what to say, repins one piece of hair behind her ear. "Are things all right at home?" She kneels in front of me and my belly drops like coming over the top of a hill so fast in the car; I could tell her anything about Mother. Anything at all.

"Your father isn't with you?" she asks.

I don't seem able to answer that. Either way. I don't think she's got any right to him, to thinking about him, to asking things and judging him. I don't say a word. Don't even nod but notice when I look at her only one of my eyes is really doing the looking. Like Daddy showed me how and Mally hated it, that we could look halfsies and she couldn't. I start with my left, then shift to my right.

"And you still say your mother's not had a phone installed yet?"

That's what I told her the day of Mally's second accident when she shivered and shook so bad, fearing that I'd really tell Mother that time. Miss Lobell gave Mally's wet jeans to the lunch lady to dry in an oven.

She slips her hand inside her white nurse shirt, above

the zipper, to tug on a brastrap fallen over her shoulder. "I suppose I'll try one more note home with you," she says. "You are giving the notes to your mother, aren't you?"

I nod halfway.

"Good girl." She hands me another folded square of paper. I get up to go, my hand on the doorknob. "Oh, there's one more thing," she says. "The slacks, Iva. I need all of the slacks laundered and back by Monday; we're getting down to bare shelf, I'm afraid. Is a weekend enough time for your mother?"

I step on only white squares back to Music. The pants. I haven't seen them, the sacks Mother puts them in for Mally to return—and she never does, just totes her Miss Piggy lunchbox and a Hello Kitty pencil box to and from school. Red corduroy. Blue and white checked. Red plaid. Blue something. Green. I can't come up with them all. I concentrate, make a list in my head. But soon as I remember a new pair, I've lost two from the start of the list. There's Mother at home moving through the house touching things, just letting her fingers pass lightly over the surfaces of what's ours: the kitchen table, three chairs; her garden bucket that sits in the hall closet; a stack of books she never opens anymore. And now this piece of paper. This isn't my doing.

I never wanted Tennessee.

❊ ❊ ❊

"You need to give back the pants," I tell Mally on the way home.

She kicks at old sweet gum balls, knocking them into the creek that runs fast and cold these days.

"Where are they?" I ask her.

"Stop it."

"I thought up at least six pairs but you've probably got twelve or twenty by now. You need to find them."

She walks close to the water's edge, lets her feet trace the creekbank, knowing I'll have to tell Mother.

❉ ❉ ❉

On Saturday Mother takes us hiking in the Smokies. She looks all right. What it is, I think, is that she's trying awfully hard. She gets excited. "We should always start our years hiking. The air's better up high."

We're standing on an overlook and she takes it all in—the view below and then above, letting her arms stretch up high over her head like a long, pointed leaf. And for a moment, because of such a soft wind, Mother's shut eyes while she's breathing, and the way, standing beside her I am entirely separate, I think maybe she'll fall.

But she turns up the mountain, keeps on.

"We'll always come hiking no matter the occasion," she says.

Mally tugs at Mother's coat sleeve, pulls her down and kisses her lips. I know what she's doing, buttering up Mother for when I have to tell her about Miss Lobell's pants. But there's more than that. At every turn on the Old Sugarlands Trail, Mally tugs Mother down for another kiss. It's as though Mally can't help kissing her, can't help knowing that Mother needs such a thing, can't help but give it over. They've had this forever, almost like Mally's still swelling Mother's belly, still sharing every thread.

Mother shakes some getting at the map, like she's nervous not to already know the paths, like she should have studied up. She fusses over the intersections of red, blue, and green lines to get us to Little Pigeon River because Mally liked the name. We stand on Alum Cave Bluff and Mother reads from the brochure: "During the Civil War, the Confederacy mined saltpeter here, which resulted in a series of bluffs."

"What's that?" Mally asks Mother.

"The salty white stuff on salami sticks," I tell her.

She wrinkles her nose. "That's dirt?"

Mother spots turkey vultures circling and lifts Mally high to see over the endless mountain laurel. When she sets her back down, Mother takes Mally's hand and holds it all the way up Brushy Mountain and then all the way down. I hang back. I watch the hungry birds.

Driving out of the park through Gatlinburg, Mally's squeezed between Mother and me onto the bump holding Mother's purse, though she's really too big for sitting on the bump. She watches for shifts in the road and pretends to tip over onto us when Mother turns the car.

"Quit it," I say, pushing her back up.

But the road winds tight to the mountain here, and Mally's back on me.

"Get off," I say, gripping her arm hard.

"Ow!" Mally stomps her sneaker onto my jeans. I poke her big toe through the canvas, hold on it.

"Enough," Mother says. "Now."

"I'm carsick and she's falling all over me," I say.

"She hurt me."

"We've had such a nice time," Mother says. "Don't wreck it."

Mally leans her head onto Mother's shoulder. "I was just trying to have fun," she says. "Iva's in a mood."

I watch hikers out the window, families with purple

backpacks, brothers tugging up groundcover to shred while walking, sisters squeezing hands, mothers and fathers.

"Mother, you know those pants," I say, looking right at Mally.

"Momma, see the pretty trees," she says. "Look at them all. There are a lot, aren't there a lot of trees?"

Mother faces out her window, takes in the woods lining our roadway. "What pants, Iva?"

Mally turns to me. Just the same way she saved Mother, she knows what I need and gives it. Her face is small and suddenly calm. This isn't the time, it's telling me. We're sisters stuck here.

Mother drives on, not asking any questions, just forgetting it all. But Mally sings the meatball song to fill up the air just in case.

"Look at all those trees," Mother says, but not like Mally who sees them once then is bored. Mother points through the windshield to the left, then right, and left again — naming each of the trees although most are leafless now. "Hickory, beech, buckeye, magnolia, sugar maple, eastern hemlock, and Carolina silverbell." She knows them by their bark and habit. She knows how they stand.

Tonight Mother removes a foil-wrapped pack of meatballs from the freezer. "A theme dinner," she announces. "But Mally has to serenade my cooking. Iva, you too."

"On top of Old Smokey…," starts Mally, and I switch back and forth between humming and saying the words while I set the table.

We eat the meatballs and Mally slurps her noodles. "Elbows off the table," Mother tells me. Mally's smeared herself good with the sauce, made a real mess of her shirt.

"Let me see it better," Mother says. She goes to stand beside Mother who dabs water on her T-shirt where the sauce has dripped.

"You've done a number on it, duck. Give it to me and go get another."

Mally lifts her arms and Mother slides off the shirt, leaves her plate to run hot water on the stains. Mally's not back yet. I pull the note from my pocket, slip it onto the counter. The paper's soft and worn now, it's been hiking and to bed. She doesn't open it. She barely touches the note sliding it into her own pocket. She won't look at me. I want to tell her it's not about me—I'm okay, I'm good.

"Iva, clear the table, please," she says.

Mally comes running in squealing about our trip. "I never seen so many trees," she says. "They were everywhere. And it's not flat as a board either! Not like Texas."

"I liked Tyler just fine," I say, the past tense of it socking me low in the belly. "I like Nacogdoches even better."

"Let's hush on that, Mally," Mother says. "Let's just all of us hush and think before we speak," and she looks right at me. She leaves the kitchen, shuts her bedroom door behind her.

Mally turns to me. She knows.

"Want me to brush your hair?" I ask, hooking a finger in the neck of her T-shirt. Needing to touch her without looking her in the eyes.

"No."

"I'll French braid."

"Go away," she says and runs to our room.

I wash the dishes. Run the water high like if it were a bath. I squirt in too much soap and then swish it around to fluff the bubbles. Spaghetti sauce bleeds from its pot and I run my fingers through the greasy orange. I'm nobody anyone wants to see right now. Anyhow, I like the suds up to my elbows.

Behind me I hear Mother's door open, our door shut. There's something happening between them and I'm outside of it again. Mother is loving Mally. Intensely, I can feel it. I hear a whisper so soft it's nothing at all. She's telling Mally how fine she'll be, how lots of girls have accidents, how maybe even she did when she was little. She's setting Mally to rights. If she's careful, and I believe she is, Mother's probably even coaxing Mally to love me still despite my siding up with Miss Lobell.

But there is a hole to all of this hushed soothing. They're not talking about him, about the move, or any of it that I can see is changing each one of us. They're leaving that outside the door, pushing it in here, in the kitchen with me. They're hugging, singing, just sorting through the night to find each other to hold. And that may do it. That may trick them both into thinking they're enough. But I'm here. In the kitchen. With the move and the voice and with Daddy, and nothing they can sing will work it out of me.

Now Mally's in with Mother in her room, sitting in her laundry basket like we used to play submarines. I slip into bed, tighten my eyes down so they know I want none of it.

* * *

I was wrong.

Monday morning Mother has boxes open in the kitchen, she's double-wrapping plates. "Morning, sleepy-head," she says, grinning and darting around the room.

I stand frozen looking at how much they've got wrapped already.

"We're moving, Iva," Mally squeals, jumping, swirling the moving paper as a cape around her shoulders.

"No school today," Mother says, trying to make friends, to cozy up. "I'll call."

"I like school just fine," I say.

"Well go if you like," she says. "There's no telling how long before the place sells. It's no beaut. And it certainly isn't on the Dogwood Arts tour. Next time we rent."

"Next time?"

"We're moving! We're moving!" Mally sings like the satin ribbon girls jumping rope on the playground. Jessica and Sue. I hate them. I hate their ribbons. I hate their noses, their pink pencil cases. I cut my eyes at Mally, hate her this instant.

"Home?" I ask.

"Iva, don't start."

"Down the road a bit. A different street. Somewhere bigger?"

Mother holds my head, bends down to kiss me in the ear. "Just away," she says.

I start for school.

I get as far as our front steps, then sit down on the stoop. I blow on my hands to keep them steamy-warm. Envelopes are sticking out of the black mail pouch beside the door. Mother says the mail comes early here, don't even bother checking. I haven't seen one of his envelopes the whole four months we've been in Hopewell. Not a single return address for me to run my finger over, match the curve of his hand to what I think I know of him, for me to know he's still out there, stuffing his envelopes with wadded dollars and heavy coins weighing down one end of the letter. It's as though no one even knows we exist.

No one calls but the PTA and Mother says, "Oh yes, I'll be at the meeting Tuesday night—with bells on," but she never goes. She promises two dozen brownies and three dozen melt-aways for the bake sale, but she never makes them. She loads dresses in the car, records and little paintings off the walls, too. Coming home from school, I peer into the way back of our station wagon and it's stark empty.

Sometimes she goes out in the day and I'm never sure where she goes or if she'll be here when Mally and I come home. In she walks with a quart of milk but the carton's soft and swollen for sitting too long in the car. Or she's found a pack of PAAS Easter egg dye pellets at the thrift store and twists our undies in twine, soaks them, and calls it tie-dye. These are her busy days. Other times we walk in and I wonder if she's even moved since breakfast.

These days, today, I look at Mother and she's pale and dry and old, the scar over her right eye from a wreck with Daddy years before me looks to have fallen lower. He used to set his finger there when they'd kiss doing dishes, he used to touch her so much. Then I'd reach up a hand to make out the lump. "Careful," she'd say, pulling back from me. "You could push the glass into my brain." I would have been just as careful as Daddy. I watched him. I was just as gentle.

The rusty lid of the mailbox makes not one sound from my hand flipping it open. I pull out Mother's letters just to see, because maybe there's more going on here than I know. But they're just bills she's paying. Gas, Water.

"Those for me?" I about pee myself like Mally. It's the mailman and he's big, blocking all the light to our front door. I nod and he takes them from me, puts two new envelopes in my hand. Looking for Pascagoula, Nacogdoches, or someplace we've never been, I read the return addresses. Tyler, the movers who brought us here—looking for their money, no doubt. Knoxville, just Mother's new Winn-Dixie charge. That's it.

I walk the creekbank, tell myself there's time to sit before school. I pull off my shoes and socks, kick my feet in the icy water. Mother says we shouldn't touch it, there's all sorts of trash running through the creek. There isn't much, really—a can every once and again. A Dilly's BarBQ napkin. But today it runs pretty clean. Now that we're going, I can't bear it. I don't want to leave Tennessee, move one more step away from these mountains and him. I lie back, watch the moon that's been left out all night. It's powdery, looks chalked onto the sky. *La luna*, Mother used to say when she saw me gazing up when we were crossing a street, drawing the curtains, or driving late—my head leaning back, my mouth hanging open. "La luna," she'd say and tell me all the world's lovelier by it, especially little blonde girls. I thought she meant Mally, but I still loved the moon.

Now I can hardly feel my toes, but something's tickling my ankle and once Mother said snakes can swim and burrow their homes into mud. I pull my feet out right quick, and there stuck in the roots and vines coming out of the creek-wall, is a bit of something, a mangled boat of paper. I open it carefully so as to memorize its folds. What it is is a slip from Benny's Drugmart on Twelfth and Locust just downtown, for something never picked up. Water has bled the ink of the name, but I can sort of make out a big J, a fat loopy G starting the last name. I roll over on the grass, spread the paper to dry before me. I watch it—for hours and hours, it seems.

I know papers like this one. I know them same as my toes or my sister's voice or my mother's way of looking without really seeing a thing. Daddy used to pace the aisles of Striplings Drug trying to decide—if he wanted what the Answer Man put in little brown bottles stuffed deep with yellow cotton wads to keep the pills from chipping to dust, or if he didn't. He showed me. 'cause sometimes he would go back to the counter when the man said it'd be ready, sometimes we'd buy the bottles. I was the one he took. Then I was the one running after him to the nearest water. Mostly the deep and wandery Angelina so near us, but sometimes east into Louisiana for the Red, or off the edge of our world altogether all the way south to the Gulf. And sometimes when he couldn't wait a second more and he was shaking and almost falling over, he settled for the shallow water in a piddly fountain out front of the bank. If he had paid for the bottle, he'd pour the white pills, the blue ones like buttons, fizzing, clouding into the water. If not, he'd fold all the corners, crimp them tight, and then it was a boat swimming away. He taught me this, where to fold the paper: starting off symmetrical, then getting tricky with creasing thirds. How to make it tight. To make it float.

It is possible. That he's here, in Hopewell. That he has sent a boat down this creek to me. It is possible. I dry my feet on my socks then put my shoes back on. I walk up the creekbank looking for him, for where he may have set his boat in. I watch for more and when I see something, anything, I lean out over the water to get it. So far only bits of Styrofoam gone murky with silt. I keep walking. I reach the schoolyard and it's recess. I see Jessica and Sue, see the sun glinting off candy green and lilac satins holding their hair. I see the girls with yarn ribbons, too, and both groups see me. He wouldn't have stood for it, for my walking around like an unfrosted cake; he'd have brought me home a length of red satin ribbon, tied the bow himself each morning before school. I turn around. I leave, 'cause she said we didn't have to go—but mostly 'cause he wouldn't want me here, not like this. I walk home feeling the press of the quiet coming over me, that something-voice squeezing the air out of me.

My sleeves are wet, my teeth chatter. Mother and Mally are wrapping saucepots and skillets. "Where's your jacket, Iva?" is all she says.

In my room I smooth the blue slip of paper again, study it, drag my finger along each run of ink. I pull my photo of him from my drawer, the one of just him and me floating in sand. It has been almost two years since I've been his daughter truly. I cannot recall the night that Mother says he came to pick us up, her included, and drove like hellfire out of Nacogdoches for no reason at all, singing the Texas river song all the way. Mother says she had to step on the brake right over his feet which were both pressing the gas. She says Mally and I were sleeping, that we didn't know what was going on and she shouldn't have said anything but Mother was so scared that night and the morning after. Mally cried all the drive back to our house. I do remember that. I remember I kept calling to him from the backseat; he wasn't up front—or anywhere—something I refused to believe, so I kept on saying, "Daddy? Daddy." And every time I said it she turned her head out the side window so that I couldn't see her and all she said was "hush."

Later, I lay pressed into the seatback and Mally's sleeping hands. I was tired and finally quiet, feeling the hum of our tires over the asphalt come up through the car and into my shoulders and head. Over and over Mother whispered, "I was scared, I was so scared for you." By the rearview mirror I saw the way her hand lay in a fist right over her heart. "It's temporary," she whispered, "he's not himself." Daddy came back so much later, stiff and purple-faced with presents for us all— pen flashlights and plastic shoehorns—and Mother sang us to sleep, bent to kiss us whispering about his being back to normal.

He's here. I can feel him.

※ ※ ※

The next day the packing's nearly done. Seems so few boxes this time. She won't say when we'll go, just whistles and tapes down lids and walks around the house swinging open cupboards to check for certain are they empty then swings them shut.

I slept with the drugstore ticket and the picture of Daddy and me at the beach under my pillow last night, have the ticket smoothed in my pocket today. Tennessee's growing colder by the minute, so I've got my jacket on. I wait for the mail again. No letters from Mother to hand over, but I'll sit on the front steps just the same, then look for more of Daddy's paper-boats in the creek. Mother's in the kitchen baking, letting Mally scrape the sides of the bowl with the rubber spatula, pretending not to notice her licking the spatula after each turn 'round the bowl. She and Mally are giddy; they like the new plan.

The mailman comes, giving me the once-over. "Shouldn't you be in school?" he asks.

"My father's coming," I say.

He nods slowly like he thinks I'm lying or I'm a fink, but

he gives me the mail anyway. A sale book for Hopewell restaurants we've never been to and three envelopes: Tyler, Tyler, Tyler.

I walk the creek anyhow. I stumble through the roots of a silver maple. I watch a crook-tailed dog skim the water on the other side of the creek. She's looking at me and the hang of her lips tells me she knows there's no hope. I walk to Benny's Drugmart. I walk the aisles as slowly as I can. I look for him. I smile at old ladies fussing through their coupons. They stop long enough to study me head to toe. I pick up a package of baby wipes so they'll think I've been sent by someone old enough to have a list that needs filling. It's mostly old people in here, especially around the pharmacy counter in back. A man asks me to reach a little blue bottle from a bottom shelf for him, some sort of special itching shampoo. I walk the aisles, I watch.

Then I go to the counter, get up the nerve to say anything to the man in a white jacket. "Yes?" he says, "Yes?" The skin on his long nose is red and thick, bumped with white scabs. He's no Answer Man.

"Have you…seen—"

"I've got no time for this, girlie."

"I found something," I start, but his cheeks are leathery and dented all over, his eyes are nothing but mean, and I worry he might take the ticket. I back away into the shelves of aspirin.

I walk the aisles, my fingertips brushing along the middle shelf as I go—touching price signs and straightening the rows of boxes so all the labels line up right. A lady in a red smock comes towards me. "Unh-uh," she says, taking the baby wipes from me and shooing me out the door. Walking home I hear the voice that's not really a voice. No words or sound even—just that pressing down on me, that forgetting how to breathe like I'm underwater. Go to her, it means.

I walk faster, Locust to Eighteenth to Palmer to Shelby Street, where we're living. Each time we move, the houses get smaller. This one barely holds us—and we're only three. It's green like cooked peas. Shutters nailed down crooked. The front steps are crumbling. When we first saw it, Mally and I thought it was a joke and wouldn't get out of the car until Mother'd slipped the key in the lock and gone inside. "We're saving our money for bigger and better," she said. "But in the meantime we can paint it whatever colors we want, even if that means swirls." Mally and I gathered fists of paint chips from the hardware store, brought them to Mother waiting in line with her furnace filters or her light bulbs, and each time she shook her head, saying, "Not yet."

I slow down because I see Mother through the front window and now I'm not certain what the voice really wants because I don't feel any calmer to be near her. I am separate from her, so very different. I am not hers. Or I am, but only in as much as he loved her.

"We can't leave," I call out.

Mother's stacking piles of clothes on the furniture. "Not this again," she says and rolls her eyes. "You home early from school?"

"You said we didn't have to go."

"Gone all day, what else would I think? You certainly don't talk to me anymore." She stands with hands on hips. She's looking right at me now, dealing with me for once. "Where've you been?"

"I know Daddy's here."

"What?" Her mouth's hanging open like she just can't make it work. Finally, she clears a place on the sofa and sits. "You haven't seen him, have you? I'm sure he's not here. I'd know it."

"He's here," I say.

"Have you seen him?"

"No."

"Well then?"

"You won't believe me."

"Iva, don't start. I'll believe you, I will." She sits me down on the pile of dresses beside her.

I take the paper from my pocket, rub it smooth against my chest and then hand it to her. "He sent this to me," I say.

She studies it, pulls it closer and squints at the faded writing, barely legible. "This is just a drugstore stub."

"I know. For picking up his pills." I feel cold. I feel suddenly open somewhere, split down some row of bones with wind blowing in.

"What do you know of that business?" She says it like I'm core-rotten. Like when I stole money for candy. Like the once I said, "I hate you"—'cause I did and she deserved it prying me off his leg when he would have taken me with him but she was screeching, saying, "If you leave, never come back." I was so little that Mally wasn't even born yet. I clawed at Mother and held on tight as I could to his knee, my legs wrapping his thick ankle. She got me loose. He left. Then she held me, hugged me. While I screamed and twisted and cried to see out the front window. She kissed me. She would not let me go.

Now I tell her what I know: "I'm the one he took with him. His pockets were stuffed to the gill with these." I push harder, push hard at what she thought was only hers. "I make them, too. I can fold them and float them. He trusted me."

Mother turns quiet. Her face is strange. I think maybe she'll slap me. "Love," she says, "this isn't his."

"Yes," I say. "Yes." Feels like the only word I know. I say it again and I'm crying.

She pulls me to her, my head under her chin, and this time it's okay. I think of Mother standing on the mountain, falling. "This wasn't one of his," she says.

"He's…pretending," I say between sobs. "It's a game."

"No, love. I know the names he takes. It's not one of his."

"But it's a boat…he sent me a boat. He saw me there at the creek and sent it right to me."

"Just one of those Lake Shore shutouts probably living in the weeds along the creek." She pulls me from the pile of dresses fully onto her lap, strokes my hair. Holds me so tight it's almost that night and almost the voice come back, too.

I fight my crying. I overtake it. I soothe my very own self.

"I didn't know you knew," she says.

"I'm his favorite."

"Yes, you are."

Something aches so fiercely in me. It squeezes me at every angle. What I want is a thing I can't always remember — sometimes a beard never thick as cake frosting, eyes I don't even know except for in my photo, the way I felt when he carried me up the stairs to bed, though I cannot picture where or how his arms took me up, a time when I could walk away from him and come back to find him there just as I left him, a time I really know nothing of.

"Where is he really?" I ask and touch my mother's face, feel it like Daddy's silk scarves hanging at his neck whenever he'd pick me up.

"I don't know," she says and because of the way her eyes shut when she breathes deep against me, I believe her.

"He's lost?" I ask, and she just holds on.

Mally's nowhere. She is disappearing into the soft squlchiness of the first bite from the center of a folded bread and butter sandwich. Or dumping out a grocery sack packed with Mother's sling-back pumps for dress-up. Or tucking into Mother's bed where she buries herself beneath the pillows and lumps the comforter over her head. She is disappearing. She doesn't know any of this. Doesn't think on him, doesn't look for him, doesn't know he's why she's hiding at school and we're moving again, will keep on moving until Mother and I can sit in a house without him and keep from trembling. She doesn't even know enough to miss him.

I spend my few days before we leave again walking the creek, looking for scraps of moon and paper lost there in the water. *La luna* and Daddy both.

to water

Daddy always liked water more than skies. Driving along, Mother'd point out the dog Sirius or the bear seeming to hang from the moon's lower lip, or maybe a planet slipping behind a wash of clouds moving. But Daddy drove with one eye on the road, or the mirror back to me for a wink, and his other eye tracing riverbanks or pondrim.

She didn't like him to drive alone. So when Mother wasn't in the car, I decided it was my job to watch him. And I did. I'd keep tugging at his sleeve to make him look at me just to know if a spell was coming on—if I could see he was different and headed for trouble, headed somewhere else. He'd laugh, saying "Quit it with the elbow; the driver needs to concentrate."

One day we stopped the car. Just the two of us, because Mally wasn't Mally yet or she was still hanging 'round Mother's neck in a scarf. He and I walked that edge of earth and water. We pretended we were wild. Like bear cubs just old enough they don't mind losing sight of their momma over a hilltop—like Sal's bear stealing blueberries from the wrong pail. Daddy wouldn't speak but only snorted and growled deep from his belly; he pawed at my hair and I pawed back at his side and we made believe we had claws and pointed teeth. A few minutes later we always felt funny. We turned red and clumsy with each other, shy for having believed we could be different, that we could be whatever it was we wanted. Then he'd lose me walking away so fast.

I was in preschool then and he walked me to the blue school every morning. Sometimes we were bears and sometimes we were tall people in striped hats. But we were never truly us. And each morning to school and each afternoon as we set out for home, he'd say, "Who are we today?"

I never knew because who we were was always his choosing and I could only fully become it if he were the one to pronounce us alley cats or woodsy owls—same as if he had a magic wand. So I'd say, "No, you," and giggle, wanting so much from him and feeling lowdown how little I could give him back.

"Okay," he said. "Today...today we are twins with fish gills." Then we both started up glubglubbing our cheeks, mushing our mouths into fish-lip puckers.

The drives were different, though. Out driving, just Daddy and me and the car. He was quiet. Like he was alone. And sometimes I wondered if he thought maybe he was. I have just one memory of him speaking. We were out pushing through heavy woods and stepping right into deep mud puddles that would never come out of the hems of his pants legs—and not minding where his feet fell wasn't anything like him. That day there was no time to look where I stepped and so my shoes sucked into the mud where it was thick enough to take permanent hold of me. But he had my hand, dragging me farther down the Angelina; behind him, I flew. We followed the run of water east till it found the Toledo Bend, and then we walked that riverbank thinking we could make out De Soto and Sabine on the other side—the low mooing of dairy cows, the stretches of cotton plantings white and brown. He pressed on and on, stopping to note the gray water washing over green-slicked rocks, the streaks of cloud off to the side, and the pushing of water against itself. I wanted to be a painter then. I tried to remember the colors and shapes, how the sunlight took bits of the treetops away into glare. I needed more time to memorize that scene— standing still, I needed more.

"It has to stop somewhere," he said, biting at the buttons of one shirtsleeve to loosen his cuff.

I refused to let go of his other arm. I think I knew he wouldn't wait or even slow down. He did not share with me what went on inside him those days. He could not. Watching for the spell to lift, stumbling across oak roots that trenched the soft ground, I kept up best I could, jostling alongside his quick legs. It was only the tightness of my grip, my hand squeezing his, that kept him with me. So I held on.

skyland for a moment

This time we don't hurry. I'm not even sure I believe there is a new house waiting somewhere. Mother's lists—of box numbers for the plates and saucers; of how many glove sets and jars of jam and honey we're leaving with, to be sure we arrive with the same number she'll check off as we unpack each box; of left-turn, right-turns along the route; of shower 5:45 A.M., wake Mally six o'clock, Iva will fend for herself—these lists which settle her brain and keep her on track, are nowhere to be seen.

I think of my bed. My Madame Alexanders sleeping on the truck, plastic eyes rolled up into their apple-round heads. No kids on the curb planning to miss us even though we never belonged to that street. And Mother kept us inside on loading day so I couldn't make Mally trip down the plank. It was a smaller truck this move anyhow. One man, who didn't talk to Mally or me as he moved through the house grabbing too many stacks of blankets and books in his arms, dropping things—letting himself drop things—on his way back out to the truck. Mother followed behind him picking up whatever it was, dusting it off, patting it like a puppy, then she set it back down on the floor for him to find on his next trip through.

I don't want to go. There's no use saying it anymore. We're gone. And Mother says she's sure. There's no undoing that.

She drives slowly, though, and the car hovers over the tip of the Smokies park. She's turned from us, looking out the window and saying, "Don't you remember that nice day? Tennessee was worth it for that one day climbing trails when Mally spied a polar bear peeking out at us."

"That was only two weeks ago," I say.

Mally giggles, telling me, "I did. I did, Iva."

But there was no black bear, no white-tailed deer, no orange-speckled cave salamander, no tree frog—not one thing shown in the brochure Mally got bored with and dropped along the trail. We didn't hear a wolf or even feel the spray of smoky mists.

Mother keeps to the right, pacing behind egg trucks and RVs. She must know if we move again so soon Daddy's letters will never track us down. But they've been missing so long now maybe it won't change a thing.

We're not making any progress. We've been driving US-40 three days already because Mother gets all turned around, sends us straight into Asheville then can't face it and we're back west to Hopewell, passing our house that wasn't really ever our house these five months. Then just outside Nashville, then back out to Buncombe County. I can hardly make sense of the signs anymore, keep straight if we've passed the borders: either passionflower or dogwood blossom; mockingbird or cardinal.

Mountain forests, tobacco, and dairy cows. Back and forth. All day.

At night, we sleep in the way back under lampposts in grocery store parking lots. Mother's face hurts to look at: her eyelids draggy for watching so much road; lips chapped for nibbling at them, one at a time, between her front teeth. Last night she pointed to the stars that were too faint for me to make out through the glare of lamplight, though Mother and Mally said they saw them all, traced one to the other to the next. "You're not trying hard enough," she told me when I shook my head. Could have just been my particular angle, but she didn't say that. So I lay down, my back up against the hump over the wheel, and Mother was no one I knew. Someone pale white, white as glue and paper and snow. Her hair a wreck on her head, strings of it shooting every which way. Her eyes too gray to bear. But somehow hopeful, somehow dancing for us—for Mally, at least.

"Sweet dreams," I told her because it was all I could think of.

She only repeated what I said, her and Mally's arms still up in the air charting pathways for stars.

Mally's in rubber pants this drive. But they're from years ago and they pinch her. She tugs at their gathered legbands. She constantly adjusts them, breaking their seal, soaking through all the towels Mother stacks beneath her. Wiping down the seat with Wet Ones, Mother always says "Thank God for Naugahyde."

But the smell. Makes my nostrils shut up tight. Makes me breathe through my mouth, my tongue gone dry, my eyes watery.

Mother tries to make us smile, saying, "Must be raining

in the backseat—what a strange weather system we've got" or "Where's the cat? Come on now, give her up." But she can't think of enough to say and just trails off asking Mally if there'll be a change in the weather, soon—"Please?"

Mally pretends not to understand that she is our weather. Outside the car, the sky is bright blue, the ground dry as dust. Mother's too careful with Mally, lets her choose not to answer. Mally knows full well she's the one making the rain, sopping her bottoms, flooding the seat, but maybe that choosing is as mysterious to her as real clouds and storms. She ignores us best she can. Even more, she ignores her very self—like she's not sitting here, not a girl in a body with all its pieces, hair and arms and toes, and certainly not coming to be a girl who knows things.

We get back on the road and Mally colors in Gingham Girls books or points at pure stands of tulip-poplars, saying she sees a moose or a wombat.

She is six now; I am eleven—a teenager I say, though Mother says that's unofficial till thirteen. I don't feel free anyhow. I'm growing fast but still have flowers on my undies, still put my hair in pigtails or braids. Mother has let me keep an old tube of her lipstick and I swirl it on some nights before supper. "It's a little heavy, don't you think, baby?" she says, so I go rub it off in a hand towel, then stand at the sink studying the color there in the terrycloth.

A few weeks ago we were in the Winn-Dixie in Hopewell—just Mother and me 'cause Mally threw a fit for jellybeans and got sent to the car. Mother walked beside me and was looking sideways at me. "Iva," she said. "Look how high you come up on me." And it's true. My shoulders are nearly to hers now. "I want to get you something," she said.

"Something meaningful. Momentous. You think it over and tell me what a nearly-grown girl wants."

I scanned every package that lined the shelves on our way to the checkout. I considered fancy curling irons, even a Sony Walkman radio though it was expensive. I thought maybe I'd like a diary or a camera 'cause Mally's always snatching Mother's and we wind up with forty-two pictures of feet and thumbs and Mother blinking. But each time I reached for a box or began to give Mother my answer, my gut went queasy and what I knew I wanted most was my own room again, like in Nacogdoches. My days steady, at least steadier. Him. Everything that used to be mine.

Mother doesn't ask and I don't tell her. The only things she can give me would come wrapped in a bow.

What I want most is a little bit of holding still. A little bit of going back.

We're moving because of Mally. When I look at her or hear her, I can't think of anything but that. Mother never said so; she didn't need to. And I suppose she would have come up with another reason if Mally hadn't kept peeing herself at school. She does it all the time now, so what's the use in moving? There doesn't seem anything we can do for her.

As usual, her right leg's bouncing something terrible.

I ask her over and again, "Do you have to go now?"

She stares out the window, still bouncing.

"Now?" I ask minutes later.

She pulls her feet up onto the seat, hugs her knees to keep them still.

"Now?"

"No!" Mally shrieks. She tugs her yellow blanket up to her lap, rests her cheek against the window. "Leave me alone,

Iva." She stares hard into the highway landscape.

But next thing is the smell, and so yes she did.

Mother passes me back the red and white towel nearly dry from two filling station washrooms ago when she last rinsed it out. "Wrap it around yourself till we can stop again," she says to Mally.

I unfold it for her, but she won't take it. She's part of the car now, frozen into the seat and door and glass. She's stone now if it will only keep us from looking at her. I tuck the towel under her hip and then watch the gravel along the side of the road.

Tonight, after walking the parking lot, Mother climbs in the way back with us. She holds Mally tight, says, "You're a part of this world, my love. I need you in it." But Mally still can't find that bit of herself that belongs. She wakes up, her rash stinging in the wet. I pretend I'm a bear or a man in a hat or a mother lying awake while her daughters sweetly dream. I nearly believe it but then I hear Mally twisting around in the covers. I'm just me. Just a girl.

❋ ❋ ❋

We're back on 40 East now and coming up on an exit for Route 26 to Skyland, North Carolina, in seventeen miles. It's still Buncombe County. So maybe this'll be it and Mother was to-ing and fro-ing just to make sure.

Skyland. I like the sound of that. It's the sort of place Mother would choose after Hopewell. She puts great store in names, same reason she wouldn't stop at a diner in Liarsfog for cheese and bacon sandwiches when Mally saw the sign and, bouncing up and down said, "I'll be good. I promise. No raising my voice. No spitting anything out. I'll eat whatever something green they put on my plate—unless it's spinach or broccoli—anything else! And I'll keep my pants dry and whatever else you say. Please?"

"Hush, baby. This isn't it. Not here," said Mother, shaking her head. "I just don't see us in a place called Liarsfog."

Mally and I looked at each other and then out our windows, knowing this wasn't Mother's time for compromise. Can't say I wasn't relieved.

Still a ways off now, Skyland looks to sit in the shadow of mountains all around. I can see myself in a cove of Skyland. I can see Daddy finding us in a place called Skyland. He'll just know that's where to go.

I want to ask Mother if this is the place, to finally be certain of something—right or wrong. But to nail her down could jinx what's the closest we've come to her making a decision in the last few days. I can't risk it. So I poke Mally, who's fallen asleep with her cheek against the window. I jab her in the ribs, then pinch her elbow, sticky with syrup and orange Fanta and everything she's eaten since we left our house. I twist that pinch of skin, feeling how easy it is to hurt her. How easy such a thing can be. Wanting her to scream, needing her to care about what's happening to us.

We three must look a sight—living, breathing, eating in this car for half of a week. Mother looks serious, studying this stretch of highway, noting everything we pass. So intent she's almost vibrating, the way she stares at trees and turns in the road, like to memorize them for telling someone later. Like pressing the gas to keep moving forward is such a hard thing she needs every inch of concentration.

With another twist of the skin on her elbow, Mally wakes, her mouth opening first. But I stuff my hand over what will become a cry.

"Quiet," I whisper. "Look around. We're almost there, I positively know it."

Mally pulls up on Mother's headrest, gripping a hank of hair by mistake. "We're near?"

"Iva, I need peace," Mother says, shooting me those gray eyes. "Can't I count on you to do better by me?"

Mally sits down on her own, looking out the window.

Mother puts on her blinker. I squeeze Mally's hand. But Mother's pulling over before any exit ramp, and now we're stopped.

"Did we run out of gas?" Mally asks Mother.

I can see the needle, and it's hardly budged since the last time we filled up at the Downey Oil in Newport.

"Are we lost?" she asks.

Mally's got more questions, but what I hear is the breeze of passing things when Mother opens her door, the gravel under her feet, the way she's breathing in, out, in, in, in. So much going on out there, outside our windows and doors. We can see it through the glass, feel the heat so heavy it hangs around the tires, our ankles—like a billowed sheet just before it'll hit the ground. We can smell the clover coming up tart through trucks' diesel. Everybody out there has a path. They're all going somewhere. While here we sit.

Mother leaves us in the car, the air conditioning still blowing. She walks down the little hill with wildflowers growing out of the loose rocks, clover and thistle. What she's doing I don't know. And we'll never beat the moving truck now, won't even have time to sweep out the corners before our furniture's dragged in and we're just stuck with being dirty forever. I roll down my window far as it'll go, fold my arms along the sill, and see Mother sit down. On this side of the car, there is no breeze; the world holds still. We face the sun that's already set for us, though I can feel it catching fire behind us, flat on the horizon and orange as lava. I won't take my eyes from her. I can't. And the way the sinking light hits Mother's cheek, her hand come up to touch her eye, feels like forever. Feels like Skyland would have been it but the timing is all wrong. Like a game of double-dutch jump rope you just can't get your feet timed in to, so you stand at the edge of the ropes, rocking forward each time the plastic beads hit the blacktop and you think next time, next time, but the ropes slap down one then the next and your feet just won't move.

If we'd found Skyland this morning, we'd be unpacking right now, picking up two pizzas 'cause Mother says moving days should be extravagant, finding the box of winter boots first and dinner plates last like every other move 'cause somehow Mother's box numbers get all screwed up on her lists or the boxes we need right away are buried in the corners. But in this moment, we feel late in this world. We just all feel far behind.

She's got no way to make it work anymore. Or she thinks she doesn't. Either way—what does the difference matter? I'd like a set of paints or colored pencils. I'd like a miniature safe for locking things away. I take Mally's hand.

"Is this it, Iva? Or isn't it," Mally says, rubbing the back of her head against the seat.

"No," I whisper and turn back to her, squeeze her to me. I don't have a word more to say to her, no hope or reason for it. Seems to me we're three people living in a car, headed three different places—or maybe only two—and that just isn't possible. Mally drapes her yellow blanket over her lap and then my lap, too. And despite the heat and dust come in through my window, I curl up to my baby sister and am cooled by the satin she's spread so smoothly.

I don't know when Mother comes back to us. I wake under the lamppost of a Piggly Wiggly—no idea which state. Mally is already in the way back. Mother is holding her. They both shake, and rock back and forth, breathing low and heavy and without any particular rhythm—thinking while they sleep, sharing a strange or lovely dream. I know she is Mother's favorite. But I believe Daddy used to love me more, and hope now he misses *me* if there's only room for him to miss one of us. I could live with this arrangement, carrying on divvied up—Mally for Mother, me for him—if Daddy were here with us. I decide not to crawl over the seat to be with them. I stretch out here, three seatbelt buckles melding to me, becoming part of my knees, side, and skull.

In the morning, Mother's cheered. She's humming. She's rested and smiling and the way she talks to us is like Mother in the Nacogdoches house. "Mornin' sweet girls," she says. And "Iva, sweetness, were you kissing boys in your dreams last night?"

My face goes hot with blushing and Mally looks at me grimacey and jealous. I check for signs, and we're just inside Tennessee, still patrolling Highway 40—west this time—but driving faster today. Mally's piecing together a magnet puzzle of zoo animals, dancing the emus all around the tigers. She looks fresh and calm, too. Rosy-cheeked, both of them.

Mother leaves off her humming, says, "Iva, you're so tall now, they may send you off with the older grades come September."

This is the first Mother's talked about the continuation of our lives.

"It's only the start of March," I tell her.

"I'm a big girl, too," Mally says.

"Oh are you?" Mother turns her rearview to catch me, says, "Some schools put sixth-graders in middle school."

"Let's stop there," says Mally, pointing to a brown Arby's sign on a pole high above its rooftop.

"But I'm not done with fifth," I say. "We left."

"Maybe we'll just tell a little tale."

"I'm starved," Mally says, but gives up on us stopping now. "What grade will I be in?" she asks.

Mother jokes: "Oh, I think eleventh for you, baby." She looks at me in the mirror again, her gray eyes blue today. "We'll work it out, Iva." She goes on humming.

I am overwhelmed, gone silly like Mally, thinking I've never seen so many trees so fast. I look straight ahead and they're slow and steady. When I turn to the side each trunk speeds by, nothing more than a dizzying blur of bark and needles. Mother pushes at the pedal and we're finally going to get somewhere. So maybe we'll be okay, the three of us. And Daddy, wherever he is. Maybe Mother has found the most perfect house in the most perfectly named town. And he'll know where to look. If he could just keep track of when and why to take his pills, he'd know everything about houses and driving and daughters and—just everything. He'd be level, Mother says some days when she can tell I need to hear about him. She says he wants us but that he can't pull himself together. She says he thinks of us every day. She gives me a look. "Iva he knows you in and out. You're so close to being him," she says. "You'll be the one he comes for. One of these days, your daddy will find you." She talks this way on her good days, when her fingers comb through my yellow hair and she kisses me goodnight. On her charitable days.

She's not talked this way for weeks.

But today, this morning, with its delicate wash of marigold light all about, Mother is transformed. She sits up straight again. She takes a deep breath. And another. She shows us the pink marble quarries in Friendsville. She teaches Mally to spell "Holstein." She says there's lemonade in one water tower, vanilla shake in the next. She says aren't we lucky for this day and this place and everything around us. She is heading for Knoxville at 79 miles per hour. And so that must be it. Where we'll spend the next five months, or six or three.

Then without one word from me, she smiles wider. "He'll know," she whispers.

"Will he?" I ask, but she doesn't seem to hear me, doesn't answer.

She's convincing herself to believe in it, to leap. Her left hand wraps the wheel, her fingers squeezing and flexing. With the other hand, she pinches her cheek redder, reddest. She takes in a big breath like a swimmer about to dive in, but this time she's so nervous, she can't get the air down into her lungs. She tries again, this time in shallow panting. Mally's silking her blanket, watching for duckbilled platypus amid the tulip trees, without a clue how this day, this very moment is different.

Mother is finally ready to stop.

Quick as Mally can soak a beach towel, Mother pulls north on 81 into Virginia. Mountains here are like velvet draped over the backs of chairs. Dark green spotted lighter, round and soft with the sweet gums just coming into bud. The highway cuts through the landscape, walled in by clay and white stone, periodic signs warning against falling rocks. The car doesn't slow until we're sitting in front of the new house on Tessle Street. No moving truck to be seen. A family of five already living there. Cousins, an uncle, Mother's sister. Blacksburg: Daddy won't think to come look for us here.

the difference

All night it felt like Mother knew he was coming. She'd been singing, leaning into the tub, shielding her hand over Mally's eyes when rinsing out the shampoo. *Don't let the stars get in your eyes*. She'd been singing when she combed tangles from my hair. She'd been singing when Mally slurped chicken noodle for supper. *Don't let the moon break your heart*. Over and over again she sang until Mally screeched to make it stop. Even then, Mother hummed.

This was back in the Nacogdoches house, our true house with Daddy. I was only eight but still, I could feel what was happening before it did. Before it was announced. Before Daddy's tires popped gravel out front. What it felt like was knowing the alphabet or standing before my whole third-grade class singing out the times tables one through twelve for a pin of the American flag. He'd been on one of his trips; that's what Mother called them. Knowing he was coming home to us was a breeze in my middle. I lost my stomach on hills all over the house. I just knew.

Mally was fussing about the lima beans, though she was eating them and I was not. Mother was singing—or humming, when Mally had had enough of her. I do not eat lima beans. Can't make my mouth open for them, no sir. I stared at the green pebbles; I don't object to their appearance. They're a nice shape. An okay color and all. But they smell so sour and squish apart under the tines of my fork, and Daddy never bothered with them anyhow. So I ate soup, Saltine crackers, and then stared at my beans.

"You'll sit there till they're gone," Mother said. But it was okay because I knew she was wrong. I knew he would save me. She went on singing, clearing the table around me and my plate.

"What's got you so smug, Iva?" Mother called from putting clean dishes away into the cupboards—first plates, then bowls, then saucers; she's always had her order.

"I just know something," I said.

"You, too?" Mother started up singing again about the stars and the moon.

Daddy did come. Soon enough, and I ran from the table. Mally whooped and called from her crib for the headlights. In he walked, *pretty as a peach in a dress*—that's what Mother said, only she pretended it was a bad thing. My daddy with his fuzzy yellow eyebrows and his darker, near goldy beard that bristled my face enough to wake me some nights he came in so late. Tall and thin as garden hose hung out to dry before first-frost can bust it open. And wouldn't you know the first thing on his mind after us not seeing him another three days or weeks—I can't be sure, though it felt like months each time he left—was to load us into the car still churning in the drive, and haul us over to the Baskin Robbins.

But just before he did, I saw him touch Mother, who waited for him to go to her in the kitchen and dropped the dishtowel just for some excuse to hold out longer. She didn't tell him she'd been singing 'cause like me somehow she knew he was on his way, didn't hum the notes to the place he'd put her face just under his own, but stood silent and still. He lifted bits of her hair back up over her ears, back up into her hair comb which had been popping out all night. I watched him flip the comb, watched his hand glide down Mother's straight brown hair. And as his hand smoothed across her shoulder, her eyes rose to his. Three days didn't matter.

Mother once said her father hadn't loved her mother. She was smiling when she said it. She knew the difference. No matter how many times Daddy sped out of our driveway, she lived that difference. When she told me, her lips curled in a smirk, her cheeks went red and round. If I'd have had that face right then, she'd have told me, "Gloating is so very unbecoming on you, Iva." As it was, maybe I was the only one seeing just how beautiful it made her.

Watching them in the kitchen a year or so later, I could not help but make offerings of all I treasured in the universe—an eraser that smelled like Coca-Cola and came in a tiny plastic box, red and see-through; all hope of ever having a pet dog; even swinging around on Daddy's elbow to "Could I Have This Dance" when really I ought to be in bed—for a love like theirs. Seemed to me then, the darkness of his goings was well worth the electricity of his returns.

This was the awful night Mother sometimes talks about. Mally must have climbed out of her crib and then run to him, ramming the backs of his legs. She was already in her sleeper for bed, the plastic feet scuffing around on the kitchen linoleum because Daddy was home again. He spun around to scoop her up. "Who wants ice cream?" he asked, so of course she pumped her little legs up and down his side.

"I want bubblegum double scoop," I said, hugging on to him. "Can I?"

"You can," he said with a slight bow.

Mother rolled her eyes and huffed: "Didn't even finish her plate at dinner, Jameson."

It was cold in the car. He kept flipping on the heat for Mally, who bounced next to me in the backseat. He was always worrying over her. She was just turning three then— I'm not sure if her birthday fell before or after this drive, though I know Daddy wasn't with us for cake, and Mother slept on the floor beneath Mally's crib, one hand up between the bars to touch her on her birthday night. But this time, right then, we were whole.

When we got to the ice cream shop, Mally chose butter pecan in a cake cone. I got my bubblegum double scoop in a sugar. I chewed and chewed every gumball while licking the pink drips. That was about all I could do, keep up with the drips starting over the rim, and suck the bottom of my cone. By the time I noticed we weren't back on our street, back on La Bega, Mally was swimming in white goo and sugared nuts, and Mother was curled up asleep beside Daddy.

"Where're we going?" I asked.

He answered me but it wasn't anything real. Him joking, really: "Fishing," he said. "Swimming, hunting foxtail ferns."

"No," I said, wanting to be let in on what he was cooking up that would top ice cream near midnight. I watched in the rearview for his mouth to move, but for the life of me my wanting could not make him speak.

Mother has said that we slept all the drive out to wherever it was he was taking us—sometimes late into a moon, she puzzles over maps and thick colorful books of rivers and lakes looking for where we were headed that night: somewhere beyond east, beyond a place wet and sticky, somewhere with the widest lake she'd ever seen. She has said he wanted to swim, though she says this on nights she's joking about everything else. On nights when she can't find a joke anywhere near, she says he wanted to lose himself and lose us with him. So the truth must lie between. She says the water was murky and strange with glowing green pebbles on the surface like lima beans, that she thought he could follow it to a town at the very least. She wouldn't say. I suppose that's where we left him.

The thing is, I woke before she noticed me. I woke and we were stopped, the engine still but their doors flung wide. I watched beneath a half-moon that, even split down the middle, gave enough light to see the way she gripped his wrist, enough to see all the paper-boats crushed in his fist. Mother kept on tightly holding him with the one hand but with the other pulled more and more folded slips of paper from every pocket on him. I could not hear them, could not make out Daddy's eyes refusing her, but I saw the way she begged. From the way he breathed, each time deep and swollen like blood to a bruise, I knew he was crying.

She came back to the car alone. He walked the riverbank with a few boats still tight in his fist. I pretended to sleep. She whispered, "Iva?" just to know if I'd seen. I squeezed my eyes tightly like Mally still does today.

Somewhere midway, I did fall asleep, woke to Mally crying for him hours later. That's when Mother could not stop talking: "He wouldn't stop the car. Wasn't going to stop it. Wouldn't have, I'm sure."

I don't think she broke once even for breath.

"I pounded the brake while he was on the gas—both feet. I don't know if it'll get us home. I didn't know what to do. I was scared. I was so scared for you. I'm not sure who he is. I'm more than this, more than the dead."

She went through the facts of the night again and again, then suddenly stopped. She didn't say another word until she had sun to stare into, and then it was only, "We'll stay home today, all of us. I think we'll sleep."

When Daddy came home the next time, Mother wasn't singing and she didn't drop the dishtowel waiting for him to touch her in the kitchen. She'd forgotten the difference.

I am shocked beyond belief. There is a moon, low and full that lights this, our next little spot of the world. A house. A white, metal-sided house, big as the Tyler house two moves ago. A yard with trees, not dirt like in Hopewell. A hillside, a rickety metal carport white with stars. But the second our Impala wagon starts hissing and spitting in the driveway, a family of five already living in our new house on Tessle Street comes rushing out to greet us.

"Who are they?" I ask Mother as she's gathering her hair back up into her side-comb.

"Who are they?" Mally's been repeating my every word since we passed through Pulaski County minutes ago.

Mother reaches over the front seat, puts her hand down on Mally's shoulder, shaking her head meaning it's time to finish the game. "You remember that drive down to Galveston," she says to us. "Three and a half years ago — New Year's Day, you remember. Spareribs on the barbecue?"

"Daddy came to get us?" I say.

"Mmm," she nods, turns frontward again checking herself in the mirror. Her mouth is smiling but her lips look too thin, stretched. She isn't pleased with what things I remember.

We pile out of the car and Mother goes to kiss her sister, smiles at the whole bunch, though it just looks like more and more of her trying.

Five of them. Five. The parents touching our faces and smiling big like cats. But I don't recall meeting any of them. Back then, it seemed nobody even lived in their Galveston house. There was the empty twin bed beside me, Mally's limp hand falling to my face when Mother leaned down to ease me awake, me holding my pillow walking the house's dark hallway with Mother warm and smelling of toast and nuts and speaking soft and smooth and lovely as a dream. And I remember Daddy tugging me out of the way back the next morning, remember the way Mother held him on the drive home—just none of these people.

"It's dark," says Mother, laughing a bellowy sound and looking at her sister to be sure, then turning back to me. "So of course you don't recognize anyone, but you'll know each and every face come morning."

I wish she wouldn't always do this; she's got no sense of what's ours and meant just for us to know. She's got no right inserting them into that dreamy night of him needing us.

Mally's slipped deep inside the flaps of Mother's wraparound skirt, hiding behind her, peeking out at the boys: two odd-looking things kicking the toes of their sneakers in the gravel driveway where we're all still standing. One pushes at the other to move him over for a better look at us. Then the first shoves him back with a squared shoulder. I'm busy studying the one girl, grown enough she must be in college but they tell us she's only sixteen.

"These little hellions," says Aunt Clea, holding the two boys by the tops of their heads, "are Samuel and Perth." Both are short as Mally, shorter maybe. Samuel shakes his head out from under his mother's hand. Perth stays put.

"And that's Holly!" says Mother, and it sounds so funny to hear her talk like that—her being theatrical again, but to someone we don't even know. "You're downright gorgeous, you." Holly looks away smiling but Mother pulls her close by the elbow, kisses the girl's cheek and then stands still behind us, leaning over Mally and holding her with both arms. "You remember my girls, don't you Holly? Mally and Iva."

"They were real little then," she says.

Uncle Davis squats down before me, puts his left cheek so close in front of mine. He smells of coffee and his eyes are solid brown. "Give me some sugar."

I've got not one clue what he means and don't like the sound of it, so I take Mally's hand like she needs me and walk her over to the car to get our stuff.

Aunt Clea shuffles and pushes her boys on to help with our things. There's not much. Each of them grabs a satchel of clothes and shoebox of what Mother calls her breakables—things she wouldn't trust to the movers this time around.

I hear Mother saying, "They're just tired. It's been a long drive."

"How far is Hopewell?" asks Uncle Davis.

"Not too long, I'd think," says Aunt Clea. "Near the

border, North Carolina. A pretty drive to be sure. Not too long."

"Three days away," I say, setting my satchel down at Mother's feet.

They look at me laughing. "How cute are you?" says Aunt Clea, taking the chance to touch my shoulder.

Uncle Davis says, "I see Jameson set his sense of humor just fine in you."

I can't help my smile.

Mother shoos us inside.

There is a room with square mirrors all over the back wall, a maroon rug on one side of the entry hall, mustard on the other. A staircase up to the rooms. Mally and I have been missing stairs since the Nacogdoches house. Aunt Clea takes us to our room, says it's really Samuel's but that Mally and I will have it now. There are bunk-beds with a slide, a small rolltop desk, some squat bookcases, and milk crates full of Star Wars spaceships and figures. My bed, my books, my dolls, aren't here. Nothing of mine or Mally's, except the grocery bags of clothes that Samuel and Perth bring up before standing in the bright hallway watching Mally and me.

"This is your new home," says Aunt Clea. "You treat it as if we weren't even here."

"How long you staying?" I ask.

Her face wrinkles, saying, "I'd better go check on Lilly."

The boys follow her. I can't tell them apart, except that one's a tad taller. That's all the difference. Both are brown-haired, brown-eyed, narrow-faced boys—like they've been sick all their lives, tired too. Both younger even than Mally.

"I've never been on a bunk-bed," Mally says. "I want the top."

That's fine by me, except that any leaking will rain down all over me. So I tell her no. There are single windows on two sides of this room. It's smaller than my room in the Tyler house, and that was my own private room. Bigger than the room we shared in Hopewell, but anything would have to be bigger than that.

I don't understand this place.

Mally and I wait for Mother, who comes alone once she's got everything in from the car. "Nice, yeah?" she asks.

Mally whines, "I want the top bunk, Momma."

"Iva will figure everything out." She smiles at me.

"What are we doing here?" I ask.

Mother shuts the door. "It's our new place," she says.

I give her a look saying she needs to do better than that.

"Sometimes, we have to make sacrifices," she says. "Sometimes, that's all there is left to do. Just pretend we're on a visit." She begins to unpack the sacks of our clothing into cleared-out drawers in Samuel's dresser.

"If we're visiting, then where are our things?" I ask.

"Let's not even think about it," she says. "Have you looked at the backyard? It's enormous, Iva." Mother unfolds each of Mally's shirts, refolds them, then makes a neat stack of them in the drawer. "You'll see in the morning. Everything will be fine in the morning. There's a pretty redbud out back. Raspberries and currants, cherry trees, too. And there're all sorts of neighborhood kids around. You'll go outside and play tomorrow."

"This isn't ours then," I say.

"Baby, we live here fair and square like they do. Now that's that. No more of this talk." She stands at the window facing out back, points to a dogwood she says is both pink and white when it blooms; a tall pine just begging to be climbed; a great, flopping hydrangea that takes up half of the property line off to the right. We can't see a thing but Mother's reflection in the glare of bedroom lights. So as she's talking, where her finger goes is really to her side, her lips, her heart, and she looks to be holding herself in the glass. I imagine she sees what we see; I imagine she likes that, likes to think the hand is Daddy's. I climb into the top bunk, Samuel's superhero sheets. Mother stays at the window a long while.

Each new place I have less and less. I don't know what to call it, what I'm missing; but it's heavy and solid, it's old and it's crumbly. All I know is that I am eleven and Mally's still a baby, and we've been living in the car for three days because Mother could not decide which way to drive—even though she must have called Aunt Clea days ago—and so we spun back and forth between Knoxville and Asheville. We have not eaten since cheese crackers at the Downey Oil this morning. We have not properly washed since four nights ago in the Hopewell house. We are in the same shirts and shorts, though Mother tied on her wraparound over hers just before a sign for Blacksburg, and made sure Mally's bottoms were dry. I have not seen my toes since last week. And Mally has cycled through six pairs of underpants several times the whole drive, with Mother wringing them out in gas station washrooms. We don't own anything here, and we haven't been near Daddy for almost two whole years.

Mother finally pulls herself from her reflection. She tucks the covers up neatly beneath our chins, kisses us both, and leaves.

Mally calls to me, "Are you awake?"

"She just left, you goof."

"Don't we need to brush our teeth in this house?"

"I guess not."

"Will you sing to me?" Mally asks.

"No."

"Will you read to me?"

"No, go to sleep."

She waits all of one minute. "Iva, I can't sleep. I've tried. Is it fun up there?" she asks.

"No funner than being down there. Go to sleep."

Aunt Clea knocks and comes in. She pulls us from bed, hurries us off to the bathroom for teeth and a shower. She has us climb in the tub together and we're used to that—but somehow it feels funny with her watching. Mally prefers baths for dumping in Mr. Bubble and now turns from the spray of water that's shooting up her nose. I scrub us quickly, to be done with this. To be done.

We stand shivering. Teeth-chattering. Twisting our arms straight down in front of us, our hands trying to keep from being seen. Mally reaches for a towel hanging on the wall but it's too nice looking—pink and yellow daisies stitched along the hem—so I swat her hand away before she can touch it.

"That's fine, Iva," says Aunt Clea, handing one to me. She pulls another off the rack and wraps it around Mally, who pinches a yellow daisy at the corner of the towel the entire time Aunt Clea rubs at her like she's a wet dog or a boy. She twists Mally's hair inside the towel and piles it on top of her head just like Mother after a shower. "You, too," she says, and smooths my hair first then makes a twisty turban of the towel. She finds our pajamas and slips us into the covers again. "Sweet dreams," she says.

In the morning Mally and I wait for someone to find us. There's all sorts of noise and commotion. Doors shutting, water running, doors slamming, cars revving.

Finally Mother comes for us. She throws open the door and near-clobbers Mally jumping on her, that's how excited she is. She's singing her morning song, "It's time to get up" over and over again, "It's time to get up in the mooor-ning."

Mally squeals. Mother squeals to find Mally's underpants dry. She'll take this as a sign.

Mother stands up to see me. "Mornin', lovely," she says, petting my hair. "Anything for breakfast you want," she tells us. "Everyone's at school for the day and Aunt Clea's out to give us some time alone."

Mally comes crawling up the slide to peek in at me on top. "Come on, Iva," she says and tugs my arm over the side of the bunk.

Mother doesn't send us to the bathroom first, but scurries down the stairs calling to us from the kitchen. She is new here.

Mally's ahead. I'm tired and lagging. "Come on, Iva," she calls again, stretching my name with too many Vs.

In the yellow morning, I can see Mother's hair is clean and pinned up with shiny new side-combs. Her cheeks are peach-glowing once more. You'd think she'd never been in our car. You'd think she'd been waking up at her sister Clea's every day of her life. She's wearing an apron over Kelly-green shorts and a blue T-shirt with green ribbon around the neck, clean white sneakers. This outfit isn't hers and I can't help but giggle thinking of Mother in checked pantsuits lent out by Miss Lobell.

"What's it to be, darlin's?" She swings a half-empty jug

of milk in the air.

Mally plops down before the pantry shelves looking at all the mixes and cereals. She hums trying to decide. "Waffles," she says and grabs the Bisquick.

"Alrighty," Mother says looking in the cupboard over the stove. "Now where is the waffle iron?" She's pulling out stacks of saucepans and skillets, checking the towers of pots behind them. "Hold on girls, we'll find it," she says.

"Just use ours," Mally calls from where she's touching every can in the pantry, adjusting and readjusting them so that the labels line up frontwise.

"I'll find hers." Mother goes on looking in plate cupboards and glass cupboards.

"I'm hungry, Momma," Mally says.

"Hush," she says, "I'm finding it."

She's nowhere near finding it. I walk to the end of the house, a large room for eating just off the kitchen. There is a wide window, a birdfeeder just outside it. Mother was right, the yard does go on forever. There is a flower garden near the back, away from the house. I see a fluffy dog in the yard next door. A hammock hanging from two old pines. And so many berries picked over by mockingbirds and bluebirds, rose-breasted grosbeaks.

It comes over me all of a sudden, like the voice taking hold in a panic. *We won't be here long enough*. This will be the one place we want to stay, the one place where we can taste what it is to settle back into having something halfway firm. But Mally will flip out or I'll get caught smiling and then Mother will say we need to leave. If I walk out into the yard, I believe I will meet it—whatever it is here that I need—a certain freedom and loveliness, a way soft spring leaves talk in the afternoon air. She will notice me not holding my breath anymore. She will see how much I'm figuring out about this world, about her. She will feel like a cornered mouse; she will shrink away from me and this place.

Behind me, Mally's far from guessing what Mother's done with our waffle iron, with our beds, my Madame Alexander dolls, my books. Our world is shrinking. It seems to me with each move, Mother slides us in tighter, smaller. I wonder how much she got for it all, and what she'll do next time now that all we've got left is what fit in the car.

"Why can't you find our own?" I hear Mally asking. "Didn't you unpack? You didn't forget it, did you?"

"I haven't gotten to the boxes yet," says Mother at first huffy then settling herself into a joke: "What do I look like, a teamster?" She flexes her muscles and Mally goes running over to squeeze them. "Don't you worry, it's in there," she says.

In there where? There are no boxes.

Over milk and oatmeal with toast, Mother says we'll have "the most fun today." She says Mally and I will be explorers. She says we're to go absolutely everywhere and report back what we find. Mally wants her to come with us. Mother says she needs to rest. This is May in Appalachia, she says, and we will love it.

I go upstairs with the word sliding side to side on my tongue: Appalachia, Appalachia, Appalachia. Like strong water coming around a rock.

Once we've found the bathroom again, dressed, and called out to Mother, who's sleeping we don't know where, Mally and I do go exploring—though it isn't one bit the same without him.

"Go on," she says, and still we can't make out the location of her voice.

So Mally and I go. Out the screened porch off the eating room, first there are trees: all sorts of evergreens sap-dripping and needle-dropping. There is a shed and vegetable garden next door. This backyard meets up with several other backyards, thick lines of trees marking property. Mally's wearing sandals, same as she wore in the car, and keeps grabbing at my hand so we'll stop and she can pick out brown needles and wood chips. I'm uneasy in strangers' yards. We move to the road, then to the next sidewalk. School's still in so we get looks from some lady clipping stinky onion grass from around her lamppost.

Quick as all I've got that voice back, just the way darkness sounds, sending me home. Making me long for Mother or Daddy, someone to look at me—truly see me—and tell me I'm all right. It's pressing my ribs so I can hardly talk. "Let's go back," I manage, and Mally takes my hand without a word, walks right alongside me without any objections at all. Maybe she hears it, too. Or maybe she's just used to following along.

I don't know if we should use the front door, so I sit us down in Aunt Clea's front yard. Beneath one of the two maples, Mally and I are quiet. This is the same sky I've watched in all these different places, the same sky that's been watching me. She plucks blades of grass and runs their tips along her toes. She laughs, then looks sideways at me. I want to tell her *it's okay, go on*, but I don't open my mouth. And the two of us are back to quiet.

"Hey you two," Mother calls from the front door. "What did you find?"

Mally drops her head backwards, leaning upside-down, She hollers out, "Trees and mean old ladies."

Mother comes out to sit with us. "And you, Iva?" she asks, but I only shrug because I just can't say anything to her, just want her near me, just want her to stay and be silent with us. She never says the right things anyhow. She never knows what it is I want.

"Oh I see," she says to Mally, "your sister's not talking again." They giggle and rock back and forth clutching their knees, laughing on this tiny, tiny hill hardly big enough to hold the three of us. But Mother puts a hand to my back, pats me there almost long enough to feel nice.

In a while they're ready to go in but I stay here, can't really see myself moving around in Aunt Clea's house yet. So I lie on my back to watch the sky through the maple leaves, my head on one root hump. I try not to, but I still wonder if I'll see him again, wonder if he wonders the same thing. I was Daddy's favorite, clearly I was. And yet, what good are favorites if he's nowhere I know?

Aunt Clea volunteers in the cafeteria some days, selling weekly lunch tickets and punching out holes for meals used up, so three days a week she drives Samuel and Perth home from kindergarten. Her car's slow up the drive, careful. When she gets out and starts over to us, I don't budge, just make as much of a smile for her as I can. What I would like to do is go back to Hopewell. At least he knew we were in Tennessee. He'll never think to find us here. Why should he if all Mother does is drive farther and farther away from our real home in Nacogdoches each time we unpack from the last move? I remember so little now.

* * *

The next day Mother sends us off on another exploration while she rests. We walk the same route but farther this time. Higher up the gradual hill of this block, there are cats skulking around all these houses, and Mally has to stop to pet each one. I keep walking. The cats gather and trail behind us. Only three more houses to pass and we'll be at the top of the rise. Mally's panting now, the slap of her sandals to the sidewalk quick as she can go to catch up. I don't know why it matters, that my sights are set on a silly brown house with short white pillars around the front door. That all I can think is to get farther away. But it does. This is a sort of mission, I guess, even if it's got no real purpose.

Cats are everywhere up here, and they're all we can hear: purring, crying, growling, hissing, meowing. And then we see it. At the end of the block, behind a wall of red junipers: one house completely overrun with cats. There must be hundreds, covering every inch of dirt, sleeping and sitting and slinking about on each gray slat of porch. We hardly notice the big girl in a rocker with a box on her lap.

"Come here," she says and Mally hides behind me. "Come over here," she says again. "Don't you like cats?" she asks.

"Are they all yours?" I say.

"Uh-huh."

Mally whispers "wow" at my side while peeking out from behind me. We walk into the yard, and instantly four cats are rubbing up against our legs. Mally's almost knocked over by their pushing noses, their twisting spines and gripping tails. There are tabbies and calicos, Siamese and Persians, blacks and oranges and splotchy ones.

"You can pet them," says the girl, still rocking away on her porch.

I crouch down and rub the sides of their faces, watch their whiskers twitch. One of them has a hole on the top of his head, a black and hairless dent the size of a quarter. "What happened?" I ask.

"Blue jay pecked him."

"Oh!" Mally gasps.

"He's fine, though," says the girl. "Come here and see what I've got in the box."

"Kittens!" Mally cries, reaching for the stripy things.

"Ask first," I tell her.

"May I?" and Mally's scooped up three all at once, put them to her chest where they grip her with fat feet and needly claws.

They're barely born, their eyes still squinty. The mother's in the box, too, and those Mally hasn't got clinging to her T-shirt are suckling.

"Go ahead," the girl says to me, so I choose one.

A white kitten with red and black splotches like a cow's. Her eyes are green and her nose pink and soft. I hold her in the cup of my hands. I think she likes me already. I cradle her to me and she sucks at my shirt, kneads my arm with her wide paws.

Mally's three kittens are losing their grip of her shirt and the girl picks them off of her, sets them back down in the box where the mother licks their heads.

"So do you want them?" says the girl.

"You mean for our own?"

"Yes!" says Mally.

I don't believe it. "You mean for free?"

"We can't keep them all," she says. "You can take your pick. I mean I'm partial but you can take your pick." She looks me right in the eyes. This is my first grown-up negotiation, so I can't pass it up.

"I'll have this one," I say, looking right at her. I put out my hand to seal the deal.

"You, too," she says to Mally who was looking worried about having to share.

Mally peers into the box again. She touches each one, pushes some aside, then finds her favorite. He's a brown kitty with an abnormally short white tail. She picks him up, flips him onto his back and carries him like a doll. She's out of the yard before me, chanting "no takebacks, no takebacks." I thank the girl and follow Mally down the street. We're chattering about names and how tiny they are. Mally's certain she'll call hers Rabbit because he looks just like a cottontail bunny. I'm not sure yet, want to think it over, not rush into anything. We're to the driveway of Aunt Clea's house before I know what I've done.

"No takebacks," says Mally, kissing Rabbit square on the nose, and I know she's right. What have I done?

Mally and I take the kittens to the backyard. Under the largest sycamore we sit with them, our legs apart and feet touching to form a diamond yard for them to play in.

Mally's suggesting all sorts of names for my kitten, sorry to be decided on "Rabbit" so soon, I think: "Splotchy," she says, "Blueberry or Towel." All I can think about now is Mother and Aunt Clea, and Uncle Davis, who, I'm convinced, doesn't even know if I'm Iva or I'm Mally. On the other hand, as short a time as she's had him, it's clear to me that Mally will never leave Rabbit behind and a cat can't live in a car.

"Callie?" I suggest, trying to get in the spirit, "for Calico."

"Or Sally," she says, "Lally, Tally, Rally, Bally, Gally."

"Mally, that's really helpful."

Rabbit doesn't seem entirely certain about his new world. But my kitten is exploring every inch of our legs, climbing up to look out, then dropping back down to the grassy pen we've made between us.

"How 'bout…what was the milkcow Momma said on our drive?" Mally asks.

"Holstein?"

"H-O-L-S-T-E-I-N," spells Mally who can remember how to spell a black and white cow but little else.

"She's not a cow, dummy."

Rabbit crawls over to be with his sister. Then they both curl up together, sleep. I push the sole of my foot into Mally's, wiggle hers, make her leg jiggle till she smiles. We watch our cats, stroking their backs, seeing how they take in so much air that their whole bodies shift forward onto their chins.

When Mother comes out to sit with us, she thinks we've found wild bunnies in the yard and are holding them hostage. But Mally pulls Rabbit from his sister and shows Mother he's only a cat. He bleats at her with his eyes shut. Mother stands over us a minute. She presses her lips one way then the other. Mally tells her all about the girl in the rocking chair, all the cats, the box full of babies with the mother who licked them smooth, the tom with his head pecked in. It hasn't occurred to my sister that we might not be allowed to keep them.

"Iva, you're supposed to know better than this," Mother says. "You just can't bring home any stray animal you find because it's cute and you want it."

"They're not strays," Mally says, stroking Rabbit from

head to tail.

"You know what I mean, both of you," says Mother. "You should have asked first. This isn't even our house. You should have asked."

"You said we're here fair and square," I say. "And Aunt Clea said not to even notice them."

"You're no slouch, Iva. You understand more than that. I know you do."

"I won't go in if I can't keep her," I say, holding my cat to me.

"Me neither," Mally says, picking up Rabbit.

Mother stands firm, her bones all rigid for the way she's keeping in something awful. She is choosing, and I guess there's not much left to try in her world. She folds up on the ground beside us. She takes Rabbit from Mally, inspects him with a hard look, fingers his stubby tail. "Let me think," she says, and I'm sorry for what I bring about, that just by being I can change her world, that I can shut it down even tighter around her.

"Yay," Mally squeals and jumps up to run loops in the yard.

"Don't do it again, Iva," she says. "I need to be able to count on you. Things are precarious enough."

"I swear it."

"You're the one I can count on," she says. "My steady girl."

Tonight while she and Aunt Clea are cooking, Mother starts asking questions about the cat house: Does Aunt Clea know of it? Does she know a jay pecked out the head of a big tom-cat? Has she heard there are kittens for the taking? Aunt Clea's smiling away answering Yes, Oh yes, and Are there now. Uncle Davis, walking through to set the table, sees where this is going. I can hear Rabbit crying on the porch just through the door, but don't see that anyone else hears. Samuel's helping his daddy place forks, saying he won't be eating the spinach and I nearly call out "me neither" just as Uncle Davis says, "Nothing more till you've cleaned the plate." Mother's fussing with the forks, checking and rechecking the number of us she counts on her fingers.

"Well the girls were up there today," Mother says to Aunt Clea, "and the gal practically begged them to take two of the kittens. Said the mother rejected them, won't let them nurse, practically clawed their eyes out. And well," she says, getting another fork from the drawer then finding she had enough the first time, "I just wonder if it's all right, you know, after all they've been through, if they could keep one. Apiece?"

Aunt Clea stops stirring the meat sauce. She looks at Mother and makes a smile and a deep breath at once. "Samuel's allergic," she says. "But if they were kept away from him, I suppose—after all they've been through—I suppose no one could mind."

Mother hugs her sister. Mally shrieks with joy, running out to the porch.

"Hush it, now!" Mother says, low and stern. "Get back here, Mallory. You will not run in here or raise your voice. You will not bring that cat in here, and you will wait until after we eat to go see it."

Mally bites her lip and stands waiting in the kitchen for Mother to be soft again. But Mother is proving things to Aunt Clea and Uncle Davis right now—that she's no doormat, that she's got a handle on us.

After supper, we go to the kitties on the porch. Mally brings a towel and shoebox to make them a bed. I bring a bowl of milk. They won't drink. Rabbit's crying nonstop. I dip my finger in the milk and put it to my cat's mouth, but she won't lick it. They're not moving much and when we pick them up from the box their big heads loll to the floor.

"They need to eat," I tell Mally. "They haven't eaten all afternoon."

"I'll get Mother."

"No," I say. "Let me think. Wait here."

We need a dropper. I've seen them use a dropper for baby bats on TV. I check the medicine cabinet: just Band-Aids and orange baby aspirin. I find a straw in the top drawer by the fridge. I snip it in half, give one to Mally. I show her how to plug up the straw when dipping into the milk so that it'll hold until she's got the bottom in Rabbit's mouth. It doesn't work at all. Most of the milk runs out the sides of their mouths.

"Wait here," says Mally. "I know what they want."

She comes back with peanut butter, puts a daub on her finger and holds it out to Rabbit. He sniffs it but won't open his mouth. Mally wants to get Mother but there's no telling what she'd do, and so I try one last thing. I dip my shirt in the milk then hold my cat to the wet bit. Her head bobbles up and down as she sniffs, and then finally she sucks. I pull the twist of cloth from her mouth when she starts making smacking sounds like a dentist's hose sucking up all the spit out from under my tongue. I dip it again and give it back to her. Mally copies me, dipping her own shirt and finally our two babies are drinking and we've done it.

Mother comes to see, to look over the cats and pretend

she doesn't think they're the cutest things she's ever seen. She's prettier now that she's decided not to be cross with us. But that may just be the moonlight, so Mally and I will be careful.

After Aunt Clea pulls us from bed again for shower and teeth, Mally sneaks down to get the kitties and a tall glass of milk. She's put them in her pillowcase and hands it up to me, then climbs the ladder to the top bunk and we nurse our kittens whenever Samuel, in Perth's room across the hall, sneezes them awake.

In the morning, Mother waits to find us until everyone else has left for the day. She smiles peeking in at us, the four of us in the top bunk. She wants to kiss Mally and me, twice each. She says my cat needs a name and that will be our project for today. On the way downstairs, she's calling out names just as silly as Mally's suggestions: Milk Glass, Peanut Butter, Side-Porch, Sneakers.

Where we are now feels better than Tyler or Hopewell or somehow even Nacogdoches. Mother sleeps while we scout the neighborhood—treelines and footpaths, a rose garden behind chain-link fence—the kitties hammocked in the waists of our T-shirts. Here a month now and she still likes to stand in our bedroom window at night and point to the sycamore settling, the patch of golden raspberries from which she says we'll make jam come fall, the zinnias we planted from seed just poking up now; one moonlit hand to her waist, her shoulder, her face.

Aunt Clea is the one who remembers we are children and comes for us when it's clear Mother hasn't yet thought to send us for teeth and shower. The shoeboxes of Mother's breakables hold photographs, I am sure. That's all there is of him in this house. Those pictures she turned down on her quilt. I've my own, of course. The beach, my beach with Daddy where we buried each other until our legs kicked up the white sand and shells. Ice cream we ate in the car because he said that was the best place to eat it. Mother never finished her own butter brickle, gave it to Daddy to free her hands for wiping Mally and me, saying "Faster, lick faster, it's dripping 'round back." The box of photographs is wherever she is, and though she calls to us each morning Mally and I leave for our walks, we still can't tell which room her voice is coming from. Some days Mally wants to try the doors, but even if it feels like Nacogdoches, we know better, just go on downstairs and start walking—Milk Glass and Rabbit hanging off of us like fat tubes of sausage.

I imagine when Mally and I leave the house, Mother looks through the photographs, spreads them out around her in bed, maybe sleeps with pictures of Daddy so near she thinks she'll dream him. I still do it, too. Pull my frame of us at the beach to my pillow, sleep with it there beneath my cheek.

In Hopewell, she said he's lost. How can that be? With both of us dreaming him—because she must be doing it, too, or trying to—he ought to feel that pull. He ought to know where we are, that we need him. It's a matter of memory, him taking his pills or not. Mother says when he forgets he doesn't know where to find us. She doesn't say what happens when he takes them regular; I don't think she's ever known. I dream of strings on fingers, of Mother's lists, of her crossing curls in her hair when there's no string or pen around.

We are squeezed tight in this house, missing everything we had because Daddy's envelopes of quarters, smoothed dollar bills, and his very own heart can't find us anymore.

like the moon

Once, when I was five, they spent three weeks not talking. Someone put little black dots on all those days' squares in the calendar that hung in the kitchen. Mother left notes telling Daddy what to pick up from the Kroger on the way home from his job stamping checkout cards at the library (though he spent most of his time, I think, selecting new books to bring home to practice my reading). She wanted cheese packs and Q-Tips. He'd answer back on the outside of the brown paper sacks, telling her things such as she smelled like the moon. And I'd catch her smiling—though she'd never admit it then—for the way he had of kissing her without even being in the room.

He'd been gone four days, not even any of his late-night calls like usual, the ones begging her to come get him. She was a wreck, rattling around the place, telling sleeping baby Mally and me we were lucky, lucky, lucky, telling us she's scared, tucking me in to bed and staying there beside me, pushing my hair around, singing and holding her sweater tight around her elbows—too tight so it was stretching out and she wouldn't ever wear it again. She was still with me when the phone rang that night and she ran to her room where I heard her pick it up screaming.

She got me out of bed. Said she had nothing to say to him. That I could talk if I wanted.

"Momma?" I said into the telephone, because she was there standing in front of me and I was still fogged up from sleeping.

"Iva, plum. It's Daddy."

"Mmm," I said, smiling.

"Put your mother back on, darlin'."

I held it out to her but she threw up her hands at me. "I've got not one thing to say to him," she said, sitting down on the bed then popping right back up. "Except, tell him he's miserable. Tell him I can't do this anymore. Tell him I'm not coming to get him, that I don't even want to know where he is."

I started to say all of this to him but Mother was huffing at the tangle I was making of her words. And anyhow, Daddy had heard it all and was beginning to reply so that I had to start giving that to her: "He says he's sorry and you know he means it. You know he tries. You know how much—"

"I'm through with it, Jameson. Through!" She pulled the phone to her mouth, hollering.

When she gave it back to me, I could hear him sad; his breaths were nighttime ocean. "I think I'll do it this time," he said. "I should do it."

"You shouldn't go away from us," I told him. I was frantic, like her—but she was yelling him away and what I wanted was to yell him home. I didn't know how so what I said was, "You're a bad father."

Mother laid Mally in a nest of blankets on my bed. She locked us in but didn't go for him right away, to wherever he was watching current move. First she made noise in all the closets, banging the doors, dragging things across the tiles. Then she drove to get him, so he must have already told her where to go. Finally I watched her taillights pass the window. His sweaters and trumpet and books were all out at the curb. For anyone to take. I could not get to them. I cried and shook but Mally slept soundly through it as though I weren't making a single sound.

That morning the piles were gone and I was certain they'd been stolen or picked up as trash, but after lunch he showed me how to finger a sheet of music on the three pearl keys so he must have brought them in and she must have let him.

Mother and Daddy were back home together but still wholly separate: him trying to find her; her trying to lose him. There were scraps of paper all over the house. Napkins and ledger pads, old bank stubs and paper towels. Everywhere I looked her notes were telling him:

> *We're over but if you're sticking around <u>now</u>, the least you could do is fold the wash.*

> *If you're planning to go on supporting your children, I suggest you show up to work today. And if such is your intention, stop at the bank to make this deposit.*

> *The baby's teething. Freeze the blue terries and <u>you</u> stay up with her tonight.*

Scribbled beneath each of these and left on the folded undershirts and sheets, wrapped flat around the bank receipt, or drifting off his lap while he and Mally slept—finally—hunched into the darkness and porch steps, were his answers:

> *I love you.*
> *My every intention is to be steady.*
> *She prefers you.*

They floated through the house in different climates of hating and being hated. Each one of them hoping for something. Promising to be over or set, steady or gone. Each of them wishing, until one morning they were kissing and holding skin, whispering, pressing close and smudging each other up with all the ways they were so near.

He let go of her only long enough to sit down to breakfast. He couldn't be near enough so he dragged Mother's chair right up against his—she bouncing along with the bowl of eggs and a potholder held up in the air. "She loves me again," said Daddy to me.

She blinked her eyes once knowing it to be the case: "You'll do better by me." She spooned a heap of fluffy scrambleds onto his plate and set down the bowl.

"I will."

I didn't get my own eggs. I didn't have eggs at all. Who needed eggs? I just watched them distracting each other into a dream. When Mally fussed, I gave her the blue teething cloth from the freezer and I sat back down across from them, smelling the cinnamon she sprinkled across his toast, smelling it all through the bright sun of that perfect completion, and hoping he'd never think to finish that plate of eggs.

I had collected some of their notes the night before, but there was a favorite on the fridge and when I checked that morning—wanting to secret it away to my stash pressed flat beneath my pillow for other nights when no one spoke at all—it was gone.

She'd been weakening; it had been nearly three weeks of nothing between them but words on paper. "I don't mean to miss you," she'd written across the top of the grocery list. "I'm right here, love," he answered down by the onions.

That's the one I wanted.

He did finish his eggs, ate them ravenously same way he was kissing Mother's neck. His eyes were black, the pupils stretching near across all fleck of green. He waltzed her in the kitchen—he pulling her away from the sink, she pretending to fuss. They whispered and laughed and talked about planting a new redbud out front to take the place of a poplar he'd chopped down one night because Mother was convinced it was leaning too far over the house.

Later in the day it was coming back, though—that rattliness in him that made his shoulders shiver and his feet start pacing. He got up from the sofa where they were reading, she the news, he a book.

"Where you going?" she asked and then looked down again.

"I want something different."

"That one's not depressing enough for you?"

"Lilly," he said, turning back. He put his hand to her face, set a bit of her hair behind her ear and touched her jaw.

"I know," she said.

He sat back down without getting a new book. Close to her, closer. Nearly on top of her. His arm around her.

"You'll stay," she said, making him promise. And he did, because he meant it and because he said she smelled just like a crooked sliver moon waiting through one last night before full-dark. "*La luna*," he said.

"*La luna*." And she let him see her smile.

like there's no tomorrow

Mally asks about death tonight; she just can't fall asleep. She lies beneath me in the bottom bunk, calling up questions, and stroking Rabbit who sometimes mews for Milky up top with me. "What will happen if I die tonight?" she asks. "Or what if you think I'm dead but I'm not really?"

"Hush," I say like Mother would tell her, because what in the world else is there to say. She is six now, too young to be thinking like this—and she's making me nervous. I certainly don't have answers.

"Will you wait to be sure," she says, "that I'm really dead? Make Mother wait. To be sure?"

"Yes," I say. "We'll wait."

"I couldn't stand it to be living all alone forever."

"Are you meaning *him*?" I ask.

But she only answers, "Who? I'm going to sleep now."

"He's not dead, Mally. He's living in Pascagoula, or somewhere."

"I'm asleep."

Now I'm up with questions. Until now, Mally's had not one thing to say about Daddy, not one thing. Every time I tried, she'd have none of it. So now I'm wondering how well she knows him after all. If she's even close to seeing what Mother's done, brought us here to live with her sister's family because of him—somehow, it's about him. Three moves now, each farther from where he is, yet I think each brings us deeper into missing him. We've been here for what seems ages—truly, only three months—but that's because we have nothing left of our own, and nowhere else to try. Mother's sold everything but our summer clothes, so for now we're stuck.

Aunt Clea comes for Mally and me as usual. Doesn't say anything. She walks us to the bathroom for teeth-brushing and a shower. Sitting on the lid of the toilet waiting for us, she looks tired. Her face is pale, the skin 'round her fingernails frayed and rough handing us washcloths. Mally and I try not to look.

I spend most days sleeping in the hammock, Mally twirling around the yard such that I imagine tambourines and ribbons in her hands, she's so pink with smiling and getting dizzy. There is a boy next door who watches us. From the thick of pines marking the property lines, he stands looking fascinated. Mally doesn't seem to notice him.

Today is Saturday and Mother's off with Aunt Clea buying groceries and the makings of pear butter she'll show me how to fix this afternoon. Uncle Davis is somewhere, who knows where. Our cousins are *out of our hair*, as Mother would say: Samuel and Perth at a friend's playing Star Wars; Holly inside fussing over herself in the mirror. Mally's spinning and I'm swinging in the hammock. It is a perfect day, never mind the bit that this isn't our house, that we own nothing, that we remember so very little, and that Milk Glass isn't in the hammock with me.

Sun scatters in the pine needles hanging over me, paints my legs. The air is hot but moving in breezes. I'm being watched again. Just the top of his hair, some of one eyebrow, peeking at me through the crotch of a thick pine limb.

Milk Glass pushes herself out through the hole in the screened porch. I'm fairly sure there was no hole before Mally and I brought home Rabbit and Milk Glass from the crazy-cat house—maybe a tiny tear is all. Now, Rabbit's bunny-brown and Milky's mostly white fur grows on the rim of the hole and each day the kitties grow, that hole edges wider. A winter muff or collar.

Milk Glass visits each azalea, the andromeda, the scraggy quince, her nose touching to sniff every leaf she can reach. Finally, she pretends a blown leaf is a shrivel-skinned mole and stalks it to the white pines and cedar tree. She disappears. Then so does the boy's face.

"Milky," I call, and the hammock sways. "Milky."

Mally keeps twirling but starts calling out "Rabbit" just after I call, like we're playing Marco Polo at the county pool.

"Milky."

"Rabbit," Mally answers, dancing deep in the sun on the yard.

I walk toward the pines calling for my cat. When I get to his tree, I'm nervous to look behind it. I creep up. "Milk Glass," I say. "Milky?"

And there he is, sitting Indian-style in the wood chips and sapped needles—what Milk Glass and Rabbit spend whole nights trying to lick from their paws. Milk Glass purrs, curled in his lap.

"You looking for her?" he says.

"Yeah."

"You have to take her?"

"Mm, no," I say.

"She one of their cats?" He throws his chin over his shoulder up the road to the cat house.

"Mm," I nod.

"Looks pretty good, though, not like some of theirs I've seen."

"You should see Rabbit," I say and his eyes get big. "My sister's cat is sort of weird."

"Yeah?"

"Stubby white tail on a brown body—looks like a bunny. He's not too smart, either," I say. "Walks into things."

"Maybe his dad's a cottontail," he says. "Maybe he got confused and did it with a cat."

The boy laughs and something comes over me. I giggle like Mally in the bath pushing bubbles. My face feels hot and I shift to standing on just one leg, my hand out for balance to the trunk of the tree, my other arm wrapped behind my waist. This boy has green eyes, is all I can think.

"What's your name?"

"Iva," I whisper, like it's a secret.

"I'm Henry. So you living here now?" he asks.

"Yeah."

"Perth and Sam are weird, aren't they? Goony," he says. "And their folks, the mom and dad, were always throwing things on the porch. Fighting. My dad says if you're gonna fight, at least have the decency to keep it on the q.t.—that's military for quiet."

"They fought?"

"Oh yeah, all summer long last year—every single night. My dad says he even saw her throw a plate at him!"

I picture a much taller, bigger Henry standing behind one of these pine trees, peeking into the screened porch, watching Aunt Clea hurl a plate of spaghetti and meatballs at Uncle Davis.

"If you wanna come over sometime you can," he says, stroking Milk Glass and studying her orange spots like maybe he's talking to her in his head. "I've got a robot and gerbils and ESP game." Then he gets up without moving Milk Glass and she rolls on her side and puts out a claw at his ankles, but he's already walking away. I don't know if he means I should come over now, so I wait here and watch for him to look back, but he doesn't.

Uncle Davis pulls his yellow Datsun into the driveway, and Mother gets out of the passenger side. I swoop up Milk Glass, carry her over to Mother whose face is pink as Milky's nose.

"Iva, baby, what's been your day?" Mother sing-songs.

I scrunch up my face trying to think of who she's aiming to be this time. Uncle Davis is still standing here, tall as the trees, and I'm embarrassed to play our game in front of him. He gives me a look like I'm very very very small today. "Nothing," I say, "just swung in the hammock."

"I'm going in," he says to Mother.

She kisses my cheek which isn't like her and what I smell is lilacs in the place just under her ear. Mother is like sunshine today.

Her hands are empty, fussing with a white thread at her hemline.

"Where are the pears for the butter?"

"Oh," she says, "you know, I forgot those, Iva. We'll just have to go back later."

"Where's Aunt Clea?"

"Speaking of sisters, where's yours?" Mother walks into the backyard. She's in Aunt Clea's clothes again, a tennis skirt, white socks with yellow balls hanging off the back to match the shirt, I know, but what I think is it's the same shade as Uncle Davis's Datsun.

Mally runs to Mother. I watch from under the tin carport. Mally spins around her, twirls and twirls like there's no tomorrow.

The boys come up the driveway, tussling for who has to carry a little blue duffel overflowing with Star Wars toys. "Where you going?" says Perth.

"Nowhere. Out," I say.

"Can we go?" Samuel takes the bag from Perth now, putting up a bit of a fight for it.

"I think your dad wants you for something."

"So," says Perth.

"I don't know," I say.

Samuel says, "You don't know our dad."

"Yeah, you don't know him," Perth says.

"You're goony," I say.

"You're jealous," says Samuel.

"Yeah, you're just jealous. You don't even have a dad."

I spit on them. I actually spit and hit them both 'cause it's not a tight spit but a loose spray. I step forward like to hit them, then mean as I can, say, "You keep your dumb old father. Nobody wants him. I'm my daddy's favorite and he sends me secret letters and he calls me when nobody's around and sings to me and I'm going to go live with him soon. On a lake. With Milk Glass and a dog and two horses."

I storm off. Go to Henry's house, feeling ugly and very quiet, about alone as the world can make me.

In his backyard, there's an oak fatter than any tree I've ever seen before. A row of boxwood to either side of the back door. His house looks like a fairytale house, with peaked roofs and cobble-stoned walls. By the time I'm to the door, he's opening it, but he doesn't say anything until we're upstairs. We're in what seems to me an attic, with low ceilings and tiny round windows up high.

"Pauline and I live up here. That's her room," he points. "That's mine."

I nod.

It's warm, bright. The walls are yellow. Pauline must be older than we are because her room is tidy, and there are porcelain dolls standing up high on shelves and thick books on a table by the bed.

"Here's 2XL." Henry presses a button and the robot rolls around, asking "Two times twelve is, two times twelve is." Henry presses 24 on the numbers. All sorts of lights flash and the robot does a dance. "It's easy," he says, already bored. "Come on."

I follow him back into the hallway. On a table just below a row of windows is a glass tank. "Here's the gerbils," he says. "The black one's Squiggy 7. The white one's Lenny 4." He pulls both up out of their cage, hands me Squiggy 7 whose claws are sharp and who does not want to be held. I have to keep shifting him from hand to hand to keep hold of him at all. Out these windows, I can see part of my bedroom in through the side, some of the hammock, and Mally spinning 'round Mother who's pinching up weeds from the flower bed.

"Don't pull on their tails," Henry says, "they come off."

I loosen my grip.

He's perched the gerbil on his shirt, and Lenny 4 starts climbing too fast for Henry to get hold of. It's around the back of his neck before he's grabbed the thing and dropped it back into the sour-smelling fish tank. "Squiggy 3 was the nicest gerbil I ever had," he says. "I could carry him around anywhere."

Squiggy 7's still going crazy from hand to hand, so I start to give him back to Henry, but he nips the tip of my pinkie finger, then leaps to the floor.

"Oh!" I drop down looking, but he's long gone.

"That's okay," he says. "Puma will find him." Henry walks into what looks like the bathroom so I stand still in the hallway watching out for Squiggy 7, wishing I hadn't worn sandals. "Come here," Henry calls. "I've got fish."

I follow him. In front of the window, there's a tank on a board over the radiator. Its glass is scum-green, so Henry and I have to peer in through tiny holes in the slime. They're pretty: a white one, a black one, a golden one, a splotchy one, a red one, all with feathery tails and funny bulging eyes. "What do you call the red one?" I ask.

"We don't name them, anymore," he says. "You wanna play Kreskin's ESP?"

"Sure."

We go into a playroom, and Henry pulls out the game. There's a white pointed egg in the box and a board, some cards, and a ruffly-paged book, but Henry only takes the egg. "Sit down, he says. The egg's on a silver chain and he dangles it back and forth in front of me. "You're getting sleepy," he says. "Very sleepy. You're closing your eyes."

And for some reason I do, but not because I'm sleepy or hypnotized. I do it because it seems to be what he wants. I listen to his voice and imagine his face and green eyes and blond hair.

"You're asleep now," he says. "Stand up."

I do.

"Touch your toes."

And I do, slowly, like I am asleep.

"Sit down."

I sit. Wishing it would work, truly.

"Tilt your head to the left," he says.

I do, though I can't imagine how much fun this can be. Maybe I'm doing other things, too. I could be in a handstand for all I know. I could be singing every time he talks. This could be being hypnotized.

"Open your mouth as wide as it goes," he says.

I do.

"When I clap my hands you will wake up and you won't remember anything." He claps once and I open my eyes. I see stars for a moment because of how bright it is.

"It worked!" he tells me.

"It did?"

"Do you remember what happened?" he asks.

I don't tell him a thing. He runs through every last little bit and he's so excited that I can't bear the truth of it and try to forget, try very hard to believe.

"Do me," he says.

"Not now," I say because I'm feeling the voice. I don't want to, but I need her. I run downstairs, out the back door, and through the pines into Aunt Clea and Uncle Davis's yard. Samuel and Perth are setting the table on the screen porch.

"We're not having spaghetti and meatballs, are we?" I ask.

"Meatloaf," Perth tells me and Samuel makes gagging sounds, then kicks his brother's shin for talking to me.

I find Mother with Mally in our room. They're napping sort of, both sleepy-eyed but talking softly like maybe they're just waking up. I crawl onto Mally's bunk with them, and Mother kisses me.

"Where's my girl been?" she whispers.

"Next door," I say.

She smiles wide. "You made a new friend?"

I shrug.

"The best move ever," she says, dreamy as all.

Mother and Mally fall back asleep. They're breathing in rhythm, shifting about in their dreams. I go up to my bunk. Milk Glass is there curled on the pillow. I slip into Samuel's Star Wars sheets and think of the dangling egg, the silver chain.

When I wake, Mally's asleep below me, but Mother is gone. Just like those first days here when Mother would send us out exploring—*getting the lay of the land*, she liked to say—and she'd call out goodbye to us from a room we never could find, I now hear her voice soft and happy, bubbling and gentle. I slip over the side of the bunk bed, step out into the hall.

Her voice is gone. Mother's quiet. I go back into our room, climb back up into the covers still warm with afternoon sleep. I hear her again, laughing. Sounding just like me at the pine tree today: silly, like someone else.

I step back into the hallway, get closer to figuring out which doors she's not behind, but still can't hear where she is. Something like water and fighting for air comes over me. "Mother!" I shout. "Mother!"

Behind me, Mally wakes, calling "Iva?"

The laughing talk stops and Mother comes rushing out of the biggest bedroom.

"What is it, Iva?" she says.

Before I can think of something better I poke out my pinkie finger at her. "I got bit," I say. The blood is dried now, and it doesn't hurt much at all, but the skin is purple.

"When did this happen?" She kneels down to get a good look.

"Just now," I say.

"Don't fib to me, Iva. This is at least a day old."

"Is not."

She licks her finger then rubs at mine, cleaning off the dried blood to see what damage there is. "That's not too bad. What happened?"

I wish it looked worse. "I don't know. I think I stuck it in the door."

"Go show Aunt Clea," Mother says and stands up. "She'll know what to put on it. And ask her nicely."

I start for the big bedroom.

"Sugar, she's downstairs."

※ ※ ※

Tonight we eat on the porch. Perhaps meatloaf is too hard to throw; there are no fights. Mother makes us put cardboard over the cat hole and leave the kitties outside because Samuel's allergies have been flaring up. Rabbit mews for Mally the whole time she's eating, so finally

Mother lets her finish on a TV tray just outside the screen door—which is fine by everyone else because fitting three more people at a table made for five, makes everyone fussy. Milk Glass is out in the yard, being a cat—sniffing, prowling, skulking. Aunt Clea made red Jell-O for dessert. She's chopped it into squares and layered in whipped cream and strawberries in fancy beer glasses.

Mother dabs her spoon in and out of the cream then sets the glass two inches away from her. "I'm watching my figure," she says.

"No need for that," says Uncle Davis, and Mother's cheeks are bright as the bougainvillea out front of the Nacogdoches house.

She looks at the Jell-O, but won't taste a bite which is good because Mally and I can take it over for her, sitting outside on the beams that run along the walk to the carport.

"Don't you figure you've got plenty enough watching it for you, Lil?" Aunt Clea pushes her own glass to the boys and then starts shrinking again. I can't stand to look. She's been working on this, tugging the words out of her napkin. We're all here like watermelon seeds in her mouth, waiting to be spat out or swallowed. And now one of us is a thief and a traitor. We know this. Some of us do at least.

The boys go in, and Holly clears the table. Aunt Clea stays a while, but then stands up smoothing the pleats of her skirt. "I don't suppose anyone in there has done my dishes," she says just like she's said every other night since we've been part of this place.

Most nights, this is when Mother offers, but tonight she's still. "You know, I think I'll sit this one out. I'm awfully sore after this morning." Mother rubs at her calf muscle.

I take the extra Jell-O out to Mally. She digs in deep, all the way to the bottom layer of clear red, being sure to capture every stripe of red and white. Getting the bite in her mouth, whip cream plops onto Rabbit's nose. He licks off what he can reach, then leaves the rest there like it's shaving cream and he's due for his Sunday morning shave.

Behind the screen, Uncle Davis sits staring out into the backyard. Maybe he sees something there or doesn't want to see what's inside with him—one watermelon seed set down on the rim of a plate, off to the side with an unchewable, unswallowable gristly bite of steak that wouldn't go down. I look him over, noting a round bump at the top of his nose, the smoothness of his hands, thickness of his arm muscles. The swoop of a cowlick starting his high hairline. Feel something like my feet wanting to push in nearer. But it's nearly dark and I can feel bedtime coming on. Mally and I make no sudden movements, slowly inch farther away from Mother.

Scratching the ground with a twig for Rabbit, Mally whispers to me, "I see the first firefly."

"I already saw it," I say.

"Not fair; you didn't call it."

I study my purple fingertip, press the gerbil bite. It stings. "Come here," I say to Mally. "Look at this."

"What is it?"

"What does it look like?"

"I don't know," she says. She grabs hold of my finger at the knuckle and brings it close to her face. "Scissors?"

"No," I say. "A bite."

Her eyebrows go up a whole inch and her mouth opens. "What bit you?"

"Shark," I say because now I'm not so sure I want her to

know.

"Cougar," she says.

"Mountain goat."

"Eel."

"Rattlesnake."

"Pig."

"Pig!" I say.

Mally and I laugh, pushing each other till she gets a little nuts with snorting and rubbing at her eyes tearing up. She falls back rolling in the wood chips. She is positively ridiculous sometimes.

Now Mother's heard us, been reminded. "It's that time, girls," she calls. "Up you go, now."

Mally fusses, "Can't we stay just a little bit more?"

"Nope."

"It was just getting good," says Mally pulling the cardboard away from the cat hole in the screen.

"Ain't it sad." Mother grins.

She calls us over to her in the dark and kisses each of us on the forehead, the sort of kiss you get in the movies, but not from Mother.

"Say goodnight to your Uncle Davis," she says.

"Goodnight," we say, and what I can see of the side of his face looks embarrassed.

"Are you coming up to read?" says Mally.

"Not tonight," she says, which is what she's been saying for nights.

Mally and I head upstairs. Perth and Samuel are already shut in for the night. Holly's humming in her room. Her light's still on. I look out our side window, see if Henry's watching from his. But his house is dark, and I can hardly make out the shine of which window's the one. Mally and I change clothes and slip into our bunks.

"Do you remember in Nacogdoches, what we'd do in the summer?" I ask.

"No." She hates it when I talk about then.

"How we ran around with a pickle jar catching fireflies?"

"We did?"

"Daddy and Mother sitting up late talking and swinging on the glider—"

"No they didn't."

"—and we crossed all our fingers till we thought they'd never go straight again, hoping they'd forget us so we could run around all night cupping the light in our hands—"

"No." She refuses.

"And when they finally remembered us, it was so late and we'd gotten so tired Daddy showed us the smeared light in our palms? You cried."

"No!" she says finishing with it. "Tiger."

Okay. "Wombat."

"Zebra."

"Mongoose."

"Chipmunk."

"Close," I say. "Very close."

Aunt Clea forgets us tonight.

❀ ❀ ❀

I go to Henry's first thing in the morning. ESP is all I've thought about since waking up. Again, he opens the door without me even knocking, doesn't speak until we're upstairs.

"What do your mom and him talk about for so long?" Henry asks me the next day.

"You saw them?" I ask, which is a dumb question. "When?"

"At night."

"Last night?" I say.

"Every night."

"Did you find Squiggy 7?"

"Part of him," says Henry.

"Oh!"

"It's my turn." Henry walks into the playroom, grabs the pointed egg. Thank God.

I wave it back and forth before him. "You're tired," I say. "So tired."

"You're not doing it right," he says. He lifts my hand, says, "Do it slower."

"You're tired," I say again. "So tired. Your eyes are closing." His eyelids shut and I about drop the egg I'm so surprised it's working.

"You will do what I say. You won't remember a thing."

He's sitting on the floor in front of me, eyes shut, maybe sleeping. And for a moment all I want is to look at him. He has freckles. His eyelashes are so light, they're almost invisible. I have to tell him to do something. "Hold out your hand," I say. He does, in a fist. "Open it." He does palm down, and his fingers are beat up with shredded skin all around the nails. He looks silly with his eyes closed and his hand out. I can't think of anything more to ask him to do. I watch him a while. I touch two fingers to his cheek, soft as Mother's. He turns his head away, a little. There is a look Daddy got when he fell asleep reading that is just like Henry now. I used to stand over him, watch his face—and though all I did was breathe, Daddy somehow knew I was there and had to work not to smile. Henry looks the same, the ends of his lips curling just barely, getting nervous to be watched so long.

"When I clap my hands, you will wake up and you won't remember a thing." I clap twice just like he did yesterday.

"What happened?" he asks.

"Were you really hypnotized?"

"Yeah," he says, but he doesn't ask me what I had him do, just takes the egg from me, wanting to go right on with the game. "Now you?"

"No," I say, "I have to go."

Mother's folding laundry in our room, putting Mally's shorts and undies away, leaving mine in stacks on the dresser. Mally has brain-dead Rabbit with her. She's got him in a doll's nightgown, dancing his feet around.

"Where've you been?" says Mother.

"Nowhere," I say.

"I wanna go," says Mally. "Take me next time. Momma tell her take me."

For once she ignores Mally. "Aunt Clea says he's a nice boy."

"Mother!" I go back downstairs.

Tonight after supper, Mally and I hide from Mother, who's sitting through the dark on the porch again. But I try to listen for what they're talking about: just the heat, just the stars, just does Mother's knee look all right after her fall on the court. Mally dances Rabbit around the yard, then sets him down in his nightgown to watch his huge head bobble with dizziness. But Mother calls bedtime, and we line up for forehead kisses, say goodnight to Uncle Davis who sips his pop staring out into the yard. There are things I could want from him, maybe do want from him. Sometimes I wonder if he could hold me once and then forget it forever.

Again, Aunt Clea doesn't come pull us from bed for shower and teeth.

"Read?" Mally asks.

"Not tonight."

"Is he nice?"

"I don't know," I say, lying on my back, stepping my feet flat to the ceiling, wedging myself there and pushing a little 'cause I like to feel how strong I am against this house. "I don't feel right around him. The whole mess of them. You ever wonder why he doesn't look at us. I mean, he's our uncle and he doesn't say one—"

"No! The boy, Iva."

"Oh." I hang over the bunk to see out our window, look for any lights in Henry's attic. All is dark.

"Remember Petie?" she says.

"Mally." I laugh.

"I think I miss Petie. He was cute, right?" She says something soft to Rabbit, probably nuzzling him under her chin. "Do you miss anyone, Iva?"

"I don't think so," I say. "Go to sleep."

* * *

I wake up early, leave Mally in bed. Still, he gets to the door before I've set one finger to it to knock. Sometimes I hear cupboards opening, shutting downstairs, but Henry may as well live all by himself 'cause I've never seen another person here at all. Never even heard voices.

We go upstairs, straight to the playroom, though I do notice on the way, there's a new one, Squiggy 8 in with Lenny 4.

"Your turn," he says. He dangles the egg in front of me and I'm so excited I shut my eyes before he's finished saying, "You're getting sleepy."

"Stand up," he says.

I stand.

"Turn around."

I turn my back to him.

"No, turn all the way around, in a circle," he says, and I feel stupid for not knowing exactly what he wants me to do. Then I feel stupid for doing it.

"Hold out your hand."

I hold it out to him, open, palm up like I want him to put something in it. And I do want that.

"Put your arm down," he says. "Walk to Pauline's room."

I cheat and squint open my eyes to get there. Henry is behind me so it's okay, he doesn't see.

"Get in her bed, under the covers," he says.

I do.

"Um, pull down your shorts."

I lie still for a minute. I wait for him to laugh or stop me. He doesn't so I put my thumbs under my waistband, lift my hips, and pull down my shorts and undies.

He doesn't say anything. Then, quickly, he says, like he's had second thoughts, "Get out of the bed."

I do. I stand there, my bottoms down at my feet. I feel prickly, warm, like maybe his fingers are somewhere on me, but when he speaks, he's way on the other side of the room.

"No, get back in the bed," he says quickly. "Pull up your shorts. That's what I meant." Once I'm done, his voice is calm. "Sit up," he says. "I'll clap my hands and you wake up. You won't remember anything. Nothing." He claps and I get stars just like last time.

"Your turn," I say, shaking. A dirty girl.

"Okay."

I dangle the egg slowly. The chain kinks, jerks 'cause my hand won't be still. "You're tired. So tired." I'm talking too fast. "Your eyelids are heavy. They're drooping."

Henry is slow to shut his eyes this time. His eyes like bottle glass. When he does, I look at him again. I study everything there is to him. His blond hair like mine. His freckles that bunch up across his nose, then spread out on his cheeks. He has thin lips. His skin is golden with summer.

"Turn around," I say. He does, all the way around. "Turn halfway," I say, and he turns his back to me.

"Pull down your shorts." He does, but leaves his underwear up. It occurs to me that he didn't say I had to pull everything down, just my shorts. "Pull down everything," I tell him.

He does, and his bum is pink and bouncy looking.

"Turn around. To face me," I say. He does and I know I've seen one before, but never quite so silly looking. Spongy and sprongy. Pale, pale pink. Still, I stare—thinking if Mother only knew, if Mally only knew. I feel like I'm burning. I feel swollen and sticky hot. I don't know what's happening here.

"Pull up your pants. Sit down." I sit in front of him. "Are you asleep?" I ask. He doesn't do anything. "Are you truly hypnotized?" I ask.

He nods.

"Truly?" I'm shaking.

"Yeeessss," he says with the letters dragged out, just like Mally talking in her sleep so I know it must be so.

"Tell me you love me."

His mouth doesn't move. I'm so scared I run out of the room, down the hall past the gerbils, down the stairs from this attic, out the back door, through the pine trees and cedar, and into our screen porch. I find Mother and Mally in the kitchen baking brownies from a mix. I try to blend in, get them some eggs from the fridge, but all I can think is that Henry will be stuck sleep-hypnotized forever. And that if he's not, he knows how foolish I am, and he lies.

☼ ☼ ☼

Mally dresses Rabbit in a swimsuit and cap tonight. She's draped him over her chest and lies balanced on the beam that runs alongside the walkway. I have Milk Glass in the hammock with me, stroking her harder than I mean till she gives a little meow and swats at my hand. I ease up and she's back to purring. I watch Henry's house. I watch for his dad spying on Mother and Uncle Davis. I'm pretty sure I know what he'll see.

There is a light on up in the attic, so Henry must be okay. I'm through with the egg on its chain. I'm through with Pauline's bed. I'm through with the new way Mother kisses us and how she talks to us here, like she's in the movies—like either she can't be bothered or we're the dearest things she's ever known.

Through the window I see Aunt Clea smashing plates in the sink. But Mother's laugh is all I hear and it's nothing like breaking china. She sounds like the color pink, like spinning, like catching fireflies for a jar. From the porch out into the night comes her voice into the trees and the sway of air. That's all there is, soft and foolish like a hand to the sapped trunk of a pine, like the way who you are isn't really who you are, and that surprise is never good.

She sends Mally to find me for bedtime, and I walk through the house without saying much of anything or waiting on her kiss. From the bunk, I watch Henry's light till it turns out. My stomach's a prickly pear. I want his green eyes, the yellow lashes like smeared fireflies across my fingertips. I want something from him.

There is a fat moon climbing into Mally's eyes tonight, keeping her up. *La luna*, I think.

"Remember to wait a while before burying me," Mally calls from below. "Just to be sure — Momma's awful confused these days."

I promise I will, then jump down from my bunk. "Mally," I whisper, feeling flight against the jar. "Teeth and shower — let's go."

nights spent floating the angelina

Anything less than a day, he knew she'd kiss him instead of holler. So Daddy tried to time these coming-homes for when Mother slept and he could climb back into her arms, his head under her chin feeling her breathe. No matter whose bed— and with Mally still in her crib it was usually mine she'd crawled into—or which sofa or what floor, he went to her.

I'd come awake between them or under one or the other's shoulder and touch my hand to his face to know for sure he was back. And to her lips to feel if she was speaking, my fingers stretched across her open mouth like spider's silk.

Breathing in his hair, she'd say like she was still dreaming, "You smell like swamp." Or river or creek or gulf or pond. She knew each one—the different ways it stayed with him, and she was never wrong. I'd smell it on him, too, be sure to hold onto the scent of that very particular wet.

So the next time, I'd be guessing: "pond," I'd whisper 'cause of the way he smelled murky and green with skim algae.

But Mother said, "Angelina," and we three went on sleeping and holding and breathing it in, pressed so tight I woke up with the river in my hair and all across my pillows.

The circumstances are that Mother used to love us right. Back before Daddy left on his drives. Back before we came to Blacksburg—our third house without him, and this one not even ours. Before Mother sold my dolls, the table and chairs, her one stained-glass lampshade she swore I can have when she dies.

She sneaks us kisses, movie-star kisses, to cheeks and foreheads and even the tops of our hands. Mally's feeling glamorous about it; I'm feeling desperate.

For the first time, Mother is making do. She's settled her whole self into this borrowed life—just like her hands these days, so still in her lap when ordinarily she's all fuss and motion, fingers picking away at her splitting fingernails. Here, in Blacksburg, she seems to have decided she can't ask for more. She never looks at the moon or aches to go back— to curl up with her girls at the foot of his music stand, lulled to sleep by a slow trumpet solo. Here, she's in love with

Uncle Davis. And it has to stop. I'm picking my moments.

Tonight is like every night this whole summer. We all, the five of them and the three of us living in their house pretending it's ours too, eat supper on the screen porch off of mixed-up china patterns with cracks wide with golden cords of Duco cement. Mother says Aunt Clea's getting clumsy; I know better. Uncle Davis grills cheeseburgers that Mother brings from her sister on an oval platter, lifting an ankle, saying, "Oh, the door caught my heel." She laughs like a crazy person, like laughing's got more to do with the air than her world. Uncle Davis has her spraying water on the fire when it gets out of hand, which seems to be a lot.

We sit down to eat and first thing, Perth knocks over the ketchup jar, letting go its salty tin foil smell.

"Watch it, please," says Aunt Clea, catching the red glop through the holes in the mesh table.

"I've got no room," he whines. Both Perth and Samuel waggle their skinny goose wings at me on one side and Holly on the other.

Uncle Davis shushes Perth, saying, "Guests, boys."

"Family," Aunt Clea whispers.

Mother goes on chewing her iceberg lettuce.

"Clea, you should have seen us on the court today," Mother says, helping Mally to another ear of corn. "I think your husband and I have finally found our rhythm. Rallies, lobs, and volleys till the end of creation."

I stop eating.

I think every single one of us is mortified. A hunk of bun drops out of my mouth. Holly sets down her corn. The table shimmies on its legs when we push away our plates.

Mother is *excitable* these days. Like Mally on Christmas

morning when she squeals and jumps on the bed waking us up for presents and stockings. Only there's nothing here to unwrap, no pretty ribbons matched up to the paper, no trash sack in the corner ready for boxes ripped open and tossed aside. No juicy-good love. There's nothing here worth a thrill. Nothing. So if the things exciting Mother now aren't good enough, I figure that's why she flip-flops from shameless to timid, red hot to powder pink. She must see what it is she's working so hard for. She must know how little it should cost. Still, sometimes I watch her and the way she looks at him, fingering the skinny chain around her neck, lifting it off her collarbone and sliding it 'round and around her neck—I might believe she doesn't see how little he is at all. So maybe *she's* just not good enough. Maybe there's a scale to weigh what's right and what's fair and it has decided that this scraped-together "arrangement" is all she deserves. I'm not sure I could argue with that.

Aunt Clea moves her chair away from Uncle Davis. We're all quiet.

Mother hasn't a clue. "Pass me the pickles for Iva, would you, Davis?" she says, even though they're sitting right next to her.

This is the way dinners go now. No talk of Mally and me starting school again in just a couple weeks. No invitations to the Duck Pond on campus or boysenberry scoops at Gilley's. No candy run to Hop-In or dirndl skirt shopping at Fringe Benefit. And surely no plans for burritos and darts at Mr. Fooz. Holly has friends we're not allowed to play with. Samuel and Perth go off for slumber parties. Mally sinks deeper into planning Rabbit's elaborate outfits. And I have Henry. And the egg. We come together for supper on the porch where we pretend everything's all right. But then one of the boys drops a forkful of greens in his lap, picks it off his napkin and flicks it to the floor.

"What's wrong with you, Perth?" says Uncle Davis, looking mean.

Perth gets out of his chair for the soppy mound.

"What do you expect?" says Aunt Clea. "Living like this."

"Yeah, Dad," says Holly who looks at Mother and then out to the driveway.

It's our fault. All of it.

Uncle Davis says, "Enough," which shuts them up and we're all stiff watching Mother make a fool of herself.

We're excused but tonight I stick around a second longer. This'll be the night. I'm looking for the right chance, checking her mood which is good, her voice which is light. But it's still too soon; I need her to be dreamy from sitting up late into the stars with him. I take my dishes in to Aunt Clea, wondering which ones she'll drop.

"I can't stand much more of this," she's saying, but not to me.

She and Holly stand facing each other. I'd forgotten the way Mother used to press in near to me when talking, hugging, smiling for me. Now when she does it I want to scream her away; I blush and fidget knowing all the things I want from her, all the ways she doesn't want me to see her.

Aunt Clea's hands are shaking in her daughter's, and I can't tell who's more upset.

"It's like you've gone invisible," Holly says.

Aunt Clea sees me, shakes her head quickly at Holly to shush her. The boys run upstairs. Everything's back to quiet though her cheeks are tight and her face looks crooked like a mask folded down the center.

On the porch Mother and Uncle Davis are talking the way grownups do when all it is is a sound, low and happy and moist. Words aren't really a part of it 'cause neither one's keeping track of a conversation. It amounts to a sort of humming. She smiles. He smiles. Her hand sits between them on the table, and sometimes he lays his right up against it—two hands on the table, side by side, touching even. But when I look at him I see it in his eyes: *What could be wrong with two hands on the table?* I walk through the mist of their voices, touch my cheeks and find them dry, step outside where Mally's got Rabbit in a sundress and booties. She's cradling him with apple juice in the baby bottle she drinks from nowadays, when she can get away with it—which seems to be most of the time.

Her accidents have stopped. She likes it here. Likes to sit in the wood chips near the carport with her cat and her bottle. Doesn't mind that the wrong thing's coming to an end.

A few stars make it through the pine branches but mostly it's just a sky deep as nothing. I go around back of the house where the hammock is, wait for Milk Glass to jump up into it with me, listen for the hum of Mother loving someone else.

It hovers like hummingbirds floating at the bougainvillea. I picture Mother and Daddy years before in the house on La Bega. Mother holding him sideways, his head on her shoulder, them both watching Mally and me with jacks or bug jars or trying to get them to play Sardines with us by hiding in the yard. My favorite spot was behind the air conditioner because that's where he always knew to look. He'd swoop down on me, then climb through our spikiest yucca plant to crouch low beside me. Mother and Mally took so long finding us that Daddy tickled my ribs trying to get me laughing. Sure enough, I couldn't stay quiet. Mally heard first and came running. Then Mother who climbed the same yucca to hide with us, even though the game was over—no one left to come searching. Daddy'd squeeze her in real close between him and me and start to tickle her. That was different. Soon Mally was bored. She'd slap my arm, saying, "You're it" and run off into the yard, singing, "Can't catch me." I followed her. The game was over so I followed her, pretending I cared whether I caught her or not.

All I hear tonight is that hum of grownup talk. I trace each of my cat's spots, the red, the black, the other black. I want to be home. I want him even if he's off his pills, I want him. It's clawing in me now, that I know she's making a choice on that porch. That this could be it. That we're losing the very last way of ever getting back to him—all hope of her remembering how much she wants him. 'cause if she loves Uncle Davis, we'll live here with them until Aunt Clea gives up and Holly drives off and the boys kill each other fighting over the one Atari joystick without the sticky firing button. And Uncle Davis will think he can tuck us in and touch our hair and sit at the breakfast table while she pours pancake batter on the griddle and Mally and I lay his silverware before him and pour his juice. He'll think we'll forget what it truly is, love. Apparently, she's already decided it doesn't matter.

Mally comes to find me with Rabbit draped over her arm. "Want to play something?" she says.

"Yes," I say but don't move. Just lie right here in the hammock swinging. Mally spins the Frisbee straight up like I showed her once, like Daddy showed me. Sure enough, the bats come swooping, snatch it for just a split second till they realize what they've got isn't tasty.

She's talking to herself or to Rabbit in sign language, which she's making up as she goes along. Her right hand flops around, bending and tugging, then sometimes both hands reach something on her body—her head or make-believe wings—and what she's saying is not of this world. Never mind that he isn't deaf—at least as far as we know—wherever Rabbit is, when Mally signs, his full attention is on her. Milk Glass just waits to pounce on her crazy hands.

Mally pulls at her shirt, her ear, her hair. Her fingers scissor and kick. She's an absolute nut, my baby sister.

"Girls," Mother calls, finally remembering us. "Bedtime."

Mally first. Then me. In a line. Just like a movie star on the red carpet. Kisses on our hair of all places, and we've never had those before, at least not as bedtime kisses. Mother's aim is off because of Uncle Davis, because he's here and something comes over her—just like it came over me with Henry at the tree, when I giggled like a goon for nothing at all.

"Tuck us in?" Mally asks, grabbing hold of my shirt.

"Not tonight," Mother says.

"Yes, tonight," I say, 'cause it's my chance at setting things straight around here.

"Not tonight," she says again.

"Yes, tonight," I say, feeling brave and very foolish. I can feel Mally's hand drop away from my waist.

"What's wrong with you, baby?" Mother asks, setting her palm to my forehead.

"I'm not sick," I say, throwing it off.

Uncle Davis puts his big face in mine, says, "You don't raise your voice to your mother, Iva."

I feel the red push up under my skin and fight to keep back the sting of my eyes. I look only at her. "I have something to say to you."

"Lower your voice and you'll get our attention," he says, butting in again.

"Don't talk to me."

"Manners, Iva," Mother says, starting to be rattled by all this.

I try to make another sentence for him. One with a beginning and an end, something to show him I'm someone to deal with, something he can't laugh at, something to flush his cheeks and make him small, small, small. Make him nothing. I don't have it in me; I don't know what those words would be.

I take her hand, tug at it, say, "Mother, please come upstairs. Please."

"Well what in the world," Mother says to him and pulls back her hand. She pushes at her forehead to hitch her bangs back up in her side-comb. But there are no bangs hanging down on her face and so she's just pushing at her bare skin to find them. "You're embarrassing your mother, Iva. What is all this?"

"Not with him here," I say, still looking only at her.

"Uncle Davis is family," she says. "Speak up now. This is getting boring." She glances at him, smiles like she might laugh but doesn't.

I can see it all over him, that he's ready to explain me away. He's studying me like I'm a dog gone foamy at the jaw, something he might have to shoot to save her from. He's got a look to his face and he's touching her arm like to pull her back, like to give her a way out.

She's not scared at all. She doesn't believe I'll do it. She's feeling strong. No matter what this is, she wants it put away. Over. Nothing can hurt her. "You want me to count?" she asks. "I'll count. One…two…thr—"

"It's wrong," I say. "What you're doing. It's wrong."

Now her eyes are pulled tight to their corners, showing too much white. She's gripping her chair arm, putting out a hand to my shirttail. "Whatever this is," she starts to say. "Whatever's got you so fussed up—"

"You're still married!" I blurt out and kick at her chair. Aunt Clea's standing in the doorway, gripping together her shards of last night's supper dishes for the glue to take. "I hate you!" I scream, feeling all the blood pour out of my head till I'm weak and pale and nothing.

I run. Aunt Clea steps aside and I'm gone. To the newel post already. I take the steps two-per.

I pull open Samuel's dresser that's been mine and Mally's for four months now, grabbing all of Holly's hand-me-downs 'cause Mother said we can't renew my wardrobe every time I decide I'm a pole bean. Shirts and shorts, undies and bras—even a padded, turquoise blue, lace number of Holly's I filched from the hamper—all into a grocery bag. I look through the trees out our side window into Henry's house. It's dark, the whole house. I can't see him in the window, but it's still possible he's there—he's always watching. He must have heard me. I stuff my backpack into the sack of clothes.

Mally comes in trailing behind Mother, who's holding her hand.

"What do you think you're doing, Iva?"

"Packing," I say. "You should know enough to recognize that."

"Don't sass me, girl."

I don't say anything back, keep working.

"This is just all out of hand. Why don't you sit down here with me and we'll talk through whatever it is."

"Whatever it is? I don't believe you for a second. You know exactly what this is. You and him."

"Don't talk that way, Iva. Nobody likes a nasty girl."

I turn around to face her, my arms loaded with all my shirts. Feel the prick beneath my ribs for what I'm saying. Hate her for making me be the one to put it all into words, make it real like that.

"Sit down here," she says and pats Mally's bunk beside her.

"I'm busy." I push everything down into the sack.

"Well then I guess it's not so important," she says and starts to leave.

No matter what the game, she'll always beat me at it. In my panic of her going, I say it: "You love him."

Mother stops, looks back. She's in our window again, reflected in its glass, but there's something off about her, something distorted now. She is entirely rearranged. Her shoulders, her arms and swan's neck fingers are not at all those of someone gone soft for being held. Her elbows are bent, one hip juts out, fingers tap-tapping her waistband.

She wipes at her face like to erase the picture of her there in the glass. "I don't love him, Iva," she says, her voice soft but certain. "Don't get crazy."

"Crazy," I say and think about that. "Maybe I am. That would make sense wouldn't it."

"Don't say that. That's not what I meant."

"Just like Daddy."

"Daddy's not crazy," Mally says and starts waving her hands around translating for Rabbit.

"Of course not," says Mother, petting Mally's hair. "Nothing's wrong with Daddy." She turns back to me. "You see what you're doing here? Just upsetting all the wrong people. You see that?"

"You can't love him," I say.

"I don't." Her face is changed, loose-nervous and struggling to keep track of how to do everything: breathe, talk, think, and be.

"He's not ours," I tell her.

"That's not what this is."

"You let him watch you. It's the same. He sits with you and it's just like with Daddy on the porch. And he looks at you. And slides himself up against you. It's the same."

"You're a baby, Iva. You're picking up on all the wrong signals. He's my sister's husband for God's sake. I can talk to him is all. It's nice to have some company, a little attention. That's all you're seeing: two grownups talking things over, trying to get to the bottom of their lives."

"At night. Alone." Always fanning and sighing from the heat. Always touching and smiling that far-off smile wider on one side 'cause one cheek gets tired of trying so hard. All the things I see and don't know how to tell her.

"You're downright ugly tonight, Iva." She grips the handle on the door. "I don't answer to you. But I don't love him, that's it." She leaves, slamming the door behind her.

Mally curls to face the wall in bed, grips Rabbit such that he makes noise breathing.

"Say goodbye," I tell her.

"You're not going," she says into the wall.

"Yes I am."

She doesn't answer.

I slam the door just like Mother but feel sorry when I see Aunt Clea in the hallway looking at me and not even bothering to wipe the tears from alongside her nose. I've got my bag and my pack and she just stands there with nothing in her hands. She looks broken. I make a racket going downstairs, out the porch, into the yard. Nobody stops me.

"Here, Milk Glass," I call. "Here, kitty-kitty-kitty-kitty." She comes running to me, that run cats do without bending their legs. I set the pack on the ground and plop her right in, though I leave it unzipped for her to breathe.

I have everything that's mine. I'm through with this house.

The porch is empty but I can still hear the hum of their words. I walk. I'm *on the lam*—like Daddy would say—so I go through trees instead of walking along the streets. I don't have any idea where to go, find myself only next door at Henry's wandering his yard—the fat oak, the sides of the house and the front I've never seen. I listen for our yard, for the screen door slapping shut after Mother come to find me. But I don't hear a sound. I can do anything I please, go anywhere I want.

This isn't how it should have gone. But I can't seem to get farther than Henry's yard. I should be marching up Tessle Street out onto Desta, and wind my way to 460 then highway 81. I am stuck. Something in me won't move. Air expanding in all the wrong places. Things replacing other things.

Daddy always knew where to go. Or maybe the place never mattered, he just knew how to move. He'd grab the keys and me, or sometimes not me and I'd run after him, get to the car just in time when I was lucky. Then we were off, on the road, listening for water, sniffing out the window for the slightest runoff from a stream. He'd tell me about when he met Mother and what color hair she had then—same as now, but he'd say brown like it was the most glorious thing he'd ever seen or smelled or tasted. He'd tell me that he sometimes lied to her and then he'd laugh about that because it was never a big lie, and always for her own good. He said she stopped coming with him on his drives when she was pregnant with me. I remember thinking I should apologize, but instead I just held his hand, feeling the little bit of electricity there in him, in us.

I stand at Henry's back door and like always, he opens it before I can knock or turn back. I'm standing straighter, I'm near stopping breathing. I feel flooded: butterflies and such. We go in and everything is dark, though I hadn't thought Mother let Mally and me stay out so late tonight. He puts a hand back to show me when to start up the stairs. I don't think he means I'm to take it. But it's there in front of me and so I do, and I can feel the way his scuffed fingers are so much thicker than mine, are gripping me in such a way that I'm tiny and safe and meant to be here.

In the attic, Henry pulls me into his room shutting the door behind us. He sits me down on the bed and I start to feel sick like when he hypnotized me in his sister's bed and I didn't do it right.

I don't know why I'm here.

"You leaving?" he asks.

"I left," I say.

"I saw."

I set my backpack on the floor and Milk Glass hops out.

"Cool," he says.

"Puma won't get her, right?"

"Naw, she sleeps outside."

Milk Glass walks the walls, crouching with her nose to the floorboards. Sniffing corners and bookshelves, researching Puma, the big black warcat who takes care of Henry's gerbils when they get lost. Milky glows bright in the dark.

"Where're you gonna go?" He asks.

"Find my dad."

"Oh."

"I don't have to leave just yet," I say.

Henry nods. "Want to play ESP?"

"Not really."

"Oh."

"Well, okay."

So he gets the white plastic, pointy egg on a chain that I see in my dreams. "It'll be freaky in the dark."

"Yeah."

"You first," he says, and frankly I'm relieved after what I asked him to tell me last time, but only a touch relieved.

It's so dark in here I can barely see him, just his blond hair and yellow eyelashes when they rest on his cheeks.

"When we do ESP," I say, "you forget it all, right?"

"Right."

"Like last time?" I ask. "You don't remember anything about last time, do you?"

"No," he says, but turns from me so I can't see his eyes. "You neither, right?"

"I mean, it's just a game, anyhow. So anything we say is

just a game, too."

"I guess," he says. "Ready?"

I nod.

"You're getting sleepy," he says, waving the glowing egg back and forth before me. "Very sleepy. You're closing your eyes."

I shut my eyes even though it never truly works for me. The house is so quiet around us that what I hear most is the way he's breathing, sort of fast like he's just run upstairs twice. But gentle, too. What I'm thinking is that I know he's older, even though if I stay we'll be in the same grade in two weeks. Still, he's older.

He says, "Iva, lie down."

I lie back on his bed, hear the box spring shift and move beneath me arranging myself. I cross my feet at the ankles. I knit my fingers together over my belly.

"Now concentrate. Say the alphabet backwards."

I start though I know he'll figure out it's regular old me, because if I were truly hypnotized I wouldn't be struggling over the order. "Z," I say, sure of that one. "Y. X. W." These are tricky. "V, U, T."

As I'm going on piecing out the letters, what I feel is the bed heavier to my right. Then the air is different up near my face. I want to open my eyes, but then he'd know.

"R," I manage. "Q, S—no that's wrong," I say. "P. O. N."

Henry is touching me. But concentrating so hard on my letters, my eyes pinched shut in the dark, I'm swimming. My skin—immersed, touched equally in all places—is delayed in telling me where I feel him, so I just don't know. Seems all over.

Now maybe something different: like a feather dragged along my whole length. But by the time I feel a shiver beneath my chin, deep into the hollow of one collarbone, inching down my sternum, his hand is gone, moved on to somewhere else and I am swimming again.

"K, J…." I can feel him breathing.

"Keep going," he says.

"I. H. G. F."

I think he's to my ear now. He's lying beside me, his mouth is at my right ear, and if he would just say it—just say what I asked him last time I had the egg and then ran because of what came out of my mouth. If he would just say it and let me stop the letters, tell me it's okay to be here with him, say someone in this world wants me.

But I'm near A and he's gone from my ear, without one word. His fingers are slower now, careless. Now I know exactly where they are. Along my side. Up under my shirt, palm hot over my heart, touching the cotton. I'm memorizing this, because wherever he is I am dented, permanently, I think. If I lie down in a storm, my skin will hold rain.

"D," I say, feeling his thumb press my very little speck of nipple. "C, B, A."

He bends his cheek to mine again and I do kiss his face. I do, and feel him pull away. I do, and am sick. And I feel nothing, not breath, not touch, nothing.

"When I say your name you will wake up," he says, "and you will forget it all."

Good.

The very second he says "Iva" I sit up and before I can get out of here explode crying, sobbing, wailing. Milk Glass comes running, jumps into my lap. He doesn't know what to do with me, but puts his hand over my mouth—his big sister's just next door, his parents sleeping downstairs.

"Okay," he whispers, burying my face in his arms to quiet me. "I love you."

But there is a difference.

In having to ask. In being the only one to want it. In striking a deal. There is a difference.

He puts my face into his pillow, holds me there bent into his lap, breathing in the salty batting. This is all wrong. Every bit of it.

My face is swollen and salty, my cheeks feel like they're cracking through the wet. I pull up my head. He turns on the lamp by the bed and he's just a boy again.

"You all right now?" he asks.

I nod, look at him. "Your turn," I say.

"Sure," he shrugs.

I take the egg from him, dangle it in front of his face, swing it slowly. "You're tired," I say. "So tired. Your eyes are closing."

He sits before me, sleeping if I'm to believe him and I think I do because he always seems so perfectly calm, so deeply under. It hardly matters anymore.

"You're in the deepest sleep," I say.

With his eyes shut, he looks frightened. Something has happened between us. Something's been happening the whole time. If the egg has any powers at all, what I make him dream as I go is that I'm still here. I'll be dreaming it too. I can settle my own hands in my lap. I can choose this. Because something is anything, can be everything.

Henry is small. But he's someone.

"So deep, deep, deep," I say. "You'll never wake up for anyone but me."

I have him stand by the big window against the wall. I

move his arms down by his sides. I inch him to the left to avoid the windowsill cutting into his back. I rearrange him, touch his hair and arms and shirtfront so that I'll remember each bit of him. So that I'll recognize him if I ever see him again—and I think I will, a boy with yellow hair like mine and like Daddy's, one who stands against walls for me, one who shuts his eyes trusting me for little reason, one who tells me to lie down on his bed, one whose mouth pulls in when I stand so close.

"Sleep until you hear me say your name," I tell him. "Only me, remember that."

I grab Milk Glass and my sack, then set his lamp on the bookcase instead of the bed table. I pull down the covers on the bed, push my hand across the blue sheets worn as pajama knees.

"Just for me," I say. "Just me."

I leave Henry standing forever waiting for me.

＊ ＊ ＊

The streets are empty. All the houses are dark. I look back to our house and it's pitch-black as well. Not one light, lamp, or flashlight searching. Henry's room stays lamplit for me. I start for Desta, but turn around and stare into that glow, think through that wall. Drop my belly over and over spelling out his name. H-E-N-R-Y. H-E-N-R-Y. This is isn't love but it's something.

By the time I've chosen to go back, I hear it. A slow *ping*, *pock*, *ping*. Slow but steady. I round the bend of the driveway and can see rocks falling from Holly's window, see the slow flash of her hand glowing white in the darkness. Her aim is true: away from the little yellow car and Clea's brown sedan snugged up under the carport. I twist my feet into the gravel drive, making noise, letting her know I'm here, I can see her. Still, she keeps on with the chinking of rock into blue metal.

I push in through the front door. I climb the stairs. All the doors are shut upstairs, even mine. Behind it, Mally lies waiting in my bunk, sleeping with Rabbit on her shoulder, her hand open on his back leg. Her face is smeared from crying, her eyelashes crusted white. She wakes just long enough to pick up her head, say, "I don't love you anymore," and kiss me goodnight.

I don't think I sleep but then open my eyes to find Mally gone and Mother's face level with my bunk, her fingers stroking my hair behind my ears.

"I knew you'd come back," she says.

I don't answer her. She hasn't any idea who I am now.

"I know you probably wish you hadn't," she says, kissing my ear, making me turn my head away. "But we need you."

Sun's come in strong and with Mother standing where she is and the glare off the window, I can't make out Henry's room, if there's a light still on or not. There's nothing to her kiss anymore, nothing much I need.

"I'll go again. I will," I say.

"We're all going."

"No." There isn't any floor to this. "Not now."

"It's too long already. Time for something new." She pretends to smile, pretends to believe I don't know she's having to pretend.

"Just because you've ruined everything here doesn't mean you get to pull us out again. No," I say, "it's not fair. Just because you love him?"

"I don't even like him."

That's the biggest lie or truth I've ever heard—I'm not

sure which.

She shuts her eyes and her eyelids are pleated crosswise. Her hair is smooth, her lips shiny and fresh, but her face knows she's ancient. "So much of love is circumstance, Iva. You'll learn that one day."

"You don't know a thing about it," I tell her.

"This stuff," she says, "making a person do things she can't understand, giving her moments of desperation, that's just the heart being weak, baby. That's all. There's nothing true about it. Real love has nothing to do with time or place. It's something you can't ever get over because you've felt it long as you been breathing. It can't be undone."

"Then why settle?" I say.

"Something about nearness. And sometimes we fall weak." She kisses what she can reach of me, my elbow, my shoulder. I like her better when she's sad.

"Weak?" I ask to be sure. "That make-do love, it's nothing honest?"

"That's right," she says. "I was only being weak."

"Me, too," I say, seeing myself in the gray of her eyes.

"Running away, you mean?"

"No. Wanting to stay."

She pulls me closer to her and I let her because I can be hers like this. I can let myself need it again, this way she's talking and touching me. I know it will not last. So I take it now.

* * *

Mother sings making breakfast for everyone, bacon and cornbread muffins from the Jiffy box. I'm setting butter knives and jam spoons on the porch table and she's humming a waltz to the one-two-three of her spoon scraping out the lumps against the side of the batter bowl. I almost start up humming with her, catch my feet keeping step to her stirring.

All of the others—even Uncle Davis—are staking out the table in the kitchen. Aunt Clea's eating cinnamon toast. So it's just the three of us, and Mother's looking pretty again. I suppose you always want to look your best saying goodbye, so her peachy cheeks and pink-pearl lips may not be real— Mother has her ways.

Mally doesn't know we're leaving yet. Without the jabbing elbows of Perth and Samuel, she's back to being chatty. She recites her list of appointments for the day: "First the tire for me and Rabbit. Then spinning. I need to dress him. Mother," she says, "where's Rabbit's swim cap?"

"You're taking that poor animal swimming today?" Mother asks.

"He's not a poor animal," she says, pounding her pudged wad of a fist on the table.

"No, certainly. Every growing cat needs a mother just like you." She pours my orange juice, saying, "Iva, you ought to be ashamed letting your naked-nudey cat run around in public."

Mally giggles and juice starts coming out her nose. She makes a horrible face, flapping her hands like she'll take off any second. "Oh! It burns."

I can't recall the porch sounding any other way than this, Mother and Mally and me talking and teasing. Even through the house door, I think they're listening to us, wishful.

Mother's the one picking her moments now. She's buttering Mally's muffin, letting her drink milk from the baby bottle even though she worries Mally's teeth will go out of whack, if nothing else. After breakfast we troop into the kitchen with our dishes and the family of five are all gone, every single one of them hiding from us upstairs.

We have next to nothing here, so we're packed by 10:30. Mally's out back with drooling Rabbit. They swing on the tire and she tells him stories located in her hands and in the air—him in his swim cap with the plastic flowers sponging right out of his head, his ears spiking up through the snips she made in the yellow rubber. Mother still hasn't told her.

❋ ❋ ❋

"I'm thinking Kentucky," says Mother, stuffing the last of Mally's shorts in a Kroger sack.

"Mississippi," I say. "Pascagoula."

"Georgia."

"Mississippi."

"South Carolina," Mother says, making a game of it.

"Mississippi."

"Pete's sake, Iva," she says, starting a new sack for shoes. "There's no chance he'd have stayed put this long."

"Mississippi," I say and walk out into the hall.

All the doors are latched shut except one. Through its crack, I see Aunt Clea reading on her bed. She looks nothing like Mother. Her hair is curly, tight to her head, short. She's tiny and pale. Younger, but older-looking. I knock.

"What!" she says, in case I'm Mother.

I push through the door. "We're going," I tell her.

"Well that's that. I'm sorry it didn't work out for you here," she says. "You two girls are fine, just fine." She's nervous. This is talk, just chittery talk that doesn't mean a thing. And it does matter who says what—whether or not being told I'm all right counts.

"Do you know where my father is?"

"What?" she almost laughs. "No."

"Last we heard was Pascagoula, but Mother says he's not there anymore."

"You talk to Lilly about that," she says, picking up her book again but not opening it just yet. "I want nothing to do with it. The root of all this mess."

"I know she's sorry," I tell her. "It was only circumstance, though. Just make-do love. Not real; she's already got that."

"Well," she says, "she's just got it all, hasn't she?" Aunt Clea springs off of the bed quick into the bathroom, dropping her book as she goes. But she does not slam the door; it's her house, after all. This is all hers. And when we leave, she's the one stuck with it.

The bathroom lock clicks. The tap opens and water rushes through.

* * *

Mother is still fussing over Mally's socks, matching them, balling them, tossing them in the bags. She hasn't made much progress since I left. I'll have to stick with her till she's through, make sure she keeps clear on our priorities. Maybe even find her a little notepad and start her up a list. I grab two of Mally's white bobby socks and turn one inside the other, drop it into the bag.

"What do you say the chances are of Mallory Mae having trouble with this? I don't think I could stand sopping up the backseat every time we get gas again." Mother hands me a paper bag. "Sugar, load up supplies—just in case."

I grab towels and all the underpants I can find, a can of Wet Ones, too. "If you think he's not there anymore," I say, "what's the harm in Pascagoula?"

She collapses onto Mally's bunk. "You are the most tenacious thing I've ever met." I don't know what tenacious means but I like the sound of it. She checks her hands, traces curves in her palm. "You wear your Mother down." Then real slow and tired, she says, "What's the harm?"

We're in the car before lunchtime: me, Mother, Mally, the two cats, seven sacks of clothes and an accident kit, Mother's shoebox of photographs—what she calls her breakables—and Uncle Davis's money. He's the only one seeing us off, she and the kids are holding their breaths and rocks inside. The blue doors and roof of our car are newly pocked, even the glass is chipped in tiny starbursts across the windshield. Uncle Davis fits his thumb to one of Holly's pebble-dings but doesn't say a word about it to Mother, who gives him a kiss on the cheek, then rolls us out onto Tessle Street. Mally and I are in back together, as always, and he waves to us even though we're hiding down low from him.

The lamp's still on in Henry's room, so maybe what keeps him standing is a touch more than weakness, a touch realer than make-do. I feel like a woman, full of air and shifting. I stand hunched forward to check my hair in the rearview, roll down my window more, enough so I can lean my whole self out.

"Henry!" I call at the top of my lungs.

Mother stops the car hard, dipping the hood for how the car wants to lurch forward. She turns around and her eyes are wide as Mally's mouth around a jawbreaker. She pats my hand, jokes, "That's the way, baby. Leave a man waiting in every state." She doesn't know I'm giving him up.

Mally covers Rabbit's ears in case I might do it again, signs something to him by way of explanation. Milk Glass is exploring the car, crawling under the seats, getting wedged beneath the pedals until Mother screams and she shoots into the backseat. Mother and I are both waiting for Mally to realize we're leaving Blacksburg for good. So far, we think she's in shock.

Mother reaches under her seat for the maps I stole on our drive from Tyler to Tennessee. She's leaning forward, grabbing far under, hardly able to see over the wheel. I'm pulling them out of my pillowcase quick as I can, tucking them back underneath her. But they're soft as cotton from lying smoothed under my cheek all these nights, me dreaming of where he's gone. So they flop and I have to reach deeper and then Mother's got my hand instead of the map.

"You little thief," Mother says, gripping me hard. She sits up straight, checks all her mirrors though there's no one else out driving just now.

I sink beside Mally, wishing I had only asked for them. Today is a good day, though. Today she is joking instead of yelling. We're okay for now.

"You must know all the routes," she says, "I guess you'd better sit up here and navigate."

"Really?" I ask and start to scramble over the seat, but Mother lurches the car to stop.

"Iva," she says, "if you're going to be a woman, you need to learn to move like one."

I open the door, stand up straight in the road, then slide in next to her in front, feeling the swing of hips, feeling tall and whole and choosy.

We find 460 which is just where I was headed last night. The wagon jounces over pavement grooves, and I begin counting the bumps already. Dressed in soft pines like velvet bunched up on a table, these low mountains tug at me; we're really going from here and I was just starting to notice them, to like being cradled in their valley. Mally's not yet said a word about leaving, though I suspect Rabbit's the only one would hear it if she did. Mother and I both keep sniffing the air in the backseat, just waiting for her to spring a leak. Once we get to the interstate, Mother's foot is propped to coast at 67. I'm studying the map, try to make out the roads whose black and red lines are almost entirely rubbed clean from the paper. I'm looking for the fastest way down to Pascagoula, and steering us clear of all circumstance.

lie

"I went to school with a kid who kept a camel in his garage and charged us nickels to brush his teeth."

"Lie!"

"Okay, it was a llama and I paid a buck-fifty."

"Nuh-uh. Really?" I could see Daddy doing it, asking politely that the llama open wide, and reaching deep in to the way-back molars, scrubbing them clean of grass and cud and whatever else might cling to a llama's tooth; he was always so thorough. "Mother, is that true?"

"What do you think?" she asked, grinning at Mally and me eating this up in the backseat.

"A banana is really a vegetable," he started up again.

"Lie."

"Porcupines have only three legs, using their tails to balance out as a fourth."

I thought about this one a second. "Lie," I said, because I've seen them at the zoo.

"Popping corn is really a kind of jumping bean."

"Truth?" I asked, unsure but thinking it could very well be of the Mexican jumping sort; and Daddy liked to sprinkle hot chili powder all over his popcorn till it was red and furry-looking.

"Gotcha," he said, checking me in the rearview.

We were out driving, nowhere in particular. Daddy at the wheel, 'cause he was going with or without us—it was just a matter of could she get us in the car before he left. She kept a satchel at the door with our necessaries: a jar of Wet Ones, cans of pop, little packs of crackers that came with their own spready cheese and a red plastic stick for smoothing it on, little-girl sweaters that zipped up the front.

It was spring and nobody knew, but this was almost it for us.

"We had a cat named Señor Don Gato," Daddy said. Mother laughed. "It's true," he said. "He fell off the roof and broke his solar plexus."

"Lie! That's the song. We've never even had a cat." I tugged at his wisps of yellow hair going every which way because they were always too long and Mother kept asking him to let her cut it, but he liked to joke that he was making a fashion statement—and besides which, he said, "Who would let your mother come near him with scissors in her hand?"

Mally started in singing about the fat cat sitting on his roof reading love letters. She made up the words once she was out of verses.

It happened so fast. He stopped talking but I didn't notice. We were slowing down, but I didn't get that either. The pieces started knitting themselves together and what I saw was Mother touching his arm and he looked over to her. I remember thinking that's the one, that's the look. Here it comes. She took hold of the wheel and we were pulling over, quickly, swerving.

Mother turned around to us, suddenly angry. "Get out of the car," she said. Daddy was hitting the dashboard with both fists and heaving his back like if he were crying hard but I didn't hear a thing except for Mother's hollering. "Now!" she screamed when I wasn't fast enough. I wanted to tell her I knew what to do because I'd been with him alone and he told me to hide in the backseat when he gets like this, so all I'd know was what I could hear, his moaning and crying. Then it would be okay. He'd be okay. We'd drive home and he'd carry me to bed slumped-sleepy over his shoulder. He'd pull off my shoes and drop them to the floor where I always tripped on them the next morning. And then he'd go back out into the hall, to Mother and the light on in their room.

Mally and I scrambled out the side of the station wagon. I walked her far from the car, and we sat amongst the weeds and waxmyrtle. It's not that Mother told us to sit facing the sun instead of the car, but somehow I knew this was what they'd both want. I was trembly, like the car shaking from trucks shooting past, like the way a moon sits on water.

I started the game over again with her. "Bees don't make honey, ants do."

"Lie," she said, nudging a rock out of the dry ground with the toe of her shoe.

"Bears eat little girls whenever they find one because of how tasty we are."

Her face folded in a little, from her forehead where she

was thinking this through, to her lips pursing up. "Truth?" So I growled and nibbled her arm. But I felt silly, like I was watching myself try to be someone I wasn't, so we stopped and were quiet and still.

"We could run away," I told her. "And they wouldn't even know where to start looking."

"Truth," she said.

I didn't know where we were, but the sun was falling fast enough that we saw it drop down below the thick of pines before us. The whole field of tough and unsteady ground broken off the highway and falling deep before us into what was maybe a river down there, glowing orange for the sun. Mally's cheeks showed it, warm and even—a honey jar on a bright kitchen windowsill. Our knees showed it. There were crows coming home now, late as it was getting, yellow-throated warblers and cowbirds, too. Wrens were leaving the pawpaw trees. I did not turn around.

"I have to go," Mally said, swishing her knees open and shut.

"Hold it."

"I've been holding it. I got to go."

"I don't know," I said. "They're not ready."

"Iva?"

"Don't think about it."

"Then I think about it even more." She folded over her lap, gripping every bit of herself tightly to hold it in.

"The sun is butter," I told her. "And every time it sets, it's really melting."

"Yes, truth." She spoke weakly, right into her legs. "Iva, I mean it."

I glanced over my shoulder, quickly like I was really

looking at the cars passing by. Mother's back filled her window. I couldn't see him.

"Iva," Mally moaned.

I left her on our patch of cooling ground and walked to the car. Standing there, hoping one of them would turn around and remember us. I looked in. Saw him dying, I thought: bent nearly in half across the front seat, lying there separate from Mother who was pushed up against the inside of the car door not touching him at all. His eyes were clenched shut, crying, his mouth open with so much sound heaving out, his legs and arms tucked up in a ball. I turned around, back to Mally. Felt my face wet and tight. He was right not to have let me see this.

Mally had tightened into an absolute stone out in the field—clutching her knees to her, using every last muscle to keep it in. I looked back to the car. The fit was ending, he was coming up out of his hole. Mother had pulled him into her lap. He was on his side facing the backseat, breathing hard, panting even. His face looked slick. Still, she gripped him: held his beard under his chin, and one of his wrists. "We're okay," she said. "You're fine and I'm fine. Mally and Iva—we're just all fine." He was looking up and out the window. I thought maybe he saw me and I should go back to Mally. But his eyes were strange and terrible. "I know, I know," she was saying. "It's over and we're fine. Rest." She kissed the top of his head again and again. He looked so very small curled up in her lap, like a woman or a boy.

Mally was hopping around. Wrapping her arms around her sides, bouncing around and kicking up dust. I led her into the trees. She pulled down her pants and I held her steady while she squatted all wobbly to the ground. Then we went back to the flattened grass to wait.

It seemed hours before Mother called to us, and maybe it was because then there was nothing around but what the headlights could find. We piled back in and Mother drove. Daddy lay across the front seat, his head by Mother's hip, our scratchy wool picnic blanket draped over his face. Mally pulled herself up by the headrest, saying, "Are you sick, Daddy?"

"Mmm," we heard from under the fringe.

"Shhh, let's let him sleep, baby." Mother's right hand was on him, rubbing and pressing him slowly.

And so we did. Mother turned the car back around and we drove. Once home, she sent us in through the dark, and Mally ran fearlessly through nighttime to the fridge for a Creamsicle before bed.

From my window, I watched Mother and Daddy in lamplight glow, heard him tell her, "It overtakes me. I can't even feel it coming most times, it just does and I'm ruined. I'm not the same. It's so dark in there, in my head sometimes, and I just need water."

"No, hush," she said. "You won't go driving tomorrow—not to the lake. Not for a long time, till you get it fixed in your head what's good here, what's alive and plenty good enough living right in this house. What's worthwhile."

"I want him back."

"Yes."

"I want to be with him."

"No. Stop it. You can say that to me?"

"I know, I'm sorry." He stood facing her, between our house and the car, and not one of us knew which it would be. "Nothing I feel is truly me. Since we were seventeen—"

"It's different with Clea. We've never been that sort of sisters. I've never had that."

"—I think I've taken on everything he'd ever thought about. He had it worse, though."

"He was sick."

"He was a kid. We were kids."

"It's different when you're twins," she said.

"It must be."

"But let me ask you—" she said, holding on to her elbows squeezing herself rigid in front of him "—what good does it do him?"

Then he was crying again but less, much less. He was flat as a bicycle inner tube run through with a nail. Limp, useless. He looked into her face, pressed his cheek to hers.

"You're Jameson not Jesse," she said. "I'm Lilly. And we're in love."

He kissed her.

She helped him to the house, her arms strong around him, one across the front, the other across his back. He leaned on her, stumbly, like how they walked after sangria made in the Kool-Aid pitcher. The front door opened, then their bedroom door shut before I could get to him, touch him—his hand or even just my finger through his belt loop. Mally wandered the halls, her blanket trailing behind her. She stood in front of the fridge peeling back the corners of plastic-wrapped leftovers to sniff at and poke her fingers in. She found a plate of Bisquick biscuits and dropped a hunk of butter onto the plate. She took her crayons and stiff paper and made a nest of this collection on the kitchen sofa. She was full of energy: scribbling away at her blue paper, holding a corner down with the elbow that propped her up—that hand holding out a biscuit she gnawed at. She bit off the pointy nubs that get dark on the tops of the biscuits, so that it was now smooth and round all over. Then she began taking enormous bites; crumbs spewing all over the cushions and her drawing, which, far as I could tell, was a camel in a dress on a hillside by a car. Her cheeks shone with butter.

I stood in the doorway behind her, rubbing my eyes for how late it was, fascinated. Wondering what sort of sisters were we.

the last bluff

Somewhere in the thirty-seven grooves of pavement between Bristol, Virginia, and Bristol, Tennessee, Mally goes deaf. She's still talking, but something about the permanence in leaving, of crossing the VA/TN border has changed her.

We're just to Kingsport and the only difference Mother's noticed is that she's having to point and repeat an awful lot for Mally who's taking this game pretty far: "See the smokestack? See it? Iva, show your sister the smokestack.... Hog farms everywhere, Mally. Roll up your window. Mally, roll it up. Up, the window. Iva, handle it."

I have to dump Milk Glass off my lap to lean into the back. Mally looks up surprised to see me reaching for the window's knob. She's cradling Rabbit, who's in an open-back bonnet and matching knit booties, her hand flip-flopping around in the pig air. I watch the way he's watching her, taking note of how she's talking to him. Like waves pushing over the sand, all it is is movement.

My birthday's going to be in this car if we drive straight through to Pascagoula. Which is fine by me. I'm turning twelve and can feel it coming on. Mally's still Mally: a baby, nowhere nearer to seven.

I'm in the front seat navigating, and Mally pokes my neck. "I'm starved," she's saying. "Rabbit, too."

Mother pulls over at the Howard Johnson's for grilled cheeses at the counter. It's September-hot and we've got the cats in grocery sacks on the floor beside us. Rabbit's still but Milk Glass jostles her bag, threatens to tip it over. Mother asks for a tuna fish sandwich hold the bread, and Mally and I dump half the glop in each sack.

We take turns in the bathroom, and when the waitress tells Mally she's cute as a rag doll, I study her 'cause maybe it's true—that she's not hearing a word. But no. There's the slightest rolling of her shoulders in a nervous shrug. What doesn't make sense is that she'd go deaf instead of mute. Mute really makes a statement. It's the silent treatment forever; no one can pull that off but the truly insulted. Deaf when the person doesn't know it, deaf just seems rude.

We pile back into the wagon and head south on I-81 a while more, Mother serving as guide, just as cheerful and finger-pointy as the microphone lady standing at the front of a Tyler rose garden tour bus. The sun bakes us, the air winds thick, tangled hanks of our hair. We're going there. Truly. We'll find him and he'll be there and all of what will happen then will cancel out these four moves away.

The way I imagine it is that he'll be reading the paper or smoking a pipe. Something with his hands, though I'm not sure these are the things he does. He'll hear the motor and get up to look out the window. He'll stand there a little too long because he just can't believe it's us, because he needs to be sure we're truly his again before his feet will budge. Mally will put her sticky fingers in Mother's hair, asking, "Is this where we live now?" The motor will chug, Mother's hand still on the keys in the ignition. I'll open my door first. He'll see me and that's when he'll know, and his feet will run. He'll run and I'll run and the air will hurt so much to breathe because of how we hold each other too tightly after not having held at all for four years.

I don't know Pascagoula at all. Mother thinks it must be muggy. That's all she'll say about it.

We're slowing down now. Pulling over. I don't say a word. I've seen this before and don't like where it's headed. But Mother does not step out of the car, plant herself on a hillside to watch the sun and make up her mind. She stays put and Mally and I both sit quietly pretending we're still bouncing up and down along the road.

"There's something wrong with the car," Mother whispers. "I don't know what."

Mally signs something to Rabbit, her hand a bird then a rock.

"We'll make it to the next town, I think," Mother says, hoping I'll answer her, tell her I believe her. "Niota," she says. "That's pretty."

I don't say a word, keep watching the cars that had been behind us pull closer to him.

She starts up the wagon again. "Hear that?" she says. "I just don't like the sound of that."

It's all the same.

※ ※ ※

We pull all our sacks of clothes from the car, leaving it not at a mechanic's garage, but hissing and spitting in the parking lot of the Always Inn—I don't like the sound of that either but Mother says *isn't that the cutest thing* and she just has to have this one over the Motel 6 across the way. She wants a bath. Mally tells hand stories to Rabbit. I stroke Milk Glass, who lies on her side flicking the tip of her tail up and down.

I don't know how much money Uncle Davis gave Mother, and I'm worried it's too much, that she'll start feeling breezy about commitments to certain daughters.

"How long's she been in there?" Mally asks.

"Too long," I say. Mally sticks her head forward to look at my lips making the words.

"No, really, how long?"

The room is done up in pinks and browns but they're all off because the pink is a red pink and the brown a yellow brown. The curtains run on a shower rod and drag on the floor. There are only two beds, though the woman at the front desk said we could have a cot brought up. Fat chance I'm sleeping on a cot, getting my finger stuck in the hinges, ripping it off in the night, waking up bloody and sore. No thanks.

I know what she's doing in there, thinking it through. Worrying over going to him. Thinking she's wrecking everything. I don't know how one person can be so wrong. We were fine then. We were all so terrifically fine. Doesn't anyone else see that?

"How long now?" Mally asks.

I'm shaking my left leg for how bad I've got to go pee. I check the crusty clock on the bed table. "Two and a quarter hours," I say.

"Oh."

Rabbit curls up on the bed where Mother dropped her sacks of shoes and Aunt Clea's tennis socks. Milk Glass is inspecting each bag, sniffing the pillows and pulling back her nose quick like if she's cut herself on glass. I pull out my maps, start to go over our route in case Mother asks, in case I have to show her in the dark.

"Is she all right, Iva?"

"It'll be okay."

Mally translates for Rabbit on the bed.

"Why do you do that?" I ask. "Neither one of you is deaf."

She pretends not to hear me, not to even know I've said a thing.

Then she looks up for a split second, just enough for me to be surprised by how blue her eyes still are. "Why are we always leaving?" she asks. "I liked it there."

"Hush," I tell her, but she's not looking back for any answer.

✿ ✿ ✿

I can't hold it anymore so I touch the bathroom door. Everything behind it is still. No splashing. No humming. Not even any breathing as far as I can tell. Between getting my hand around the doorknob and pushing in the door, I wonder about being the child of a lady drowned in a motel tub, being the one to find her puckered and blue and so sorry for everything. Official types would set Mally and me on a bus then, get us to Daddy fast as rain. Maybe even give us some money to see us through—after all we've been through, our mother dead and us traumatized, maybe not even speaking anymore because of the way her neck seemed snapped with how loose it was leaning on one shoulder, over seeing her dead, truly dead like a dog in the road but one you've lived with for years.

"Iva." Mother groans it, her neck straight as swamp-cedar. "Can't I have any privacy? Can't I just have one minute to think?"

I step back out.

"I wanna go," says Mally when I swipe a key from the top of the TV.

"No," I say.

"Please, Iva. I'm coming." She's standing right there, Rabbit dangling over one of her arms, Milky curling around Mally's left ankle.

"Can't you leave me alone?" I slam the door on her, or try to. It's on a spring arm that's too strong and slow to shut. I don't know why she doesn't just come out after me, but she doesn't and I'm glad.

I follow the balcony wrapping around the building down to the parking lot. I walk a gravel road away from the motel. Queen Anne's Lace lines the path and climbs tall as Mally, up through trash and worn tires in a field beyond. The highway is behind me but I can hear it, all the ways we're stuck.

The gravel peters out and I'm on loose dirt getting dust inside my sandals. I keep going. There's nothing around just the path and the flowers and some cloudy, gray weeds ugly as all. I wade into the grasses and pull down my bottoms, pee in the orange dust, feel spray on my ankles. Walking back I tug at the Queen Anne's, start to our balcony with seven stalks. But I drop them when the dirt becomes gravel because it's risky to pretend this is any sort of a home.

She's right there when I open the door, fiddling with the

television for Mally. "Where were you?" she asks, but not like she's mad. More like she's sorry.

"I had to pee," I say.

"Why didn't you say so?" she says. "What are you scratching?"

"I don't know, something's just itching me." All down my back and bum.

"Let me look." She tugs me over to her by my waistband, turns me around, lifts my shirt, and pulls at my shorts. "You've got chigger bites, darling," she laughs. "Go peel everything off in the tub—make sure they're off of you."

Little raised, pointy bumps all over my bottom and my back. They sting and itch and I can't quit scratching.

Mother comes to stand in the doorway. "What am I gonna do with you two? One girl's scared to hear, the other's scared to speak. What has your world done to you?"

"We're okay," I tell her, because getting on the road is all I want right now. And because *she* is my world.

"You're not okay, Iva. You're not." Mother pulls her hair back with both hands, grabs a rubber band off the bathroom counter and ties up a ponytail. She pieces through my clothing, checking every stitch.

"I just want to go," I say. "Can't we just go now?"

"The car."

"I think the car's okay."

"I'd worry the whole drive. I'd just worry till I was sick."

"So no difference."

"You don't know what he's like," she says, rubbing her cheeks and looking at herself doing it in the mirror.

"I know I don't."

❁ ❁ ❁

Early in the morning we're on I-75, making our way to him. The cats are curled together in the foot well behind my seat. Mother's quiet. Mally's deaf as all, now pretending trouble at reading lips. She leans forward, her brow pulled taut between her eyebrows; she even reaches out her hand like she'll put her fingers on my lips to make out the words better when I speak. But she doesn't actually touch me. Then she sits back against the seat, lips pursed, brow still grooved.

I'm running the tip of my finger along the armrest, down into the ashtray, over to the light blue window knob. "Pretty drive, yeah?" I say, willing to try anything.

"It all looks like the same highway brush," Mother says.

"It's greener down here. Grass-green. North was more forest-green. It's yellow, too."

"Are you talking?" Mally asks no one in particular.

Mother tips up her chin into her rearview. "Greeeeeeen," she drags out, letting Mally read it in her lips. "Iva's saying it's a different greeeen here."

"You don't believe her, do you?" I ask, looking out at the rows of corn drape together then pull apart, making sure Mally can't see my mouth—which is silly to be hiding if *I* don't believe her myself.

Mother doesn't answer me.

We cross Tennessee into Alabama and Mother's suspended in a state of completely rattled nerves. She turns the radio on, then punches the buttons but we haven't had accurate preset buttons for eons so all she gets is static. She turns it back off. The wipers start going and she pulls the lever to squirt washer fluid. Done with that, she flicks on the right turn signal, then the left. Just checking. I'm getting dizzy with all her fiddling, even dizzier watching the lampposts and telephone wires that hang low then tug up, then low then up.

We're getting so close to the bottom of America, Pascagoula straight and a little to the right below us, that I can't sleep or talk or even think clearly. All my innards are getting jumbled, swelling and thumping and knocking around in me at once. I have my own list and the closer we get to him the more pages it covers: Daddy in my picture, or singing "Slip Slidin' Away" over and over again, just that one line down then up because he can't remember anymore of the song; Daddy on the front lawn in Tyler, falling asleep hoarse from hollering for us; ice cream and crawfish moque chou; his beard bristling me awake at whatever hours he'd come home — 'cause first he'd come to me, show me he's back — then slipping into Mother's arms. That I'm his favorite.

Late lunch in Greenville at the Too Damn Hot. It's really Darn but the customers and waitresses and cooks are all saying some damn ribs, a damn pulled pork sandwich, one damn slice of peach pie. Our waitress has something wrong with her face, black patches in front of her ears, one stretching as high as her forehead. "You know what you want?" she asks.

Mother's giving Mally a *Don't even think about staring!* glare. But I'm the one can't pull my eyes from her. At first the spots look scabby, but once I'm used to them they're like rocky terrain. I can almost imagine a bird perching there by her eye.

"Iva," Mother's saying. "Order or I'll order for you."

I scan the menu fast. "Cheeseburger and fries, please."

Her name's Fran and she smiles at me even though I can't stop looking.

"What's wrong with her?" Mally asks after Fran has gone back to the counter.

"Looks like melanoma," says Mother. "Sun cancer."

"It's gross," Mally says after making a show of studying our lips.

"I think it's kind of pretty," I say.

"Well whatever it is, it's serious." Mother peels her straw wrapper and starts sipping at her orange pop.

Mally and I eat our damn burgers and fries and Mother picks at her damn cheese and tomato melt. Mally adds damn to whatever she's saying and Mother gives up on shushing her, just rolls her eyes.

This is my birthday and I only now remembered. I make a little deal with an imaginary cake and its candles: get us to him and I won't put up a fuss that they've forgotten I'm adolescent today.

We're back in the car and Mother says, "Let's drive around Greenville. Have a little look-see." We pass the churches with high steeples, the fruit-stands kept by leather-skinned women with sagged-out bosoms, sitting in lawn chairs, mason jars of change in their laps.

"I'm buying a lemon of all things," says Mother, "because I've never seen one so huge and perfect yellow. And besides, I have a craving for something tart after that greasy lunch."

Not even any sugar to dip it in like Mally and I used to suck from them back in Nacogdoches with Daddy. Mother plops herself on a bench and digs her thumb up under the rind. She slurps and swallows each section and even sucks on the seeds before spitting those out on the sidewalk, saying "whoopsie." Then she eats the strips of peel sitting in her lap.

Mally and I just gawk along with the fruit-stand ladies and the passersby.

We get back in the car and Mother smells so good, all bright and tangy. I'm not sure how she does it without me catching on, but she gets our sacks of clothes and the cats and Mally and me into another motel—it's a cute building and we're just in it to sightsee and it's too hot for the cats so we'd better take them in with us and we'd better take all our sacks 'cause one of the doors of the Impala isn't locking right anymore. And then here we are, staring at blue and green curtains in a room just like the Always Inn, only this is the Last Bluff and it's got decks of cards in every drawer and sleepy jacks and spooky queens painted on the ceiling.

Mother's in the tub again and this time when I think about being half an orphan I like the idea. Mally and I lie on our backs on top of the one bed's coverlet. There is no TV, so we're just watching the ceiling fan. Milky and Rabbit are bored out of their gourds, like Mother would say, lying like sacks of potatoes on the foot of the bed ready to claw at anyone who moves past. Mally lifts her arms in the air and starts telling herself a silent story. Her fingers walk along a trail, then stop to meet her other hand moving past. Her hands hold tight and sway left over me, then right over the floor, then back and forth again.

"It's my birthday," I tell her.

She pretends not to hear but hugs me anyhow.

I wake to Mother combing out her hair on my side of the bed.

"My two sleepyheads," she says.

I nod, watch the bend of her wrist, how it turns to comb behind her. "Want me to?" I ask. I sit up and take the comb from her, start pulling through her brown hair long enough to just brush her elbows.

"I could really go for another lemon. You could walk down for me."

"A person can't eat plain lemons," I say.

"Oh can't she?"

"Can I get something?"

"Get whatever you like with the change," she says. "Just get me a sack of lemons."

"A whole sack?"

"A whole sack, button." She gets a five-dollar bill from her purse, folds it up for me and sticks it in my shorts pocket.

The sun's getting tired. Just a haze of light on the street. I turn right, then another right, pass a dark window for bus tickets, see two men with bottle bags sitting on the bench where Mother ate her first lemon. The stand is still there, the old thick-skinned woman dark as a chocolate orchid Daddy once brought home to Mother from one of his trips; she threw it in the trash the next time he left. I checked on it but the neck of its stem was snapped, the roots torn clear off the stalk, its sandy soil scattered. The lady is sitting, saggy as ever, sleeping almost, with her arms folded across her chest as a droopy shelf.

"What'll do, child?" she asks me, barely opening her eyes.

"A sack of lemons, please, and—" I'm thinking what I want, looking all the pears over, thinking maybe I'd like a red Seckel pear.

"Your mother having a baby?" she asks, handing me the heavy paper bag.

"No."

She gives me my change and I go without my pear, walk

the other side of the street, slowly. All the windows are pitch black, a flower shop full of brown-edged pink roses and gray carnations, a hardware store, a tiny bank. The ticket window's light now, with a sorry-looking man reading behind the desk. Out front, a man sitting on his duffel bag looks up at me coming near, smiles then looks down again. Farther down the street, past the hotel steps, people are heading into nightclubs wearing purple and maroon and velvet shoes. I can hear the music, the distant hum of it, anyhow. I can hear it moan.

I make my way back up to our room, find Mother and Mally playing Spit on the bed, the cats looking up supremely disturbed each time one throws down a card and the bed shudders on its casters.

"There she is," says Mother, grabbing at the sack.

"What'd you get me?" Mally asks, hoping for candy I'm sure.

"Nothing. Unless you want a lemon."

Mother tears into the skin of her first lemon, slipping her finger under the rind to loosen the flesh. "Mmm, it's so good," she says, her mouth all juicy and squishy.

Mally dumps out the rest of the lemons onto the bed. She holds each one to her nose and lips, sniffing; she's a bee tucked all the way down inside a honeysuckle bloom.

I tell Mother, "Here's your change."

"You keep it. You'll get something tomorrow, maybe an apple."

"I don't want his money."

She looks up from her lemon, though she goes on tearing at it. "Whose money?"

"The money Davis Neale gave you."

"*Davis Neale*," she says throwing back her head 'cause she thinks it's such a hoot. "Well la-di-da. Since when do you call him that?"

"He's no relation, and I don't care to talk about him," I say.

"He's your uncle."

"Not blood."

"Well," says Mother, chewing. Then quietly, just to herself like she can't resist it but isn't willing to make a show of it either, she says, "Isn't that a good thing."

I want to scream. I want to tear at her hair and call her names. And if I were to touch another living person at this precise moment, I'm sure my slightest finger's-press would send them flying across the room.

I check myself. I rein it in. Shut my eyes and try to think.

I have a list. I have a photograph. I'm on a mission.

I make my voice soft, sweet. "We're leaving here tomorrow, though, right?"

"Tomorrow?" she says, chewing a bit of rind.

"Tomorrow."

"Maybe," she says. "Gotta make sure the car's all right. Don't want to run it into the ground. It's all we've got now."

"The car's good," I tell her. "It was fine coming down from Niota."

"Well it could start up any minute again, that pinging. I don't like that pinging."

"You could have a shop look at it, just tell us if it'll make it down is all."

"That costs money, Iva."

"Well, you've got some."

"You mean I'm to use Mr. Davis Neale's money after all?"

Anything I have to say to that won't get me to Pascagoula

so I'm quiet.

A short while later Mother says, "I just think we should wait it out."

"Wait what out?"

"This feeling I'm having that it's the wrong thing for us all."

"Maybe for you but not for me."

"I don't want to rush this, you see?"

"Rush what?" I ask her.

"I've got my reasons. There are reasons."

"What could they possibly be? You told me you still love him. Daddy. That he's the one. The real one."

"I also told you that's not enough."

"If you would just try," I say, grabbing hold of her hand, feeling the sting of pulp and juice there in her palm. "I know it'll be different."

"I can't go back to him now, Iva."

"Why not now? Now is perfect."

"Not now, baby. And that's that."

"That's not that. You said we were going to find him. You said what's the harm. You said why not Pascagoula. What can happen in only two days?"

"Hush now. Enough," she says.

Her eyes are gray today. Gray! Doesn't she understand who she is and who she's got every ability to become? I've seen her pink-cheeked. I've seen her red-lipped. Blue-eyed and smiling because she wanted to—not because she had to convince anyone, but because *she* was convinced.

I'm desperate: "Two days away from Davis Neale and you can't think straight? Is that it?"

"That will do, Iva Giles. Don't you think you can talk to me like that."

"You want to go back there for your sister to throw you out again?"

"You better watch yourself, girl," she says, sucking at a hole in the skin of her third lemon. She's staring at the floor. "You were about as wanted in that house as I was. You and your damn cats that *I* convinced Clea to let you keep. You remember that? Of course not. All you think about is your goddamned father—"

"Don't say that," I tell her. "Don't curse him!"

"He doesn't love any of us—no, let's say *either one of us*, 'cause that's what's going on here, isn't it? That's what's always been going on between you and me. And oh, you put up quite a fight for him, missy."

"I hate you! You're a horrible, horrible mother." I scream it. I see stars and the red bubbly insides of my eyelids. I am shrill, saying 'horrible' over and over and over again. I go hoarse.

"That's right: I'm the horrible one. He doesn't love either one of us enough to stick around. And I'm a horrible mother. He drives day and night to water. Any kind of water. For God's sake, he's too scared to do it, to finally do it and be done with it like his brother. Have you ever asked yourself, Iva, how much a person is allowed to get of you, of your soul, before you get something in return? Have you ever counted up all the nights you got nothing, all the nights you weren't enough to make him want to live? He doesn't give one goddamn for you or Mally or me. Not one goddamn. Not enough to take a pill so he can behave like a normal person. Or just to stick by you. To remember we're in love. It's not possible a person can be so sad that remembering how much he's loved wouldn't matter. It's just not possible."

She's shaking now from saying so much. She gets up and starts looking through her sacks, I haven't any idea for what. The way she's still taking huge bites from the lemon, letting drops of juice fall into wherever she's holding over, makes me say it.

I whisper so quiet I hope she won't hear me. "Are you pregnant?"

She spins around at me, clenches her jaw hollering: "How dare you!" Her veins bulge out over her ears, where our waitress had all her trouble and rocks.

She digs her teeth into the skin and sizes me up. I stop believing there is an end to this, stop thinking that anything I say or keep from saying will have anything to do with us always leaving and then, when we need to go, being stuck. I am beginning to think Daddy's had nothing to do with her running for years.

"Every single one of you is selfish," she starts up again. "So why not me? Why don't I get to slip? I'm not budging, Iva. You want to learn how to drive? You're a big enough girl. Steal you a car and pull out of Greenville. Better yet, feel free to take the keys off the nightstand. Otherwise, darling, you're stuck right here with me eating lemons."

We're quiet for seventeen number flips of the crusty clock. After seventeen, I'm pretty much through.

Mother's dumping out her sacks of blouses and skirts, of shorts and underpants, folding every piece then putting it in the motel dresser.

"You lie," I say.

She goes on folding. "That's right, bluebell. I lie. I said we'd go and now I'm chickenshit. I lie. Mally lies. She's the farthest thing from deaf, sitting over there playing Solitaire so she doesn't have to know we're screaming. She hears every single word, just doesn't want any of them. And you, my dear, you lie. You're the biggest liar here, 'cause you're lying all these years to yourself. You were there, Iva. Nothing special, in fact entirely irrelevant—just there."

She comes to sit near me on the bed, but doesn't touch me. Only breathes here like air is enough. "Circumstantially his, not chosen. Just his because you happened to be his and so that meant something. You really believe that he's been looking for us all these years, that he's wanting us, missing us, hoping we'll show up one of these Tuesdays so we can be a family again? You're too old for that anymore, and I'm sick of it." She stands up and looks at me. "You're a liar big as they come," she says and then slams the bathroom door behind her.

Mally still won't look up. She's shuffling cards, intently studying her own hands—how she handles each half of the deck, the way she blends them. She won't lift her head for anything.

I grab my one sack of shorts and shirts, leave my toothbrush in with Mother. I take the change she said I could have, then go looking for more of his money in her wallet, take six of the fifteen twenties and a ten. Last, I pull Milk Glass from sleeping with Rabbit, dump a last sack of Mother's blouses on the floor just for show, and put Milk Glass in my backpack.

I'm to the bus station before any of it's sunk in, ask for a bus to Pascagoula or anywhere near and am told to wait out front where the man's still sitting on his duffel waiting for my same bus. I lean into the windowsill until the ticket man bangs on the glass for me to get off of it.

The guy on his bag tries to talk to me, but I can't hear everything, I've got so much in my head right now. "It's late tonight," he says. "The bus. You're lucky to've made it."

I smile but then pull off my backpack to check on Milk Glass.

"Better not let him see you with that cat," the guy says, motioning to the ticket man. "Driver won't let you on either."

I zip her back up with just enough of a gap in the zipper to breathe but not stick anything out. I check the steps across the street, check the fruit-stand now packed up and empty, check the men pouring into the club down the hill. She's not coming for me.

I memorize the sign, where Mally and Mother are. Last Bluff. I memorize the street and the color of the shutters. I memorize the woman with black shale growing across her face. I memorize the twingey itch of chigger bites and then scratch my knees now that they're on my mind. I memorize the way it feels to have ninety-two dollars in my pocket, and the way there isn't any moon tonight just street lamps. I'm standing under them just like Mother used to in the Piggly Wiggly lots late at night while Mally and I slept in the way back. I memorize the way it feels to think things through in light electric-yellow and too bright to ignore what's here to be seen.

I'm going to see him and it's the last thing I'm thinking of. I'm stepping on a bus for the first time, praying Milk Glass won't cry or yowl because she hates being shut up in a moving car.

I'm that girl who found her mother drowned in the tub and they couldn't decide if it was an accident or not, the one with money because it's the least they could do, the one with a white spotted cat but no sister because she wouldn't hear her calling, the one they think is ruined by the sight of a mother with her neck snapped over because what's the use in holding it up anymore if you're dead anyhow, the one who'll live with her father who smiles and buys her ice cream and forgets her name by morning, the one they'll send the news clippings about her mother's depression and hopelessness and careless words—like liar and suicide—and the poor baby inside.

I'll be that girl.

He was out when we left Nacogdoches forever—but only at work, not gone. Not gone. Just going to the library, planning to come home with pizza or burgers afterward. And maybe he did.

It was a Thursday. I remember because I dressed for gym in shorts, my Boss Hogg T-shirt, and my ugly blue canvas tennies. Mally was wandering around in the hall, quick-footed like she knew a secret. I saw the truck first. Out my window, a long orange truck swinging its doors and dropping its ramps.

I found Mother surrounded by boxes in the bedroom, each one labeled with a number and the room checked off the preprinted list on the sides and lids: 4, kitchen; 5, master bath; 2, hall bath. I wanted to tell her about the men coming up the walk, but she spoke instead. "It'll be hard on us all, Iva. Please don't make it harder."

They were knocking now. We couldn't keep them waiting.

"We have to do this. You have to do this." Mother stood up and started to the door. She opened it and stepped outside with them, talked quietly with her knuckles at her mouth.

"Come here," one of the movers said, kneeling down, the cloth of his blue jumpsuit stretching taut over his knees. "Come on out here with me."

Mally went first. He lifted her up onto the truck. He plunked her right down on the metal lip of the truck's back end and she ran around calling for me. So I went, too. He lifted me up and she was flopped into a cavern of dirty brown quilts and flat-folded cardboard boxes. I ran after her and tried to tip over the stack of blankets, tried to topple her off her tower. But she held tight until I started tugging and she came tumbling down onto me.

"You're gonna get it now," I told her. "You're my prisoner. You'll walk the plank and then I'll leave you here."

I pushed her on at swordpoint, pushed her to the drop-off and then pushed her out onto the plank. She jumped off sideways pretending to drown and then I jumped off to be the shark who eats her. She squealed and ran tiny circles, waving her arms in the air and making gulping noises like she was going under.

"Okay, then," Mother called to us. "So let's us go on ahead. They'll manage the rest."

She gathered a satchel, her notepad, purse, and car keys. She turned to look at the house, and laid a piece of paper on the hall table. That's when she told us not to worry about a thing and then she took each of us by the hand and led us to the car. I watched our big silver-legged sofa being wheeled out, Mother and Daddy's bed, and saw both things pushed up the ramp, looking tinier out here on the street. I wished they'd leave the sofa because I hated its woolly pillows that scratched my neck when Daddy let me start to sleep downstairs while they read or played records.

We'd been to Tyler before on day-visits: to drive the streets gawking at the rose gardens, to visit nurseries for the newest variety of color and form. Once we side-tracked at the Caldwell Zoo, watched a lady milk the one cow. I got tipped over by knobby-headed baby goats in the petting zoo when Mother funneled feed pellets into my palm. Mally loved it, let the goats climb her once they'd pushed her down, let them lick her face and chew at her hair. Mother said, "We're going. Now, Mally. Right now. You need me to count, Mallory? I'm counting. One. Two. Three. Four." But Mally stayed put, giggling and cupping her hands out around her nose and mouth so she could get enough air to breathe beneath the goats' nudgings and licks. Mother fumed. She slapped at the dust on the seat of my shorts, too hard at first, then went on brushing the hoof prints from my front more gently. "You all right?" she asked.

"I'm all right."

"We're leaving you," she called back to Mally, and putting her arm around me, she let me lean on her all the way back to the car. Still no Mally. Mother sat there with me in the front seat. We waited, not saying a word. Finally, "Oh! That girl!" and she swung the car door shut behind her. She didn't come back till after I'd sung "There's a Hole in the Bucket" twice. On my last "Well fix it, dear Henry. Well fix it, dear Henry. Well fix it, dear Henry. Fix it!" there she came, dragging goat-slobbered Mally who was limp in a tantrum of refusing to put down and use her own feet.

❖ ❖ ❖

This time Tyler was different. No garden paths, no goats — good or bad — no salivating for chili and cornbread at the end of the drive home to Daddy. Sitting in the car watching the streets, the turns Mother made and corner shops we passed, was like being in a dream that isn't going right but can't be fixed because nothing's truly out of place, yet. Not wrong enough to wake you up anyhow.

We pulled up to the house and I couldn't feel the tip of my tongue for chewing on it the whole way — two and a half hours. I remember that, the way I couldn't taste a thing for days, the red bumps bruising it on every side.

The house was brown and single-level. Wide brown doors. Brown roof. Brown chips of bark around the foundation. High windows on the front. A wall of windows and sliding doors to the back alley. Mally ran in noting all possible improvements on our real house. She cobsed her room, the best room, first. I was checking doors, found every single one. Tried them all. Pulled them open so fast, steeling myself for him jumping out hollering "Surprise!" Because this had to be a joke. I lost track of the doors I'd already opened and shut, began leaving them open so I'd know. Every door in the house hung open.

Then I got it into my head that he wanted me to hide. So I chose a closet in the back part of the house, the darkest one, the one I knew he'd think made me smart for picking it, and I hid. Beneath stacks of summer quilts and extra sheet sets and towels Mother'd already unpacked, I held my knees to myself and I waited.

I didn't know it was possible. That any part of our life could change, let alone near-everything. They were always shrieking and then making up, leaving and returning home, hating and coming to terms with each other. And sometimes I shrieked, too. Because he was flip about some things. Like suppertimes he'd miss without even a call and she liked to make that point with us so we weren't allowed to touch our plates until either he was home or she heard from him. Some nights we didn't get to eat at all. And on occasion he'd put Mally and me to bed in the full sun of afternoon, swearing up and down it was well past midnight. "So far past your bedtime," he'd say, "and you don't want Momma cross with me, do you?" Of course not! So Mally went to her room and I to mine. When Mother did come home from her errand, she found us alone, sleeping, or trying to, though the light fought through the thin cotton sheets she'd made into curtains, and our bodies knew enough not to be tired.

He made promises toward permanence and we all knew they'd break. So sometimes I hid lengthwise under the silver-legged, yellow sofa hollering for them to get a divorce.

This wasn't what I meant. They got to scream and not mean it. I should have, too.

I wrapped my favorite quilt, the one pieced by Grandma from Mother's baby dresses, around me. Sniffled into it. Hating myself. He'd come in last night reeking of water and silt. His ankles and middle, socks and a sweater still dragging low with the weight of dampness, falling away from him. His hair slick and brown. It was so strange, that this time Mother was calm and easy with him. She didn't yell one bit, just let him hold her on the porch steps while Mally danced around the willow tree and I slid under the sofa, gripping those silver legs and screaming with every bit of lung, "I want him out of here! He doesn't get to do this! He doesn't get to do this to us! I want him out!" Maybe because she was so quiet with him, and maybe because I'd always been so quiet before, she'd stood on tiptoes leaning in to him and kissed and kissed him: his cheeks and forehead and nose and lips, his hair and each ear, right down his neck to his heart.

❉ ❉ ❉

I stopped waiting in the new closet. Instead, I pulled all the folds of sheets and blankets down onto my head. I smoothed them over me, over my face to be tight across my mouth and nose, to make things difficult. In the darkness, I set my hand in a fist over my own heart. I tried to go away.

But I woke up. Mother was cooking beef Stroganoff and singing and there, for a moment, I thought the dream was righting itself—he was coming to us and I'd been wicked to think he might not. It all came clear: Mother had been the one to handle the move because he was never any good with details and she had all her lists to keep her straight.

So I pinched Mally's side every time I felt my stomach tip over with looking at the clock dial on the oven. And I pinched her every time I thought I heard the door push in.

"Ow! Quit it!" she kept saying, scootching her chair away from mine.

But I couldn't stop. I had all this energy in my fingertips, electricity shooting through me, and it had to go somewhere. So I grabbed hold of her Special K pinch-an-inch at her middle and twisted it.

"That's enough, Iva," said Mother, getting up with the dishes and putting her hand over mine. "We all have to be brave and act our age and be good about this. Each and every one of us."

"How many are we?"

"Tonight will be the worst. So we should all just go easy."

✻ ✻ ✻

In bed, I listened for the telephone. But he did not call. When she came to tuck me in I asked her to tell me the truth.

"We're on an adventure, Iva," she said. "Be brave."

It was real this time. I couldn't breathe through so much crying, the entire day's sad terror I'd been shutting my eyes to. "I don't want this," I tried to say. "I didn't mean it."

"No, no," she said, pressing her face to mine, two wet faces plying together. "Nobody meant it. This is all wrong. I know."

"I just hated him for one night. Only that once."

"Sweet," she said, "not even that."

"No."

"We all tried so hard."

"I tried," I tell her, sniffling, wiping at my face.

"Yes. We all tried."

"We can go back. We'll do better. Be better."

She looked into her lap, at her left hand, her rings. She shook her head.

✻ ✻ ✻

It didn't occur to me then that he didn't even know our new number or address, that he wasn't in on this plan of hers. What kind of a night he must have spent worrying, frantic — all of a sudden alone in a house he'd always been the one to leave, the one coming home to the fact of our patient waiting. I stayed up, sitting if I had to to stay awake, listening for his call. And when it didn't come, when Mother began opening and shutting cupboards the next morning and I knew I hadn't missed a sound all night, I crawled under my bed and ripped at the hem of my nightgown, even the arms of my favorite cloth doll, and cried. We were abandoned.

light as moon

Night is the way the bus aches. Swollen and terrified. Half empty or slightly more. Following telephone wires south south south through Alabama from Greenville to Monroeville to Evergreen and Brewton to Bay Minette, Mobile and Foley. And not one person climbs on at these. And not one person gets off. We're just rolling through the darkness that's temporarily spotlit by one sorry lamp hanging over nobody at each stop. How it feels that Mother's not phoned ahead to stop me, raced the Impala alongside my bus to catch me home, is night.

We make one pit stop for bathrooms and cheap cheesemelts and because the break is scheduled for the driver no matter what. Here's where I lose her: Milk Glass prefers mayonnaised crawfish to cheese, and so she walks 'round back for the dumpster's sogged-out scraps, while I'm waiting on my check, which I don't think I can step away from even for my cat walking off—because I'm not a hooligan, and I'm not a thief. So I stand here waiting to know how much of Davis Neale's money I'm to give the waitress. And she is slow, with nine or ten others grumbling for change.

I am wrong about cats and mothers both, thinking love means anything close to needing nearness. When the driver calls, I'm lifting myself up on the huge trash bin, calling Milky, Milky, into the sting of old tin cans and eggshells, but nothing.

"I'm pulling out," he's hollering at me. "Come on now." Whooshing the door open, shut, open, shut.

There's nothing so tight can bind what's already gone. I leave her somewhere around back of the Sand-Hopper Diner. She's probably tired of the trip and of our life; just wants a break; misses her brother, Rabbit. Must be she's sick of this. I walk away, my pack light as moon, because I can't blame her. And because I can hardly feel a thing now my nerves are so frazzed. I am her one true thing, her shepherd, and I've chosen to leave.

The driver's taking I-65 so slow and with each town we sit waiting seventeen minutes for passengers, and I'm going crazy hating him and his stupid blue cap with the gold cording dragging over the brim. Crying is expected; I don't cry. I'm shaking, though. I wedge my head between the seat and window, watch how many ways the moon can make shadows out of nothing, out of boring-old-cornfields-nothing. *La luna*, but she's weak above clouds tonight.

The moustache man from Greenville with the duffel bag heading for Biloxi, comes sit in the seat across the row. "Where's kitty?" he asks.

Now I could cry. Think if I have to open my mouth I will. I just look at him, study the way his moustache is a whole finger's width wider to the left, the way a patch of red skin just barely sticks out from the longer side.

"You mind?" he's tapping out a cigarette and pulling a square, silver lighter from his front jeans pocket.

I shake my head, watch how he flicks the flame and pulls in hard to make the end of the cigarette burn hot and red at first, then settle on making soft, gray ash.

He lets out a long stream of smoke, aiming only slightly over his shoulder for the window. "My name's Chet."

I nod.

"Well what's your name?"

"Iva," I whisper.

"Who's in Pascagoula?" he asks. "I heard you at the counter."

"My daddy."

"He know you're coming?" Chet takes in more of the flame.

I nod but can tell he sees right through that.

"You on the run?" He winks at me, fiddling with the hang of vinyl piping ripped down from the seat in front of him. By the way he's placing the lit end of his cigarette so near I think he's toying with the idea of melting the seat.

I nod again, keeping one eye on his hands.

"Well, how old are you?"

"Fifteen," I say.

He looks up hard, cutting his eyes at me. "Tall as fifteen maybe, but all the rest—" He drops his head to the side and if he goes on with this sentence I don't know what he says. Then, like he needs me to know it, he turns back to me saying, "I was fourteen the first time. Couldn't keep it together anywhere I went. Kept going back until I wound up drunk and stupid on a bus to Keesler last year—'Sustain the wings!'" He looks out his window. "Nights were bleak then. Nights are always bleak."

I wait for him to tell me the secret answer. The one he screwed up in his own life but knows enough now to give me straight. When he looks back he's different, smiling. Looking past me. "Your cat'll be all right," he says and pats my shoulder once, "I saw a mouse out there by the cars along the side of the place."

We lumber down to the rim of Mississippi and Gulf and that I'm going to him isn't on my mind at all. Instead of thinking on the beach, missing him and the sand dunes, wondering at his favorite color or bird or if he still sissy-whistles with his tongue to his palate—instead of wondering anything about him like I've done all these years of wanting him back, instead of anything-Daddy, I'm asking myself will Mother go out into the streets after me, will Mally cry for being alone in the motel's second double or slip into Mother's bed tonight. Are they sitting up waiting still, only on the verge of uneasiness, not believing I could be gone from Greenville—just thinking I'd walk off the fight like in Blacksburg, bring back another sack of lemons for Mother to eat, peel and all, as an offering.

But then there's a moment of slipping the name Pascagoula between my teeth, of being his favorite, of knowing I'll be held tonight. I can make my stomach flip with any one of these promises, and I do—over and again just to work it through my skin. I pull my feet up sideways on the seat, hold my knees under my chin. I cannot help it, this way I am: a little mad, a little stumbly in my own self, in my world.

I don't know who I am. Whose daughter I am.

No matter which, in my head I hear Mother telling me I'm too old for this, too old for acting on hopes, for stepping on clouds. Now I'm falling through, sinking my toes right down into space. And I'm just too old now not to notice I've got no footing.

It's evening-dark so this qualifies as my birthday still. I wonder if he'll remember it. If maybe each year he bakes something, slathers it in pink for me, just in case, then eats the whole thing driving, looking for whatever it is we weren't.

In Mobile we head west on I-10. And aside from glimpsing the bay, we're in the land of trucks and farms. "You're next," says Chet. "Closest thing for you is Escatawpa. You ever hitched before?"

"No," I say, feeling like I'm about to parachute out of an airplane.

"Don't take a van," he says, "and don't ride with anyone who gives you the creeps. Pickup trucks are iffy. Eighteen-wheelers are almost always good—long as the outside's clean, you can be pretty sure he's got a life that won't mess you up too bad. Women are, generally speaking, good. Trust your gut; it'll almost always know."

He hands me his silver lighter and a knife with mother-of-pearl handle, tells me they're for light and for keeping whole. "Look me up if you're ever in Biloxi," he says and slips a piece of paper into my backpack. "Be careful, you."

There are no trucks, no cars either. So I start walking. I know 613 to Telephone to US-90.

The gravel's killing my feet so I step into the road. Then I start worrying I'll be run off the pavement by a semi before I know to step back. Here, on bare highway, the sky glows heavy with moon and stars, the way nights lit up in Nacogdoches. I wonder how close I am. An inch or so on the map. Mississippi was pink, Louisiana yellow, Texas green.

This is right, that I'm here, coming to him. That I'm the one to find him.

Slow behind me comes light and then sound. A single motor trundling along, rubber tires slapping pavement. Not a van. Not a filthy truck. I move aside and face it, put up my hand and stick out my thumb. It's a sedan and it's slowing. Dust bunches up at my ankles. It's a man, young, maybe even a kid.

He leans over to the passenger window, says, "Where you wanna go?"

I am struck dead with stabs all over me, imagining blood and myself trying to scream from a ditch. "Pascagoula," I manage, feeling that little flip of my world.

"Cool," he says. "Get in."

He's in no hurry it seems, driving close to my walking-speed—more time for him to murder me before getting to town. We're almost there and I realize I'd rather be on my way than arriving—'cause now I have trouble picturing it, how it'll go, what I'll say if I have to say something.

I'm frozen looking straight ahead up the road, like maybe once I see he's an ax murderer he'll have to hack me up.

"What's your name?"

I don't move. "Iva."

"I'm Perry. Where're you from?"

"Texas, originally. All over, really."

"Oh yeah? You hitch everywhere?"

"Mmmhmm." I nod.

"Cool."

We're on Telephone then 90 before I know it. Everything's white here. White boards on houses, fences, signs for all kinds of rabbits — *feeder, eating, or pet* — and I think of our cats. All the white is falling apart, dragging off the walls, yard posts falling over but not quite ready to drop. Peeling and cracking in the moonlight. This is inland Pascagoula, away from the Gulf and all the places anyone cares about.

"Stars are brighter here," says Perry. "From the water."

"Seems so," I say, and then I turn to him.

He looks somewhat like Henry — whom I've barely even considered since leaving the house on Tessle, so it must not have been love after all — same feathery eyelashes floating up or resting on his cheeks. But Perry's hair is medium brown and his eyes are too dark to know in this car. His lips are shiny because he keeps biting at them. I put that detail in my head, for telling somebody if I need to, can even hear myself reciting this boy's entire face for someone holding a pencil and pad of paper.

I give him the address and he knows just which turns to make, says he lives pretty near so he'll take me the whole way. He pulls up in front of some houses on the block because we're having trouble making out the numbers in the dark.

"That one, I think. They expecting you?" he says, pointing to a red shack of a house, real skeptical. "In case things don't go how you want, remember 44 Patch Street."

"Okay," I say, getting out of his car. "Thanks very much."

He leans forward, over the passenger seat and into its open window. His arms hang out over the car, his neck's stretched long and he looks like he forgot something or thinks I did. He's smiling, kind of toothy in a grin that's more left than right. I try to give him back some of this funny looking, that seems fair, but I don't know what face to make and my eyes hit all the wrong spots—go to the tip of his nose, the corner of his mouth, lobe of an ear, then give up and go down to looking at the sidewalk.

"44 Patch Street, okay?" he asks.

"44 Patch."

Then he's gone. Faster going than our whole trip from Escatawpa. No brake lights at all. I hoist up the slip of paper and all the emptiness in my backpack, turn around to face the house.

worlds away

We were on Padre Island, though I didn't know it then. What I knew was the water far as gulls could turn, the sand swallowing Daddy's toes faster than mine under each wave, that we were the only two. My hair blew so I could not see through it or hear a word, just the sand and the birds and girls chasing boys with little plastic pails breaking under the weight of sandy water.

Years after, I believe I only remember him—not Mother, not Mally—because he was the only one who mattered. But when I pull hard at the truth of that day, I see they've never really been a part of our world at all.

This was one of Daddy's trips looking, and he'd chosen only me because Mally wasn't here yet and there were times he had trouble breathing around Mother. I was four then, nearly five—a bit younger than Mally is now—one third of who I am today. I was a piece of him pedaling fast to keep up with his legs. I was an arm so long it drags, a gorilla arm hardly noticed in spite of the strength in its knuckles.

This was the first time he pulled a paper-boat from his pocket. There would be many times more from then on. Both of us squatted down at the rim of where the earth broke away for Gulf. He set a tiny blue boat down in the waves, watched it knock against the shore as far down the coast as we could see the tide.

He took another slip of paper from his pocket, this one white. He laid it smooth on his thigh, then showed my fingers each fold to make. He tucked in the ends too thick for me to fit, and I set it in the water just like he had. I did not know these slips were for pills.

My boat was gone so fast and I wanted it back. I walked alongside it at first, put a finger to its pointy top, holding it still while the water pulled away and back.

"It's not for us, plum," he said. "They're love letters we're sending to secret islands for spells and magic potion. They're just wishes."

I tried the pocket in his swim trunks for more slips of paper, spent the day launching his fears.

We were in Galveston for the week, staying in what must have been a motel room. Separate cars because he couldn't ever feel stranded. Daddy went places early in the morning, came back with a quiet face. He slipped out of his sandals, positioning them just so at the side of the bed, then lay back with his arms making a square pillow over his face.

"Play cards with me?" I asked, setting the deck on his chest. He didn't move. The cards were fresh, slick, and the pile scattered down his sides to the quilt. I giggled. He was motionless, silent.

Mother came out of the bathroom folding our swimsuits

from yesterday that she'd hung to dry on the shower rod. Mine was red with white polka dots. His was orange trunks with blue stripes up the sides and a white cord to cinch up the waist. Hers had a belly pocket because Mally was growing inside her. There, in Galveston, Mother woke up on the wrong side of the bed every day. She was mad at him and mean there. But she'd stopped yelling. It was worse than if she was yelling. Her voice was like finding out I ate the last sugared pecan from the tin even though I said it wasn't me: *I'm disgusted with you, Iva; I'm simply disgusted.*

She stood at the foot of the bed, swatted his feet, their white sandal-stripes glowing in the dank gray of the room. Our windows faced the parking lot. The highway overpass hung in the sky over us like a stuck cloud. We were a long way from the beach.

"Lilly," he moaned. "Lay off."

"I can't stand it," she said. "Why do you think we're here? This isn't a vacation, Jameson Giles. You said you wanted to do this."

"I do." He shifted one elbow so he could halfway see her through the dark of his arm-pillow. I laughed for the way he looked like a furry thing peeking out of its winter den. Then I was sorry for laughing 'cause maybe he'd think I was ganging up.

"You're no good," she said. "That's all there is to it."

His chest sank a little, his ribs flattening out like when I fell from the monkey bars flat on my back and he said I had the wind knocked out of me; I thought I would die. I put my hand on his arm to see his face and his lips came faintly apart to tremble.

"This is the time," she said, 'cause she never knew when

to quit. "We're here and this is the time. You've got to get something to fix it. Didn't they write you up a prescription?"

"They said I'm fine." He was talking to her but looking at me, his pretty eyes blinked away their green on me like a kiss.

She didn't speak. But oh, her breathing made a racket: sucking up balloons of air then sighing it out loud as she could through her mouth. Then finally she quieted down. "Please don't do this," she said. "Don't lie."

He sat up on the bed. "I don't feel it all the time."

"You feel it often enough."

"And if I don't feel it all the time, then it doesn't make sense to swallow something that'll change me *all* of the time."

"You're so sad. It could help you, Jameson. It could keep you from being so sad."

He got up off the bed, started walking around the room, touching his hand to things but not picking them up. "I'm not always sad—"

"You never hold still long enough to know that's what's pushing you out the door." She shifted her weight, her eyes followed him around the room.

"—and if I'm not always sad, well maybe the times I am sad it's for good reason."

"Of course there's a reason," she said, putting one hand to her back which pushed out her big baby-belly. "We know the reason. It's too hard a thing to lose a brother—"

"You make it sound like he's out there wandering."

"Well, isn't he? To you, I mean?"

He took a glazed doughnut from the box that'd been sitting on the kitchen counter all week. "I just want," he started, stuffing the stale, crusty mess into his mouth. If she had manners she'd know not to make him talk about it anymore. Crusty glaze fell down his shirt and all I could think about was picking off each flake of sugar to eat. "Myself," he said. "My-fucking-self!"

"Don't you talk foul to me like that." She sat on the bed with her stomach taking up all her lap. "You've got a daughter, plus this one," she said and grabbed hold of Mally inside her, round and low like a kickball she was taking away, back home after being tagged out.

I wondered if they fought when I was inside her. I imagined he was the one holding on to me then. She must have been putting her hands anywhere else but on her baby-belly.

I went to her, climbed the bed to touch her belly as I'd been doing ever since they explained that Mally was coming to live with us just as I had. I lifted Mother's blouse, smacked my mouth and nose and cheeks to the streaky skin, kissed my whole self to it. I was a daughter. I was a thing that stirs up worry, and I wanted to show them I wasn't so hard to manage.

"Iva," Mother said, snugging her seersucker top back down and not even looking at me. "We're talking here."

I sat still beside her instead, unsure which her eyes were that day, blue or gray. Even so, I wouldn't look. I was being good. Being good was my mission. I would prove to them how very still I could be.

Daddy rubbed at his hair so hard I thought he'd make bruises. "What use am I to her if I'm not human?" he asked.

"You'll go again tomorrow." Mother left for the bathroom where she'd been spending so much of her time peeing or soaking.

He grabbed two towels and our freshly folded swimsuits. "Change in the car," he whispered to me. "Come on now, hurry."

I thought it was a game. I followed him into the parking lot, climbed in beside him. I let myself forget her back in the room, that maybe she'd come out of the bath scared to find us gone, not even a note. I took him over her.

Forever was what I wanted. He held my hand like that there.

We didn't swim. We floated and bobbed, hopped up with each wave to keep from going under. But I was small and there were times he was too far away to lift me over. Then it happened. My legs were sucked out from under me and I went down. I tumbled to the floor, gulping saltwater in a panic because I couldn't tell if I was up or under and all I wanted was air and for him to find me. The wave flipped me upside down, dragged me 'round, my head in the sand, fingers grabbing up grips of water until the wave carried me in. Gobbled up by the ocean, I saw my feet and the churned up floor. Finally, I broke loose in shallow foam, back into regular motion, slow motion. On my knees and elbows, a pile of a girl; I dug my suit out of my bum, scooped out the sand tucked there in the lining's crotch-fold. The shells so near shore, crushed and spat by birds, sliced my toes. I coughed up sand and water, my nose stung with bubbles. I grabbed hold of him.

We planted ourselves far from the water just long enough for my ears to unpop, for me to get back my balance, to know I was meant for land.

Then came the drying out: our bellies pressed deep into white sand, towels wapsed up under our heads for pillows, our toes sinking down into crabs' houses. Sun like that was real sun, all orange and wavy when I looked. The heat did it so fast that I could feel the prickle of my suit drying, lifting from my skin.

We bobbed and floated and baked on Malaquite Beach, well into the stiffest heat that came hours into an afternoon. Every time I looked up into his face, I saw the sun instead. I did not know to take that face with me, to hold on to its every detail: his brow Indian red, hair yellow like banana taffy, and beard same as the color of Mother's favorite copper-bottomed skillet. Instead, I smoothed the rumples out of my towel and dreamt of limeade, pulled pork barbecue, and ice cubes slipped inside our clothes.

There, beside him on the beach, I didn't know his face. Just his hand. I knew that precisely. Big as my entire head, rough as asphalt to a knee. He stretched out his arm in the air for me, made it seem the ranger stations and visitor decks so far off now sprouted right out of his palm no larger than apples.

We moved farther down the beach. Over to Laguna Madre for wading and to keep from swallowing anymore waves. We bum-floated, seated and swaying in the gentle water same as how kelp swishes back and forth but doesn't quite go anywhere. We spat up salt with white pelicans. We climbed through the sea oats tall as me.

"They're what hold the sand together," he told me. "Their roots."

"Silly," I said. "Sand holds *them*."

We sat on the dune, oats scratching every inch of me and rattling their dry hollow sound in the wind.

"If you sit in that bare spot," he said, "you'll fall in."

"No!" I told him. "It's earth. It holds up the world."

He smiled. Lips dried white, pulled wide. He lay back, elbows propping him. His neck went long and thin, relaxed when he stared up into the blue sky. "Wouldn't that be wonderful," he said.

I watched the water because I'd never seen anything so clear and blue at the same time, and I wondered how something that wasn't glass could seem it so. Where the dune dropped away to quick shallows beneath us, there were fishermen yanking up sheepshead and croaker and occasionally flounder—he knew them all. I heard frogs but Daddy told me it was only the fish.

He ignored the sign trying to keep the dunes from collapsing, telling us KEEP OFF. I read it over and over again until the letters were just shapes, like all the books stashed under my pillow for nights when Mother and Daddy were late coming to sing me to sleep. He pulled a tall stalk of grass over in front of him and looked at it so close to his eyes I doubted he was seeing anything but blur.

"We're not supposed to be here," I told him.

"Aren't we?"

"Maybe it isn't safe," I said, meaning the way he claimed roots were binding things as tiny as bits of sand.

"Well, we're worlds away from anywhere safe."

He stayed sitting and so we hid in the grasses a while longer.

❈ ❈ ❈

All of it, the smooth heat and the way I thought he was looking at me, truly—that this sturdy, smiley man was who he was, who he could be—it all went on too long for him. Carriage to pumpkin. Sturdy to fearsome. We tired, or he did and maybe who we were at that very moment was the actual game, and it was over. I thought about Mother, wondered if she knew where I was that time, wondered if she was grateful or hating us, if they'd fight that night because of the way he did things, if he'd know the way back to her.

We started to go and the sky was dark, a shifting dark, for the moon shining in the tide. Not even the stars were steady. We stepped through ghost crabs and blue crabs and felt the salt marsh mosquitoes nipping. I was the only child out so late.

He didn't say a word but my hand in his found him shaking. I walked beside him, taking three steps for each of his. I stumbled in old footsteps left out on the beach.

He could not find the car. Anywhere. He wrapped me in our towels, and I was so hungry I could feel my belly grinding away at its own walls. I sucked on the terrycloth, worked the sandy grit between my molars as we walked. Then I was the one feeling what she must have felt, being gone for a minute or a whole day. Being invisible there with him.

We stopped in the sandy gully alongside the road, and though he stood over me, dragged the sand lower in a rut of his pacing around me, I knew he was different from what I'd always believed. I knew he was broken. Not over the car but over things so much bigger. Over losing things and never getting them back.

I woke in the way back of the Impala wagon, Mother slowly driving the drags of pavement that ran between dunes and boat ramps looking for Daddy's green Pontiac.

"They took it."

"Hush," she said. "No one's taken it. You've just forgotten

where you parked."

"This looks right. This was where it was. See? It's gone."

"Jameson, these turns all look the same. It's around here. We'll find it."

Their windows were open and the night sang with crickets in the dunes. Daddy's arm was out the window feeling for his car.

"It was a corner, though. I know that."

"Okay," she said. "We'll look at all the corners."

"It was a corner."

"Okay."

"It was."

"I know," she said, slowing so she could touch his face.

I knew they wouldn't fight about it that night. But soon. I could feel all the breaths she was taking in, how she was holding on to it all, building and building. "You'll go again tomorrow," she said.

He didn't answer, just extended his arm far as it would go, spread his fingers in the breeze driving gave.

I forgot the day. I went limp and dreamy. The moon out the side window was on me. I still felt the easy waves lift me up and tug me back down from their foamy crests.

Mother found the car. She pulled alongside it, and Daddy said over and over how he never knew anything for certain anymore.

"Go ahead," she told him. "You two tail me to the motel. We'll all be fine."

He opened the tailgate and reached in for me to go with him, his fingers light on my back. We could have sung sleepy-tongued, me stretched long on the front seat like how we'd driven down from Nacogdoches separate from Mother days before. Or the car might have been quiet, his face sad. His hand might have pulled mine away from twirling the long hair that curled over his ears. I might have disappeared again.

Such a short drive back to the room, but she was the sea oats and he was the dune.

I grabbed one last look at the moon then closed my eyes before he could see me. My face was tight from burning, my cheeks and eyelids salt-dusted. I wanted him gone for the certainty of it, wanted his trips and his missing face and his paper-boats gone.

"Iva-love," he called in to me.

I squeezed my eyes tight pretending sleep, picturing the water and the dunes and where we belonged if not there.

"Iva-moon," he whispered, stroking my hair.

"She sleeping?" Mother asked. "Pick her up. It's okay."

"No," he said. "She's dreaming."

There was no sound for a moment while he decided, then I felt the suction of the door shut down soft. He went without me.

"Be safe, Lilly," he said, kissing Mother through her window.

Soon as we were moving, Daddy's headlights were on us. Even with my eyes shut I was blind for the glare, could feel the way he'd seen me there with my legs curled up into the corner lying on my back to keep feeling the current. I propped up on my elbows to look, be sure it wasn't the moon playing tricks, to keep track of him.

It wasn't long before he turned off down a road unpaved, just a path sending up dust in the red of his taillights.

I sat up, all the way up. Because I didn't believe it. It was too much. Something in me took in all sorts of air, breathed in deep as it would go, held on to all of it like water when the waves crashed me under. I felt the endlessness of that tumbling again, and of the night and walking on the beach not knowing if I existed. I believed in forevers.

"Momma?" I whispered, knowing she'd hear me no matter how soft I called her.

"You had a good day though, right," she said.

I couldn't open my mouth or I'd lose every trace of voice and seams holding me together. I'd lose him.

"That's got to be enough."

* * *

I have my picture of him and me half-buried in that sand, our knees cracking the surface.

It is a mystery to me who buried us if we both were perfectly under. It is a mystery who took the photograph. And a mystery that he did not lose me there—despite how tightly I held on—walking, walking, walking over so long a shore.

What he's been looking for all this time I don't know, though it must be a place where something stronger than sea oats holds ground. That night, we believed he'd find us. And he did. He just never stopped looking.

For years I've dreamt of that place in the road where Mother and I stayed on track and he turned away. In my dream, I am there in the dark standing somewhere on the unpaved road. The green Pontiac's coming, slowly. Windows open, radio humming, kicking up dirt in the red glow behind it. Daddy's arm is out the window, opened wide in the fog and dark. He's so near I want to tell him to stop, so near I almost see his face. I reach for him. The Pontiac's crawling and his hand's suddenly got mine. His eyes are shut. I walk alongside the car that inches its way closer to me. I hold his hand which my own hand knows precisely. I tell him slow down, he's found me, slow down. But he won't look. He won't open his eyes. He's so afraid he won't find all it is he's lost that he doesn't even see me. And his hand doesn't tell him who I am. He isn't sure I'm the one. Isn't sure he's not worlds away from anywhere safe.

That's the night I started memorizing him.

saying to myself that what I hear next will be him waking and finding me, and I will remember it forever. But I wait a good while and there's nothing.

I walk along the front window of 13 thinking maybe he's hiding. Everything's dark and the sorry moon and my one flame to the glass prove nothing.

I press the door, which is about all it needs to open. I hold my breath as I go in, start to breathe inside and it's nothing I know. Stiff and tired air. Like sick people. Or dogs out in the rain.

"Daddy," I whisper only once because the sound hits the far wall and bounces right back at me.

He isn't here.

It's just a room with a sink and toilet. A mattress on the floor. A bureau. I sit on the edge of his bed. I lie back to feel it like he does because I think it matters, that somehow my cells that are truly his cells will wake up and figure out who I am just by sitting the way he sits, sleeping the position he sleeps. I rub the wheel of my lighter again and watch the long flame eat the air. There above me, carved into the battered and grimed and sooted-out plank board ceiling is a whole series of names, rivers and ponds, lakes and reservoirs: ANGELINA RED WOLF BRAZOS MISSISSIPPI PEARL TOLEDO BEND CATAHOULA SABINE CALCASIEU GUADALUPE NUECES ATCHAFALAYA PECOS TRINITY. Some I know because we've walked them together. Some I think I've only heard him say. Others paint our driving maps blue with their squiggly pathways. Run around the base of the walls, scratched into the warped and chewed strip of wood, is one more: PONCHARTRAIN PONCHARTRAIN PONCHARTRAIN PONCHARTRAIN PONCHARTRAIN, over and over until there are no spaces and I can't make out a single word at all.

I've heard him say this one at night. In the Nacogdoches house. When he was just going or just coming and Mother couldn't bear it. When she stood with a hand on Mally's head, her fingers winding Mally's pigtails, and shook like a cartoon cat sticking his finger in the electric socket. "You can't have it back. You know that!" she hollered. "So you're choosing something that doesn't exist over something that does." Mally tipped her head up 'cause her hair had twisted all it could; her eyes welled up and she began to squall. But the crying, that wasn't for the pinch of her pigtails—it was for Mother. On those nights I stood in the hallway by the little glass dish where they tossed their keys. I staked out the dish. Wouldn't leave my spot by the front door for anything. It simply wasn't possible that I was a part of what he was choosing to leave.

I hear something. Think maybe I do. Hold extra still. I don't hear it again. I go to the door. Open it. Nobody. I think maybe it was my own feet or maybe I was whispering to myself. I don't know, but here I am alone.

None of this is real anymore. My head hurts from so much trying to figure out who he is, who I am, what we're doing here. Mally's with Mother pretending she can't hear a thing, the two of them holed up in Greenville, Alabama. Both stuck there because who's to say where I am is right. Searching him out after four years. Mother's sucking at lemons all day as her one craving. She didn't love Davis Neale but that wasn't enough to keep her from him, his money she seems pretty satisfied to be living on. And I know it's too early for cravings, am certain she just needed someone to know about the baby. None of it is any sort of real.

I never imagined Daddy living like this. He'd never abide dust and peeling linoleum squares. He'd never live in so horrible a place as this. He wipes his teeth clean when he can't get to the bath for brushing; he cuts French fries with fork and knife to avoid the grease, eats popcorn with chopsticks. These aren't things I remember from him being my father, but from Mother—times she was feeling brittle, times she needed to turn Mally and me back to her.

I walk the dim edges of the room. Follow the names up top that never end, that are so perfectly measured it is impossible to say where he began or where he ended carving. I trace the spines of a few books stacked under a lamp in the corner, the shade of which is bashed in and melted on one side from being pushed up against the wall too long. I walk around the tiny sink and scruddy toilet bowl, stand a minute in front of a small square mirror. I'm not who I think I am. In the last year my hair's been turning from his yellow to her deep brown. It used to glow at night, now I can hardly see where it meets the dark. My shoulders are squared, broader. My T-shirt binds my chest, cuts tight up under my arms. My legs shoot long and full out of my shorts. My hips have emerged as strange curves where once I was straight and knew how to run fast without my own self getting in the way.

I'm looking like a woman. Like Mother more and more even though she always told me I was his spitting image. I feel for the knife in my knapsack, run the back of the blade so cool along my thigh and roundy sides, up my soft front. Then I pull the true blade against my hair until one hank comes free in my hand. There, it just covers my ears and I'm looking more yellow. Just the one cut, though, because I can barely see. My hand is wobbly for how hungry I am. And I need hair long enough to braid with a red ribbon running through it. I finger the blunt ends of the section I've cut. Smooth them down. Know I can be his again easily enough.

I like the mattress the best. It's where I think I can smell him. It's where I think I should be when he walks in. But I can't sleep, I'm back up investigating everything, putting my hands all over wherever his have been. I'm careful, though, not wanting to rub away his fingerprints, rather to press mine into his.

I start with a rickety card table, lay my hands one after the other in horizontal rows until I've touched the entire surface. Then the wall by the bed. The top of the bureau. And then I pull open the bureau drawers looking for a sweater or T-shirt to climb into. The top drawer is empty. The second drawer is empty and my stomach drops; this means something, that it's empty, that they're both empty. I wait before opening the third drawer. Maybe this has all been wrong. 13 Fay Road. Maybe he's not living here anymore, this is someone else's house now who'll be back soon and I'll be here. Or maybe he's gone but coming back. I don't open the bottom drawer, instead ease into his water, my fingers pressing the wall.

I don't know what time I wake. Still evening-dark. Before I can stop myself, I'm pulling open that last drawer. And it's empty all except for a piece of paper. I hold my lighter close to it, see our names in a list.

Lilly

Iva

Mallory = Mally

I fall back into his pillow, his bed. I fall back into dreams, knowing. 13 Fay Road.

* * *

It's morning and there's no change. I pee in his toilet, quickly and sort of standing, my fingers gripping the waistband of my bottoms for when there's a footstep and the door'll push in—it's not how I want him to see me first. But the place is stone-quiet. I go sit on the stoop out front. In daylight I can see this row of painted houses goes on for the whole block. Even colored so bright, it's plain they're all falling apart. My head feels like it's caving in with hunger. The juices of my stomach are fighting over how much of my innards to devour. My right ear itches with bits of hair tugged away by the knife. Milk Glass is gone somewhere in Bay Minette and now I know I had the time to go after her, wait the night for another bus. I think of rubbing her cheeks, how she loved me to pick at the flea-scabs she'd get deep under the fur around her ears and just beneath her eyes. How she'd purr and get tiny drool bubbles on her lips and the tip of her pinky tongue.

There're a few people out on the porches, rocking with iced teas sweating drips down their knees. They're all staring at me. I look at the dirt.

When it seems the entire row can't stand it any longer, a pink lady in a green housedress and canvas slip-ons marches across the road. She stands before me a while, her nose crimped on one side and swollen on the other. "Who are you?" she asks.

"I'm waiting on my father," I tell her. "He lives here."

She's shaking, puffing on her lady's cigarette. "Jameson Giles you're after?"

"Yes!"

"Long gone."

"When?"

"Near a month now."

"Where to?"

"Who could say with him? Half the time he's lived here he's nowhere to be seen—never gone so long as this time, though, and never without paying next month's due. So I declare he's officially broken lease."

I wrap my hands around my ankles. "But he left something behind."

"You seen it then? Well, how could you not," she says, and I follow her inside because she's still talking. "Seen what he did to my house? I mean, it's *my* property—all these houses are—all sliced up to Sunday."

She means the carving not the note. Not a girl. I set my fingers to the words, trace them, imagine my father with a knife. There are too many ways to be left.

"I mean, you'd think he were a land surveyor or something—well, for water, you know. Lived here all my life but I seen a good handful of these." She noses the soft toe of her shoe to the baseboard, then teeters one-footed to tap each of her rivers and lakes up top. "Now that's some strange fascination he's got. Whoever heard of such a thing? Sweet as all, though," she says. "If he was a little off." She starts to loop her finger around the side of her head like the kids in school when they say *loco en la cabeza*, but then she thinks better of it. "I can't hold a thing against him," she says, putting up her hand.

I sink into that bed, sink, sink, sink. I'm out of ideas.

"How'd you get here?"

"Where's he gone? Do you know where he's gone?"

She's bent over, her head studying the words like she'd

never laid eyes on that particular set before, or just was having trouble keeping on believing it. "Like I said, haven't the foggiest."

"Do you have a phone?"

Her mouth folds in on itself while she considers.

❊ ❊ ❊

She stands over me making snorting noises when I ask the operator for The Last Bluff Motel in Greenville, Alabama.

When Mother comes on the line, she won't talk. We're quiet for such a long time that I start carrying on a conversation in my head of what she's supposed to be saying.

She doesn't say it, any of it. I give in.

I tell her, "I'm sorry."

"Hmmmp."

"I'm okay. Safe."

"Good, fine."

"If you're worrying over me, you shouldn't. I'm in Pascagoula. You've probably been searching."

"I know where you are."

We don't talk a while more. I nod my head like I'm being told things because the lady's antsy, gripping the rim of her table for how long I'm taking.

"He's gone," I say.

"Yes, well. I told you he would be."

"Nobody knows where he is. And he's not coming back."

"Well," she says, and I can hear Mally humming "Lida Rose" in the background.

"Put her on," I say, suddenly longing to hear Mally's voice in the bunk beneath me, her squawks when I poke her for stepping on me in the car, feel her sticky fingers wind through my hair while we sleep in the way back of the Impala.

"No use in that."

"She *still* claims not to hear, making signs to Rabbit? I didn't think she would be."

"Mmm," Mother says, and I picture her giving a slight nod.

"Oh."

"And completely unmanageable, blaming me for you leaving us."

"How's Rabbit?"

"Is this really why you called? If you're so interested in this family, you should have stayed with it."

"No," I say. "I bought a one-way."

"Oh, that's it. We're only *almost* irrelevant. A sort of convenience-factor in your world. How nice for us."

"I know the directions. It's not very far."

"You're not getting me down there."

"But we were all coming anyhow. We just got sidetracked. You just got sidetracked."

"No way. No sir."

"You just got scared."

"You done, Iva? Someone here needs the telephone."

"I had to try," I say. "I had to try to find him."

"I can't bear it, Iva. I just can't bear it. I won't have you people leaving me and then dragging me down to find you. You're with *him* now, Iva. You made your choice."

the breeze of passing things

I follow what the lady told me. Down the road, then to the left, and it's not far before I see Patch Street. The house is bigger and slightly less run down—for a few obvious repairs like plywood boards on the roof, bricks thrown under sagging porch steps, and duct-taped screens. I don't have much else to do. I knock.

A small lady with big, pink-red hair opens the door. "'Morning," she says.

"Um, Perry said —"

"Still sleeping, darling. Go on back." She motions to the back of the house then goes off to the kitchen.

I wait at the bedroom door making up my mind, open it when I'm sure he hasn't heard my knock. He's a log in the bed which takes up the entire room so there's just a slim path hardly enough to walk around from one sagged-out window screen to the other. I don't want to wake him, don't think I should, so I just stand there. When I can't take it anymore, I sit on the floor to wait.

He turns in his sleep. He makes breathing sounds like suffocation, then shifts and goes easier, quiet for a few minutes. Then he starts the upset and relief all over again. I can hear his mother in the kitchen, moving things around on the counter, shoving the dishwasher racks in and out. I can hear someone just outside the window dropping things and cussing. I can hear someone turning on the shower. When morning's gone, Perry starts waking, blinks his eyes open, shut, open, shut, sleeps more, moves around some. And finally he's just staring out the side window, doesn't even see me.

"I hope it's okay," I whisper softly so I won't scare him.

But he's not startled one bit, looks down toward the foot of the bed where I'm sitting on the floor, says, "You." He sits up and his hair's spiky to one side. "You could have sat up here."

I shrug, thinking about who I am and what I'm doing here. I stay on the floor.

He reaches down and touches the side of my head. I'm pulling back. "What happened here?" he asks. I remember the inch of short hair over my ear and turn my head feeling stupid and ugly. "You go to sleep with gum?"

"No," I smile.

"No one hurt you though, right?"

I shake my head wondering what's he thinking about me.

"You hungry?"

"Dying," I say.

He walks me into the kitchen in just a T-shirt and his drawers. The house feels empty which makes me nervous. He grabs a sugary cereal box Mally would go ape for, and the milk and two bowls.

"Sylvia let you in?" he asks, scooping huge spoonfuls into his mouth.

"Your mother?"

"She's *not* my mother," he says, looking hard at me. "*Step*mother."

I nod and shovel so maybe I'll finish my bowl same time he does.

He looks at me and I can't stand how long his eyes are stuck on me. I press my fingers to crumbs on the tabletop. I make a pile of them between us.

"I know what it's like, when they don't want you around," he says, not even trying to shut his mouth to chew or swallow; puddles of milk like gutters of cloudy rainwater line his bottom teeth. "My stepfather's the meanest sonofabitch you ever saw. Militant and Mormon and shit if I'll go back out to Reno where my mother's at, until she leaves him."

"That's not it," I say. "He just wasn't there."

"When's he coming back?"

"Don't know if he is. The lady across the street said he's not. She seemed pretty sure. But he didn't know I was coming either."

"Oh."

Perry and I leave our mess in the kitchen and he parks me facing out the window, sitting on his bed while he gets dressed in the closet. My skin feels slimy but I don't press my luck for a shower.

"I'm gonna take you somewhere," he says.

"Where?"

"It's a surprise."

We drive and in daylight I can see that Perry's glovebox well is stuffed with maps. A week ago, half a week ago, I would have been itching to touch these maps, study them, sleep with them beneath my pillow, trace the greens and reds to blue where maybe my father's dreaming of me. Now I know all the routes and not one is any good.

September heat's getting to me when we stop for crossings. Perry's driving faster today. Where we're headed I don't know, but there's a narrow slip of water to one side of us growing wider as we go. Water oaks and tupelo gum on the other side. Perry pulls over in the gravel and leads me down a steep bank.

"Careful," he says, planting his feet and putting his arms out wide in front in case I start to tumble.

At the bottom is the water, now grown about as wide as half a football field. Across it is a plank bridge held by nothing but ropes.

"Come on," Perry says. "Isn't it great?"

He's to the middle of the bridge and I'm just stepping on. The planks give a little, the ropes are worn, the whole thing sways. Perry sits smack dab in the middle and I make it to him, first in cautious shuffles then trying to walk, even jog but it's all in slow-motion so I'm not fooling anybody. He yanks me down and I sit right in front of him.

"I come out here all the time. I love how the wind pulls at the bridge."

I smile but I'm still gripping the ropes.

"Now lay down," he says.

Mother would correct his grammar. I don't, though I'm itching to.

"That's the only way to get the full effect." First he turns me around, then pulls me down so he's kneeling over my face. "Feel it?"

Then he lies down and his head's by mine. He has a mole on his earlobe and in the sun his hair's got red strands.

"I love it," I say. I do. I love everything about it.

The bridge rocks with his shifting to look at me and my shifting not to be seen so close, feeling like both commotions might tip me out. Now we stay still and the bridge calms. We lie like this, shutting our eyes to the light piercing the trees overhead.

This is nothing like ESP with Henry. Nothing like pretending to be hypnotized then feeling him look me over. Telling me what to do, making it ache in me. Henry touched me and my skin wore away beneath his fingers. He didn't have one thing to show me.

Perry's hand touches my face and I keep my eyes shut tight. My skin feels dizzy, good. I like what a hand on me means. It slides down my cheek and then we're still again. Feels like turning on tiptoe in ballet before I learned to spot, when I'd fall out of a spin all wobbly because I hadn't kept my eyes on a single point in the room.

His hand is more than breeze so I believe it.

When we get back to Perry's house his sister Lynna's watching television. She's between us in age is my guess. She likes my name and wants to do something with my hair to fix the hole. I ask if I can take a shower and when I shut off the water and step out of the tub, there's a stack of fresh clothes for me to choose from. I comb through my hair and slip into a pair of Lynna's jeans shorts and a green T-shirt.

I find Perry and Lynna in his room listening to Air Supply.

"Great getup," she says and then launches in to a whole host of questions leaving no space in between for answers. "Where're you from? Did you really hitchhike the whole way? Are your parents remarried? Where are you going? How old are you?"

Once Lynna is done Perry says, "Yeah, how old are you?"

"How old are you?" I ask.

"Asked you first."

"How old do I look?" I sit up posture-perfect and look him square in the eyes.

"I dunno. Sixteen?"

"Yup. What about you?"

"Sixteen—just turned."

"You hungry?"

"Tacos," he says. "There's a place; Sylvia doesn't cook."

"I'm coming, too," says Lynna.

With one pointed finger, Perry sends her to the backseat of his car so I'm up front and I bite at my lips to keep from smiling. Abuelita's isn't far. We get a sack full of tacos and three extra-large orange pops and sit on the hood of the car making a mess. It's coming on dark. Perry keeps running his hand through his hair and Lynna keeps giggling at him doing it. We pile back into the car. This time when we make our first right turn, Perry slips his hand onto my hand—like it's just keeping track of me.

At the house Lynna disappears. Perry and I sit on the couch in the front room watching reruns of *Alice*. He takes my hand again—measuring our fingers palm to palm—and we sit quietly, not saying a word because who can talk with as big a thing as this sitting in the room.

When Sylvia comes home with their dad Perry's hand drops to his side. I am semi-properly introduced. Sylvia offers for me to sleep over and I'm wondering which room she's thinking of because she doesn't say and Lynna's nowhere to be seen. Where I've come from or where I'm going, they don't ask and we don't offer. Sylvia struts through to the back room on the other side of the house and Perry's dad, who first looks at me smiling and sweet, follows her whistling.

Perry grunts. "They creep me out."

"Your dad seems nice," I say.

"Vacant."

"He's here," I say.

"Sort of." He takes my hand back and we go on measuring and watching the *Alice* marathon quietly, not even laughing each time Flo says "Kiss my grits." Lynna comes back and sits on my side of the couch. After four more episodes, she's ready for bed and so I go with her. She gives me a big T-shirt to wear and an old toothbrush and comes talk to me while I'm peeing and brushing.

"You like Perry?" she asks.

I shrug and roll my lips under in between my teeth, feel my jaws clamp tight.

"He likes you," she says, giggling some more. "More than this weird, kind of mentally troubled girl in my class last year who never talked—and he liked her a lot."

Lynna drags all her sheets off the mattress and tosses them to the floor where she makes a bed for both of us. She just won't shut up until I pretend I'm sleeping: "Have you ever kissed a boy? I've kissed a boy, but only once and it was just out back of the Burger King one night and it wasn't anything, just a dare. Some of Perry's friends. You know, hand stuff, too—but that doesn't count, right? You have a brother? I've never been in love, have you? I thought so once but I was wrong. It's one of those things you can never be sure of. What's your middle name? Are you gonna start school Tuesday? I guess you'll be in ninth not eighth with me. Does your mother know where you are?"

I wake and Lynna's clock radio reads 3:47 A.M. She's rolled off the bottom sheet and halfway under her bed. The house is quiet. Outside the night is still but for crickets and the whir of highway a little too near.

I am alone and maybe an orphan.

I walk light as I can to the kitchen, take down the phone, even though it's middle of the night, and ask for the motel again. I tell the clerk it's an emergency, but still he says Lilly Giles is checked out—took the towels and bedsheets to boot.

We're truly lost now.

※ ※ ※

I get up and go to Perry's door. It's a crack open and I push in, latch it behind me. I stand over him, watch him sleep, then climb onto the far edge of his bed, my back to him. I don't believe he wakes, but his arms slip around me, his face nestles into my shoulder and neck. And I'm crying. Soundlessly but sobbing. My whole body convulses with too little air and too much of something else. Needing not to be separate.

"Iva," he says, and he could be my father in the red house on Fay Road for how good his holding me feels. He kisses my hair, his fingers stroke my face. He squeezes me and tries to turn me around to face him. I don't know, I don't know. I can't be sure what I want. I don't know who anybody is anymore. My skin's so hot it's burning right off me.

I won't turn. I stay staring out into the driveway and night, at the way everything is so dark and still. Then I sit up and watch the sky. He sits up behind me.

"See?" he whispers. "Stars are brighter so near the water."

I'm a mess of tears and trying to catch my breath. I don't see the night, its clouds and stars. "I'm not sure," I say. I don't see and I don't believe.

"I'll show you."

He slips into his jeans. I grab Lynna's shorts, thinking we're headed for beach. But we drive back to the hanging bridge. Lying on our backs, this time beside each other though there's hardly room, his arm beneath my head. Both of us feel the sway of the breeze and our eyes are open this time to be sure.

"Brighter?" he asks.

"So much brighter." There's a new moon tonight, a no-moon. Even without her, under a sky tall as this I'm halfway to believing there's no such thing as lost.

Perry picks up his head and kisses me on the cheek. His mouth is moving toward mine and his lips are soft like earlobes and I'm feeling the bridge give out beneath us and the stars spin 'round and I'm kissing him back and I'm feeling it swallow me up—the everything of want, the everything of need, the everything of leaving and replacing.

A kiss can be so much. A kiss can be the universe. It can simply be enough.

Perry lies on his side, his head on his arm, watching me. There is nothing more than this.

"What do you see?" I ask.

"You."

"But what is that?"

"I don't know," he says.

The water's running fast beneath us.

"Polished bottle glass like you find in the river?"

"What?"

"Shut up," he says. "I'm not a poet. I don't know. Fire?
Birds? I don't know what I see."

His hand on my arm suddenly feels strange, his skin
heavy and hot.

"I *think* I see you," he says.

I sit up because the breeze is turning back against us. It's
blowing into my eyes. "And what is that?" I ask.

"Well, it's like you're kind of hurt. Like if you're limping.
It gives you this quality that's hard to explain but if I have to,
well, it's like you're—don't take this the wrong way—but it's
like you just don't know stuff. Like it's all new." He stares
straight up into the night. "It's like you've just woken up."

"And you like that?"

"Yeah, I like it. I like you. So I like it. Or I like it, so I
like you." He sits up, too.

"I guess that's good," I say.

"Yeah, it's good." He leans forward, takes my whole face
in his hands and starts kissing me again but this time it's
different. Strong and a little bit queasy. One of us pushing.

We drive back. Perry's hand is on my knee and
something somewhere inside me wants it gone, says it's got
no business there. I'm quiet, staring at his hand. He pulls
over in the car. He's practically turned around the way he's
half on me and half over the brake lever. He's kissing at my
neck and my ear. That side of my head is soggy, gross. I'm

gripping the door handle. He wraps himself around me, his hand coming up my leg, and for the way skin on skin feels now I have to concentrate to keep from biting him.

Still halfway sucking on me, he says, "I don't know. I think I love you."

This I don't know. This isn't anything I know. If a person stops saying "I love you" to someone — either because she isn't sure she wants to give so much or because they're no longer there — there's not much to be done to put those words back in her air. They don't fit in the mouth anymore. They're not my language.

"I love you, Iva," he says, but he's begging it. "I want you," and his hand's up my shirt.

I throw open the car door, push him away. I say nothing but start to walk up the street, feel the air sticking to my wet neck.

He's coming after me. "Iva," he's calling. "What's wrong? Get back in the car."

I can't answer him.

He catches up to me, but stays back. "I don't get you," he's saying. "I thought you liked it."

I stop walking, turn around to face him. I look straight up into the night. Perry was wrong: I can hardly make out any stars at all. He's no part of me truly. He knows nothing of the sky, nothing of *la luna*.

He takes my hand. "I won't do it again — whatever it is — I won't do it."

"Okay," I say but keep on walking.

"Come on, let's go."

"No." I pull my hand free of his.

"Iva, where are you going?"

"Back down Lovell. And Turner. To Fay."

"But he's not there. You said so. He's not coming back." Perry grabs hold of my elbow to keep me. "Tell me what I did, Iva. I won't do it anymore."

"I'm not what you see. I'm not clumsy or retarded." I start walking again. On Fay Road now, looking for the bruise of a house two blocks ahead on the left.

"What do you mean?"

"I mean I can talk. And I'm not like your sister at Burger King. I'm not like that."

He calls after me, "Whatever she told you, it's not true."

"I don't care. Just get away from me."

"Well you can't sleep in an abandoned house. He doesn't want you, Iva. You can't choose someone who's not even there and doesn't even want you over someone who does?"

"You don't know anything. Get away from me!" I yell.

A dog about three streets deep starts up yapping. Another after it.

"Just wait a second," he says, his hands up in the air like he means to surrender. "I could go to my mom but she takes Big Jim over me and Lynna any day. They're the ones who get to make choices. They do. They choose. We can't change their minds. We just deal with it best we can and then get the hell out. Slow down and listen," he says.

I keep going.

"Listen. Listen to me. Don't get *crazy*!"

"Fuck you!" I scream back at him. I run ahead and he gives up by the middle of the block.

I'm to the house. It's the same as last night. Pitch black. I don't have my lighter or knife so I feel my way to the bed, first knocking into a chair I thought was farther to the right.

When the toes of my sandals stop at the mattress, I sit down, lie right on the edge because I'm feeling dizzy. I recall Mother setting her foot to the floor New Year's morning to keep her head steady after too many champagne refills, so I hang one leg off the bed. The air feels different tonight. The sounds of the room are like Perry's breathing this morning, like I'm holding a shell to my ear, I hear waves of breathing.

Sleep comes easy. I'm in and out of the black of it, my head still tiptoeing through today, and then an arm falls heavy over me.

"I don't want you! Get out!" I scream half awake and half dreaming, and I yank his arm off me.

The whole bed shakes. Something's got hold of me and hauls me up and over to the wall. The lamp flicks on in the corner, its light shooting through my eyes, burning them before I adjust.

A naked lady is crouching in the corner, and he's got hold of me. It's him. His yellow hair, his copper beard, his hazel eyes, his eyelashes like smeared light. He is smaller than I remember. His skin is golden with summer, his cheeks white-creased where the sun hasn't found him.

The woman is trembly. "Who is she?" she asks.

He's looking me over, still gripping my wrists. Seeing my yellowish hair, the place I'm scarred over my nose from chicken pox where he secretly scratched for me when Mother tied the socks over my hands, my eyes. I'm big now, but I'm me.

He stands here, his mouth ready to say if it'll just come to him. But he can't answer her; it's clear he does not know.

"I'm Iva," I whisper, not believing it has to be said. "I'm your girl."

I see him hear the name. I watch the letters go through the air to him.

"Iva?" he asks. "Iva?" He pulls me to him, lifts me off the ground, spins with me. "Iva! It's Iva," he tells the lady.

She grabs a shirt from the floor and slips it on. "You have a daughter," she says, stepping into the back corner of the room. There's nowhere for her to go in here. She sits on the toilet, pees right in front of us like a dog at a tree.

"When did you get here? Is your car out front?" he asks.

"I can't drive yet, Daddy. I came on a bus."

"Oh, a bus. Well, that's too bad. You're tall, though, bet you're a hotshot driver."

"Your car's not out front," I say, thinking we'll just talk about whatever he's interested in. "Where is the Pontiac?"

"Bet it and lost, baby-doll," he says. "Worst night of my life."

I'm wondering about him being without a car; he never could be stuck anywhere without his car to get him free. "You hitch now?" I ask. "I hitched from the bus."

"In a manner of speaking," he says, winking at the woman.

"In a manner of speaking," she says from on the bed now where she's slipping on her cut-off shorts and shoes. "Well, it's been fun Jameson. See ya now."

Daddy follows her to the door, whispers something to her. Her mouth turns crooked and her eyes glow bright. She gives him a deep kiss and squeezes her hand on his backside. I look to the bed, then hating the idea of what was in it, I look to the wall, see the bathroom, look to the floor, see the lake ringing the room. Nowhere left to look.

"We've got all sorts of catching up to do, now haven't we?" Daddy says, turning back from seeing her out.

"I've been trying to get down here for over a year now. We didn't even know if you'd still be here—"

"How's Lilly?" he interrupts.

"She's all right," I say.

"Where's she hiding?" He starts looking around like there's anywhere she could go unseen in this one room.

"She's not here."

"Oh. She'll be back, though. Took Mally for a drive? Mally used to love a good drive with a bottle. Warm milk. Soothed the savage beast in her." He talks so fast. "Lilly ran up to the corner Shell station for something? She's always on the ball, that Lilly."

"No," I say, racing to figure out how to be enough for him.

He wants Mother. He can say Mally without pulling open that bottom drawer, tracing his finger along the equation: Mallory = Mally. I may as well be a niece he's never met. I stand here. Just stand and am his girl, his four-years-older girl, and see that the fact of me being his means so little.

"No Lilly?"

"No."

Daddy's cheeks fall flat, he blinks some, his mouth pushes tight. Like Mally before she knew words, when everything happening in our house was secret from her. This is how he stays: cheated.

"I rode a bus all by myself down here."

"That's great, bug," he says. "You know, I'm pretty zonked. Let's pack it in." He turns out the lamp that's melted more of the shade up against the wall. I nearly go to it, adjust the books beneath to a safe distance from the wall. This is something he would like me for. It is something he would do. But he doesn't, so I don't either. The smell of plastic burning feels like bugs crawled up my nose, and it goes on long after Daddy's in bed tugging me down beside him. I kiss his cheek and I can feel him smile, but then he's sleeping. Breathing waves of sound and heat like Perry or Lynna, or just plain anyone else sleeping in a room. I am here and his arms are at his sides.

He's up long before me, though I swore I'd stay half awake so I wouldn't miss a thing. Then he's in mid-sentence so I look around for that woman crouching in the corner, but there's no one here but us: "… that way you'll have a place to stay while you're in town and no squatters can take over while you're on duty."

"Daddy?"

"Yes, sweetness." He's sitting at the card table, writing something.

"You're going so soon?"

"I'm off," he says like it's a mission to Mars.

"I just got here."

"Well," he says but doesn't finish.

I sit up in the bed. "Can I go with you? Like before. You used to take me with, remember?"

He's at the sink, smoothing his hair in front of the mirror where I cut mine off yesterday. "I'm afraid, buglet, that would complicate matters—you know, getting the right ride and all. You ever want to buy me a present, baby—get me back my car."

There's bees in my stomach buzzing a panic, stirring up desperation. I'm slipping on my sandals to be ready to run. He's back at the table writing some more, so to show him I can rough it on the road, I'm peeing in the corner toilet. He doesn't even notice.

"Besides," he says, "haven't you got school starting up?"

"Not yet."

"Just stick it out here for me. We'll catch everything up when I'm back."

Then she's at the door, that woman.

I've got no choice.

When she's kissing Daddy on the chair, laughing about where they're headed, saying Ronnie will flip when he wakes up, I slip out the front of the house and into the backseat of her car. I squat in the footwell beneath the pink and purple pairs of side-zipper and ankle-zip jeans and her pile of off-shoulder peasant shirts and fuchsia bras. When they climb in, Daddy taking the wheel, and Coral sliding up next to him on the bench seat, I feel like throwing up.

The first couple of stops, for gas and for Coral's Slurpee and corn nuts, are too soon. Once we're out of town, I figure it's safe—too far and too much trouble to take me back. Besides which I'm starving, I get out of the car and walk into the I-HOP behind them. I sit down like I've been with them the whole time and had just gotten up to use the bathroom.

"Goddamn, Iva. You scared the shit out of me," Daddy says and slides over in the booth to make room. "Long as she's here, Coral…," he says but doesn't finish whatever it is he's requesting of her.

Coral's face plumps up into a taffy-pink smile but it's one of those puppet smiles with the strings still attached.

I eat pancakes, French toast, hash browns, sausage, and Coral's bacon which she says is too wiggly. Daddy laughs at me and says I'm wolfing everything down. We're back on the road and heading west on US-10 into Louisiana. I watch his hands on the wheel, hoping we'll stop to see him shimmy the lever in and out of reverse, watch its pearly green knob sparkle in the heat; itching for Daddy to pull us into somewhere secluded and teach me how to drive.

We pass turnoffs for Biloxi and I think of Chet, and how sure I am Perry's already gone through my pack, found Daddy's list of us three, Chet's knife and silver lighter and number at Keesler A.F.B., Davis Neale's money. Daddy's not looking at me, not talking to me. All he's concerned with is the road and Coral and her left leg thrown across his lap. Wriggling up there like Mally stuck in a turtleneck, Coral's making a to-do out of getting comfy in his right arm. Each time she decides she's not truly settled after all, the car veers and my feet go tense as if I'm the one with the pedals and the wheel. Maybe I wouldn't mind Perry so much if he were here in the backseat now, sucking on my neck right in front of Daddy and Coral.

We head through Slidell, then find a little road that follows shoreline. Coral's sleeping now, her mouth hanging open with a catch of drool off her bottom lip.

Daddy's driving slowly, taking things in. "You remember this place?" he asks, checking on me, finally, in the rearview.

I look around. The deep green of draggy trees leaning out over the thickest water I've ever seen.

"That's Lake Ponchartrain," he says. "Brought you here when you were—" he wonders a split second "—hell if I know."

"Not this again, Jameson. You swore off this route last time." Coral smacks her mouth trying to work up some saliva after it's all dripped out of her face. She puts her arm over the seat turning to me. "Your father's positively obsessed," she says. "Comes here any chance he gets at a car."

"I want to take her over the causeway," he says.

"Well *then* let's get out of here," she says.

"Patience."

We drive the long bridge over the lake and I don't remember the water being so deep and wide. I don't remember the sun off it making the world seem a green glass bottle. I don't remember other cars whizzing past. The bridge lasts near to an hour and once we're through he turns us back out of New Orleans to take it again. Coral protests that she didn't volunteer her car for this. I kind of like what we're doing—that he's happy about something, that he's needing to show me. Finally back on the other side, he pulls off the road onto a boggy half-road, cuts the engine and gets out. This I remember.

I get out behind him and am glad not to hear Coral's door open, glad this is special for me. Daddy's up ahead, leaning against the tallest baldcypress I've ever seen, must be over a hundred feet high, with dozens of knees rising up out of the water all around it. There are redbays wearing Spanish moss and so many warblers trilling that their songs echo like cavecalls. The air is spongy-wet as my forehead when I have the flu and Mother's hand insists on checking my fever every hour. I am discovered by fat mosquitoes too quick for me to swat.

Daddy's just standing here, leaning to look out over the lake. I recognize this spot now in its angles and lighting. Nothing more definite than what's seen in a blurry picture— a thumb over the lens, a girl skipping by at the closing of the camera's shutter. In its pieces, each tree and vine and bird and weight of the air—in its pieces, I would never know where I stand. But this is the place Mother first left him. This is where she's said he wanted us all to swim and she was terrified, screaming and pounding her foot over his on the brake. He was driving the car straight at the water.

Coral's come up beside me saying, "He says it's the last spot he ever understood the world. Anywhere else, he can't be sure of a thing."

She's being sweet to me now and what she's saying seems deserving of a response. And so I say it, what I've never really known until this moment: "He tried to kill us all here."

Coral backs away, goes to the car to wait, sitting rigid in her seat. I go to him, balance my feet on two cypress knees beside him, feel the straps of my sandals near snapping for the way their soles curl down over the spikes.

"You know what I'm wondering?" he asks.

"No," I say.

"What happened?"

I set down a syrupy napkin-boat I folded beneath our table at I-HOP this morning. Let it tap against the rim of mud and roots.

He can't take his eyes off it. "No doubt you're mine, love."

No.

He's wrong. We are separate. All this time I've been carrying him along with me he's been someone entirely different.

"This is where my brother went in," he says.

"Your brother?"

"My brother."

"I didn't know." Though that's not entirely right. I didn't know it from him, is what I mean. I didn't *know*.

"I had a brother."

I wonder at this, why he's telling me now. What else he's kept for himself.

I watch a black and white woodpecker take perch and peck a hollow tupelo. Then he flies again, white underwings flashing me blind. If he stepped down now I wouldn't see him. I would hear the water move around him and I would know, but I wouldn't see a thing but the whiteness of the sun off those wings. I could forget it and go on looking.

"Head back to the car," he tells me, but the idea of it makes my stomach fall. I tell him no, but he tells me again. "Go on, girl." I do.

Coral's picking at her hair, lifting the layers of fluff higher again. I lean over the front seat trying to keep from blinking. What he's doing out there I don't know, dipping the toe of his shoe in and pulling it back out, laying twigs and washed-up debris back in the murky water. He sits now with his back to us. I can hear him through the trees and air and snagging of Coral's pink nails in her hair. I can hear him calling "Jesse, Jesse." I can hear him believing he's losing it all again.

❈ ❈ ❈

"Sug, why don't you take a rest?" He pats Coral's thigh.

"I slept the whole way to New Orleans. What more do you want from me?"

"You look tired, baby," he says. "You look like you could use a rest."

She pulls at the rearview mirror, centers it in front of her face, and presses her bright pink lips together while tipping her head up. She runs her fingers into the corner of each eye, pulling out tiny crusts of sleep, and pats her cheeks. "I don't know what you're talking about, Jameson, you lousy bastard. I look good." She runs her lipstick around her lips once more for good measure and then falls dead asleep.

"Are we near Nacogdoches?" I ask, thinking what he needs is the way things were for us then. "We could go see our house."

"Sure, let's go. Just don't wake Coral. I swore myself to craps on the riverboats with her."

I wish he would put the mirror back not for driving purposes, but so I can keep an eye on him. We cross the Mississippi and he gives me thumbs up. Then I sleep.

I wake in the car, a stiff note tucked into my shirt, the same writing as his list of our names, saying, "ROOM # 7." It's night already, deep night, and the parking lot's flooded by one sorry lamppost, the brightest bulb ever. Room # 7's door is propped open with a pink flip-flop. I turn the lock behind me. They're in one bed, I'm to be in the other. Coral's naked again and he's sleeping with his head on her boobies, her fingers wandering through his hair. I use the bathroom then slip into bed, listen to the window A/C blast all night long.

In the morning, there's another note tucked into my shirt, saying, "*Noona's Café, across the street. Leaving at* 8:15." I check the clock: five minutes to eight. I step into the shower but can't concentrate with so little time. Get out after only wetting my hair. I comb it with my fingers, put my clothes back on and slip into my sandals. Coral's paying the check from her fat wallet and when I come in she takes pity on me, tells the cashier to add in a sack of beignets. She hands over the whole sack for me to eat in the car, powdered sugar slicking my fingertips for the rest of the drive. I fold the paper napkins Coral hands me just like all those paper-boats

Daddy set free in the gulf waters years before.

"Cutting it close, kiddo," he says.

"Why didn't you get me up? Next time get me up." I set one of my boats on the top of the front bench seat, then think it might upset him so I take it back down.

We head up highway 49 then over on I-20, and by the time dark's coming on, the names are getting closer: Natchez, Zwolle, Sabine, Natchitoches Parish, Negreet. Daddy guns it to get us there before too late. Through Shelby County into Nacogdoches, and to our house on La Bega. None of it is the same now. I don't know the turns or names. Each time we're to the middle of a block I call out, "There it is!"

But Daddy finds our house. He pulls up in front and while I'm stepping through Coral's mess of skirts and underpants to get out the door, he turns around to look me straight in the eye. "It's not a good idea," he says.

So I stop. Because I know. This was where we were last whole and so maybe he needs to just take it in a minute. But that's not it. Instead he starts the engine again and we're gone out of Texas faster than I can spell all our names he set down in order and equation, plus his.

Coral's putting up a fight in the front seat. "I did not come all this way for nothing, and I did not let you take Ronnie's Plymouth Fury for no chance at making some cash at the slots or on dice."

"*Ronnie's* Plymouth Fury!" cries Daddy. "You mean if we're stopped I'm driving stolen property?"

"Ronnie wouldn't do that to me. He's not like that. He's considerate, and—"

"If he's so considerate, what're you doing with me, sugar plum?"

"Shove it up your ass, Jameson Giles."

I sink down into Coral's outfits to get myself out of here, make like I'm sleeping. Last time I was sugar plum was in the Tyler house when he sang and called to me from the front lawn all night. I pressed my fingers to the window, watching him pull at his hair screeching he wanted us so bad. Mother had turned the lock on my door. I held my hand to that glass all night, woke up with her shooting the hose at him.

"You aren't real, Coral. Never have been."

"Oh here we go," she says.

"You're stealing from me."

"Ha!" she laughs. "What do you have I want? Your car? Oh that's right, you lost your car."

"Shut up, Coral."

"Your gorgeous red shack? House, I mean, house."

"Bitch."

"Your peach of a daughter trailing along behind us? Sleeping in the goddamned next bed while you're fingering me?"

"Shut the fuck up."

She turns back to me, making it a joke. "Your father is a volatile man, Iva. You know that don't you?"

He pulls over to the side of the highway, leans across her and opens her car door. Then he starts pushing.

"My breath, Coral! You're stealing my breath. I can't breathe around you."

"Don't touch me!" She grabs hold of the dashboard and bites at his wrists.

"You're the one with nothing," he says. "You got your tits and your ass and your car—no wait, I've got your car! And your tits and ass, well I've had those too." He starts kicking her, batting at her till she's out.

"This is it! After this, nothing," she says. "And I'm calling it in, the car! I'm calling it in!"

He locks her door and pulls away.

"Give her some of her things," he calls into the backseat. "You keep whatever you like."

I pick up the pink jeans and they're the first thing to fly through the night to her, but not the last. I hold on to a few pairs of cutoffs and a slew of peasant shirts because I'm thinking more and more of Perry and skin and that maybe I should reconsider what I think of a soggy ear.

We spend the night in the car and I'm glad for that because it means I don't have to worry about him being gone before I even see a note tucked into my clothes. But he's crying, I can tell by the way the front seat shakes. I put my hand to the vinyl and feel the way it moves.

In the morning, he's not talking and I feel sick. I duck down into the footwell, slip into one of Coral's off-shoulder peasant blouses and a pair of red shorts. We're back on 49, then 10 and I'm hoping we'll pass right under Lake Ponchartrain, leave Louisiana for Pascagoula or anywhere else. But Daddy's driving slowly again, like he's hypnotized to go right there.

I ask him, "Are we going to leave the car somewhere? I've got some money back in Pascagoula. We could borrow on it for bus tickets."

He doesn't answer me. He drives, his hands at ten and three. His wrists, smudged with her lipstick, are purple-mooned but not bleeding. He keeps to the same left lane even when trucks come up hard behind, honking to move us out of the way. We're less than an hour away from that big bridge when Daddy has to stop for gas. He's angry about it, tossing around the nozzle, slapping the handles up and down on the pump.

"I'm gonna find the washroom," I tell him.

He doesn't even look up.

When I pull down my shorts and underpants, there's slick red everywhere. Soaked right through and I wonder about the boy who watched me from the pay-up booth, hope red through red just looks like shadow. Mother said Aunt Clea got her period at twelve so I should be ready this year but she never said what to do.

I wipe myself and my underwear, make wads of the awful toilet paper that's stiffer than newsprint, press it into my clothes, each layer. But it keeps coming. And I'm instantly wet and pulling out the sticky wads for new ones. I flush the toilet to get rid of so much mess in the bowl and sit back down over it.

I need to hurry. He won't like waiting on me. I pull on the toilet paper, keep wrapping it 'round my hand till it's about an inch and a half thick and stuff that in my underpants, take another pull at the roll and put that stack in my shorts. I flush, wash my hands, take the extra roll from the top of the toilet, and unlock the door. That's when I see them: his notes slipped under the door, hand steady as it was writing his list of who we are because he needed to know us, or at least our names, by heart.

The paper on top says, "you'll be alright." The one beneath, "5 minutes."

I open the door, step out into the glare and the streaky smell of gasoline. Of course he's gone.

This time I'm not scared to hitch. I'm scared not to.

Scared I won't catch up in time. I take the first ride I see and it's a pickup truck and even with what Chet said about trucks and instinct, I'm grateful and hop in wishing the seats were vinyl not velour. It's a man with white hair and a beer gut.

"Lake Ponchartrain," I say.

"Top or bottom?"

"I guess top."

He nods, offers me a cigarette without saying a word. I shake my head 'cause there's no time to explain that we are fastidious and even scrub our teeth clean after eating pizza. The guy's giving me sidelong glances the whole way. It's not that I ignore him, it's that there isn't any room in my head for dealing with him at all.

We're there fast. But I don't see anything, not that I know what I'm looking for.

"Can you take me across and back?" I ask.

"If that's what you want."

Still, there's just the water and the cars, lazy trees where it's shallow or shore. No Plymouth Fury. No flashing lights.

"Thanks," I tell him when I can see the end of the bridge. I jump out before he's decided to fully stop and his hand's grabbing at my butt. I kick at the rear bumper while it pulls past, hope to God I stained his upholstery.

I walk back and it takes years. So much bright pavement hitting my eyes. I count the bars of the railing. I lose track, start counting the rush of cars going by, separate tallies for blue ones, for red, for white and black. I reach the end of the bridge and step down into green. Keep going until I'm at the water. I stand in the trees. I listen for him breathing, him cussing, him calling "Jesse," him anything. To see deeper into the expanse of water, I step off the shore, balance my curvy soles onto a cypress knee then another. Going quick as I can without falling in. One sandal strap finally gives up with a snap.

He's not here. I start for the road and see the car, tucked into a thick stand of swamp tupelos. But he's gone. I check the water. I check the road. There's no way to know which.

The doors are unlocked. The key's in the ignition. Coral's clothes are still in the backseat. I open the door and get in. I slip out of the red shorts and underpants. Grab a pair of shorts from Coral's pile, and a jeans jacket to wrap around my waist. I climb over the seat, check the glove box and find her lipstick. It's brighter on me. There's a box of rubbers and her wallet. Only it's not hers, just what she used wherever we went. It's Ronnie's and his I.D. is in it along with a photo of Coral and him sitting in a booth at some Winn-Dixie. There's still some cash so I take it. A fifty and some twenties is all. I leave the car and Lake Ponchartrain, grab rides from Madeville to Alton. From Alton to Gulfport, and there to Pascagoula. The whole way I clutch my sides and wonder at this new throbbing in my belly—if it's me or if it's him.

I don't go to 13 Fay Road, but instead to 44 Patch. It's Lynna I want first, though Perry's talking to me nonstop through the bathroom door while she's showing me what to do.

"Whatever you want, Iva," he says.

When I open the door I tell him to shut up. Then I kiss him and I can't be sure, of course, but with my eyes closed it sort of feels like the universe splits wide again. Or sort of. It's nice, anyhow. I laugh at Coral's pink on Perry's lips. I check on my backpack and the names, the knife, the address and lighter—everything's right there. I put away the money and lipstick.

"I'm going home," I say.

"Home, where?"

"Home, Fay Road."

"I'll come."

"No, that would *complicate matters*," I say, thinking of Daddy. "You want to see me, come by later."

I walk to the red house just to be sure. I can smell the lipstick on my mouth and feel this new pair of Lynna's shorts—black, which she says is best.

I am different now.

Walking up the block looking for the house, I don't even recognize our car, the Impala, until I'm near enough to make out Mally, too. I stop, then start up again. She's out front of the house, sitting on the stoop facing away, holding Rabbit on her lap.

I shout and run, calling out to her. "Mally! Mally!"

She hears me, comes running, her sandals slapping the pavement, Rabbit flailing in her arms. I hug her. I hug Rabbit. I think of Milk Glass living off the dumpster.

"We drove straight through once Momma stopped crying," Mally says.

"She was crying?"

"We've been here all night."

"I called. When did you leave?"

"Just after Momma saw the doctor."

"What doctor?"

"I dunno—we went, I sat in the chair a minute, then they wanted us to go but Momma said she had to know and anyhow we'd checked out. Then the man came and took her over into the hallway and it was just her back to me so I don't know, but her cheeks were hot and she kept yanking at that patch of hair—she's gonna go bald if she doesn't quit it, Iva. Then we started driving."

"Didn't you ask her?"

Mally's eyes bunch up, puzzled. "Ask her?" she says.

"Never mind," I tell her. "Where is she?"

"Sleeping." Mally points to the car and I see the seat reclined, Mother lying in it, her whole body taut.

"She still mad?"

"She's been pulling out her hair, I told you. There's not much left 'round the side, behind her left ear."

"You slept in the car?"

"Sure."

"You didn't go in, right?" I ask 'cause I need some things to be just mine.

"Yeah," she says. "Where've you been?"

Mother sleeping is an old, worn-out woman. Her face is paper-thin, her eyelids swollen, her lips cracked and covered in rips and chunks of skin I can tell she's been chewing on. I knock on the glass and I can see it isn't me she expects because for a split second I find her face moving from one sort of panic to another. Then she's out the car door, hugging me to her.

"Iva, oh Iva." She squeezes me so hard I want to scream. She gives me the once-over, once she gets a hold of herself. "What are you wearing?" she asks, lifting one of the shoulders of Coral's peasant tops back up off my arm. "And where've you been? I'm not taking my eyes off you."

Now after four days not seeing her, I think Mother's started to show.

"We've been waiting on you," she says, stuffing some

clothes from the front seat into pillowcases I know she's stolen from The Last Bluff Motel. "Let's step on it, babycakes. We're expected."

"Wait," I say, sitting on the hood of the car trying to be agreeable but knowing it's all wrong. "I don't want to."

"Me, neither," says Mally, climbing up after me.

"Get used to it. We're going. You can't like it here so much, Iva. He's not even coming back—you said so."

I don't tell her he didn't really know me. I don't tell her he lost the car. I don't tell her he said I'm tall and thinks I'll be a good driver. I don't tell her any of it, not even that I've seen him and been with him—though anyone with half an eye could see it in me. It's mine. I don't even tell her he's swimming.

"I'm sick of you pulling us around," I say.

"Mother's going to take good care of us," she says.

"You can get a job. You can find a job anywhere."

"First you need money to get a place. She's letting us stay with her. Iva, there are things you don't understand about the world. Let's don't fight now. We'll go to Okaloosa and get you two settled into school and we'll just cozy into life down there."

I start into the house.

"Iva," she calls, "where are you going? Don't go in there."

I keep walking. She won't follow me inside.

"Don't, Iva. Come on now. I don't want you in there."

I shut the door behind me, catch Mally trying to decide between us. She's still sitting on the hood but now her legs dangle from the near side of the car, my side. I'm after what he was writing, find it there on the table, see her name and figure he knew she'd be coming for me.

Lilly,

Darling, it's all gone wrong. You're real and all these years I'd been hoping you weren't. This child comes to me and is tall and grown and I'm so fogged I can't even be sure if she's the first born or the baby.

I tried doctors. Everything they wrote just swam the Pearl River til the folds soaked through and the boats sank. You know I'm not whole without him. We were kids and everything he was I am too. So why didn't I walk in behind him? Why didn't I swallow the lake too?

You should have let me do it that night, bury us all. I try every time I pass through. But someone's always standing in the cypress knees watching, and I'm so weak.

There'll be water and stars and moon there. La luna. Jesse and you too.

Jameson

Mother's hollering for me outside. And so I go to her, tell her I'm hungry and can't we just cool off over tacos. I tell her the turns to make. I smooth his letter between my shirt and skin and check what few stars are early tonight to see if they're brighter for the water. I can't be sure under the parking-lot lamps.

Mother hardly eats a bite, slips into the car beneath her Florida map, checking over routes. Mally and I are sitting on the hood, just like with Perry and Lynna. Mally's nibbling her taco, then daubing refried beans to Rabbit, who's sitting on her lap.

I take a deep breath, then say it quietly. "I'm not going to Florida. You want to come with me?"

Mally looks up, her gray eyes big, her whole face

swollen with this possibility.

"Well?" I ask.

But she starts up with Rabbit again, signing to him, her ears failing her, shutting up, saving her from choosing. Her right hand waves in the air making all sorts of breeze for him.

I hop off the car, grab my backpack through the side window.

"Where're you going?" Mother asks from her map.

"Stock up on napkins. Ketchup and mustard. Bathroom too."

"Get salt and pepper, baby," she says. "And Iva?" she looks over to me but can't lift her eyes. "There's no more trouble from before—never was. Just a fluke. Just a sad sad thing is all. And we're fine. Everything's fine. It'll all just be fine." She touches a hand to her stomach, then moves it away to set on her thigh.

I nod and brush my hand over her arm that's resting on the door. I drop his letter onto the backseat hoping she's the one to find it—not Mally. Around the side of Abuelita's, I'm in a blue Chevy in no time. We make New Orleans in just under two hours, and I send us up the causeway for one more chance to see him. We're so fast because this guy's putting his hand on my thigh and each time it moves I dig my fingernails into his knuckles. I have him drop me at the end of the bridge, hoping to God it's still there, and I walk back into the thick of trees. I have every reason to limp, what with the swampy ground sucking at the heel of my broken shoe—but I don't.

It is here. Ronnie's Plymouth Fury and I'm in it before I know. I touch the key, start her up twisting the ignition long enough to grind all the metal, pat the wheel in apology. The shifter won't move till I remember and press the brake pedal, see the red of my taillights glowing through the green behind. I check my lipstick in the mirror like Coral. I'm all new. I'm Iva Giles: tall and soft-full for my age; an orphan with a sister who'll flap her hands like birds taking off the minute she hears my name; sunny golden, and a little bit crazy.

I lock all the doors, lay Coral's daisy tube top beneath me on the seat, set my paper-boats on the dash. I ease my foot off the brake and the car's rolling back a little. I stomp the gas and skid some, then ease up and up the bank it goes. Through the back roads. Onto gravel, then road.

The first place I head is Bay Minette. I've got choices I'm making and they're coming pretty easy right now. I hit US-10 into Mississippi, feel a hit of heat thinking what if I pass the Impala. But the road's pretty clear and the night's heavy with stars brighter for all the water. I've got the air of night coming in on me and things are looking good.

I've been chasing him since I was born, needing him near me just to know who I am. I never even heard his question. Didn't see that we were asking the very same thing and that up until today the answer's that I was a dream. I didn't understand that some people can choose what to know. And what to forget, no matter how many times they write us down in lists. I thought there were pills for being so wrong, but Mother's the one with anything worth wrecking, not Daddy.

I've been smiling with strings.

What I'm feeling now—in Ronnie's Plymouth Fury, gassed to 39 mph because anything more makes me nuts for

the shaking, doors locked, and all four windows rolled low,
paper-boats flying out the car worthless as pink and purple
jeans—is the breeze of passing things, what I've been feeling
all these years, only this time I'm the one moving.